Crimson Buccaneer

CLEO CORDELL

BLACK
lace

Black Lace novels are sexual fantasies.
In real life, make sure you practise safe sex.

First published in 1995 by
Black Lace
332 Ladbroke Grove
London
W10 5AH

Copyright © Cleo Cordell 1995

Typeset by CentraCet Limited, Cambridge
Printed and bound by Cox & Wyman Ltd, Reading,
Berks

ISBN 0 352 32987 4

Chapter One

Carlotta Mendoza lay back against the embroidered linen sheets and watched the young man dress himself. The morning sunlight sent a glow to lighten the rose-wood panelling which lined the walls and struck glints from the leaded windows.

With his back turned to her, Hernando pulled the loose shirt over his head and tied the laces at the neckline. Now and then he glanced over his shoulder as if expecting her to comment on his prowess as a lover.

Carlotta decided that she would not give him that satisfaction. He was conceited enough already and there were women enough to flutter around him and feed his vanity.

She yawned and stretched, lifting her heavy hair away from her neck and leaving it to lie in a dark plume across the pillow. A sweet langour spread through her as she relaxed the tension of her limbs. She could smell her own body. It was ripe with musky odours, but she wouldn't bathe for a while. She liked to smell the mingled juices of sexual pleasure on her skin.

Her eyes swept over the young man's body, admiring the wide shoulders and slim hips. His legs were long

1

and muscular. Not many men could still look potent and desirable whilst wearing nothing more than a baggy shirt which reached to his upper thighs, but Hernando did.

'Do you mind me lying here and watching you?' she asked him, her voice low and husky with a teasing note.

She already knew the answer to her question. It was evident in the set of his shoulders, in the way his face was now turned resolutely away from her.

'No, I do not mind,' he lied.

Carlotta's full red mouth curved in a smile. Most men found her directness disconcerting. In Catholic Spain a woman had few choices. She could be the personification of the virgin Mary, a respectable God-fearing widow, or a whore. Carlotta was none of those things, or rather she was a mixture of all three, a fact which both attracted men to her and repulsed them at the same time.

Perfectly aware of this and accepting the fact as something she could not change, Carlotta lived by her own set of morals. As a rich widow she could take her pick of personable young men, all of them hopeful of becoming her next husband. It amused her to have them dancing attendance on her – they were moths to her flame – but she had not the slightest intention of re-marrying. One arranged marriage had been enough for her and it had been no loss at all when Charles Mendoza – forty years her senior and a cruel and miserly man – had died two years since of the bloody flux, leaving her everything he owned.

'Will I come to you again tonight?' Hernando asked, a self-satisfied smile on his lips. How can you refuse me? his eyes said.

'I'll send a message to tell you when you may next attend me,' she said coolly.

She could have told him that she had a portrait sitting with the Greek artist who was much in favour at court,

2

but decided not to volunteer any explanation. To give an excuse was to suggest that she regretted spending the night without him. Hernando was a pleasant enough young man. Good-looking certainly, and intelligent. He was an ardent if unpractised lover too, but she didn't want to get to know him too well. That could lead to a dangerous intimacy and then he would get delusions of ownership. Carlotta valued her freedom above all else – being married to Charles for four years had taught her that.

Lifting her arms she interlocked her fingers behind her head, lifted her chin, and continued her examination of the handsome young man who had shared her bed.

Hernando's profile, clean cut and silvered by the morning light, was as pure as the saint in the stained glass window of the cathedral. He turned towards her then and she saw the flare of heat in his eyes before he could disguise it.

Slowly she pushed the rumpled sheets down to her waist, amused by the fact that he couldn't keep his eyes from straying to her high round breasts and fixing on her large, rosy nipples. Despite his annoyance at the way she was dismissing him, Hernando could not help but react to her beauty, to the earthy sexuality which she knew oozed from her every pore.

'You could do me a further service if you've a mind to,' she said huskily, holding back a smile as she noticed the sulky set of his mouth.

She could see that he was tempted. His eyes were glazed with lust, but the fingers of one hand were clenched into a fist. Throwing back her head she laughed, a rich rippling sound which was infectious. It was always this way. Her lovers never knew whether to cover her with kisses, beg for her favours, or stride angrily from the bed chamber.

Hernando was too smitten and too inexperienced to storm out and risk offending her.

3

'Well then?' she said huskily. 'What's it to be? Have you yet some ink in your pen?'

Hernando's mouth twisted in a wry grin as he capitulated.

'Witch,' he murmured. 'What gimcrackery have you used to enslave me?'

Leaning forward, he covered her naked torso with his partly-clothed body. His fingers tangled in her unruly black hair and he pulled her face close to his. His firm young mouth covered hers, his tongue pushing hotly into her mouth, lashing against her own. Carlotta responded readily, clutching at his broad shoulders and breathing in the fresh animal scent of him.

The flare of lust took her by surprise. This had been a game – she had wanted only to tease him – but suddenly she needed to feel him inside her. Sometimes she thought that she was only truly alive when she was making love.

'Do it to me now,' she ordered, twisting sideways and pushing the rumpled sheets aside. Lifting her legs, she parted her thighs. 'I'm ready for you.'

Her coynte was wet and swollen from the night of shared passion, the thickened sex-lips bedewed with a slick of sperm and female moisture. Her bluntness shocked him, she saw, but his fine young cock sprang up potently before him.

Sitting back on his haunches, Hernando looked down at her exposed sex, so shockingly red and glistening against the silky black hair which covered her pubis. As he ran his fingers down the inside of one firm white thigh, Carlotta shuddered. Slowly he moved inwards towards the pulsing centre of her, all the time watching the progress of his fingers across her skin.

'What is it? Have you never seen a naked woman spread before you?'

He shook his head. 'Before last night – no. It is unseemly. My wife has never stripped naked in front of

4

me. She is a God-fearing, virtuous woman and even bathes in her shift.'

'And your lovers?'

'They ask me to blow out the candle before they even raise their skirts. None of them would lie thus before me, even were I to ask them.'

Carlotta chuckled. She knew that this was normal for most women. The church taught that the female body must be kept covered lest men be inflamed unduly by gazing upon the fount of their bodily wickedness. But she had never cared much for the idea that women's bodies were inherently sinful. It was the minds of men which were at fault.

'Poor Hernando,' she said, not troubling to disguise the amusement in her voice. 'So that is why you are so fascinated by Eve's furrow between my thighs? Look your fill then. Taste me again if you wish. You relished the flavour of my coynte last night.'

He cursed softly, a blush staining his cheeks. 'You should not say such things. It . . . it is not right. I've never met a woman like you. You're so beautiful, so fascinating. But you're bad.'

Carlotta shrugged and her breasts jiggled. 'I've tried to be good. But it's so . . . dull. I cannot believe that it is bad to share such pleasure. Is it so wrong to ask for what I want just because I am a woman?'

Hernando shook his head. 'I don't know. I think it is wrong. But when I'm with you it doesn't seem to matter. Oh, I know that you don't love me. But I can't resist you.'

'Then stop trying.'

With a groan he slid his hands under her buttocks and lifted her up to meet him. In a single smooth movement he sank his cock all the way inside her.

Carlotta arched under him, loving the way his thick shaft filled her and thrust so strongly inside her. The rigid flesh stretched her, knocked against her womb, and sent little ripples of sensation coursing through her. She clenched her inner muscles around him and tipped up her pubis, grinding the head of her erect and aching bud against the base of his belly.

'Sweet Jesus, Mother of God,' Hernando gasped as he surged against her, his taut buttocks clenching with each inward thrust.

He took a long time to come; she had ridden him hard all night. Grasping her breasts, Carlotta pinched and rolled her nipples. She knew that the sight of her caressing herself maddened him. The first time he had seen her stroke her breasts he had been so shocked that he had reached his climax at once, spilling his seed into her rucked up skirts.

Hernando plunged against her, his balls knocking softly against the base of her upturned buttocks. Carlotta moaned, grasping his slim hips so that she could direct the pressure and depth of his thrusts.

'Oh you wonderful bitch! You wanton!' he groaned as Carlotta arched her back and worked herself back and forth on his shaft.

The damp blond curls at Hernando's groin tickled the bead of flesh which was at the centre of her pleasure and she felt the strong internal pulsing begin as her crisis swept through her. She cried out and her nails dug into his muscular buttocks, raking at the warm golden skin. He grunted and pulled out of her, his semen spattering her pale belly before he collapsed shuddering against her.

Carlotta stroked his tumbled blond hair, smoothing it back from his high forehead. She held him until his breathing returned to normal. After a while, Hernando eased himself away from her, the love-lock hanging over one shoulder brushing against her cheek. Slowly he pushed himself to a sitting position.

Reaching out a hand he stroked the damp curls that covered her mound and then ran a fingertip down the slick parting of her sex. His touch was tender, wondering.

'I could stay a while,' he said.

She shook her head and pushed him gently away.

'Better that you do not.'

Hernando pushed himself to his knees and took the hand she held out to him. His fingers were warm against her skin and his mouth was soft as he kissed each long pale finger in turn.

'Your nails are like almonds,' he said. 'Do you know that I adore you?'

'Beautiful boy,' she whispered. 'Go now. I have work to do this day. I'll send my messenger to you, soon.'

If she had not been expecting a visit from Don Felipe Escada she might have been tempted to spend the forenoon with Hernando. He was so lusty and energetic and so deliciously easy to shock.

As he pulled on his hose she stifled a yawn, the warm after-glow of her last orgasm already fading. Her mind ran on ahead. The French fencing master would be here in an hour to give her her daily lesson. There should be time for that before Don Felipe arrived, then she would put on her finest gown to receive her guest.

'I'll take my leave of you and await your message with eagerness,' Hernando said, breaking into her thoughts. He was dressed now in a quilted leather doublet and breeches. When he bowed his single pearl earring trembled. 'God give you good day, Donna Mendoza.'

Carlotta's mouth twitched at this formal leave-taking. 'And good day to you, Hernando.'

As soon as he had crossed the bed chamber and gone out of the panelled door, she picked up a bell and rang for Juanita. Her maid appeared almost at once, tray in hand.

'I've brought your morning hippocras and there is new bread and honey,' Juanita said. 'I heard your guest leaving and I thought you might be in need of something . . . strengthening.'

7

'Don't be impertinent,' Carlotta said mildly and without rancour. 'Set the tray down beside me.'

Juanita had been with her since they were both children and she had no secrets from her companion. It was, however, sometimes necessary to remind the other woman who was the mistress.

'Draw a bath for me, Juanita and lay out the plum velvet gown and silver under-skirt for later. I'll change after my fencing lesson. I want to look my best, Don Felipe is an important man.'

Juanita bobbed a curtsey, her pretty oval face lighting up with a smile. The prospect of a visit from such a man was exciting. Perhaps her mistress might consider him as a suitor. To Juanita's mind it was high time that Carlotta re-married.

'Is Don Felipe a handsome man?' Juanita asked innocently.

Carlotta flashed her a grin. 'I don't know. I can hardly remember him. We have met perhaps thrice, and the last time I was thirteen years old. I cannot imagine what he wants with me.'

I can, Juanita thought. I'll wager that he wants what they all want. Sometimes, for all her fiery independence and worldliness, Carlotta could be quite naive.

'There surely cannot be any red-blooded man in the whole of Castile who has not heard of you,' she said. 'You are the most beautiful and eligible widow in these parts.'

When Carlotta did not reply she was emboldened to continue. 'It's one thing to take lovers, but tongues will begin to wag if you do not seek to re-marry. It's been two years now. A year since you were out of mourning. It's not . . . respectable to stay as you are . . .'

Under Carlotta's glare, Juanita faltered.

'You mean that I shouldn't act like a man and take lovers whenever I choose to? But it would be permissible to do that if I had the protection of a husband? Someone who would expect me to wait upon him, play

8

fast and loose with my money, and force me to be discreet. Is that it?'

Juanita nodded, but did not reply. She knew when she was beaten. Carlotta had a knack of making the most normal laws of society sound ridiculous. Inwardly she shrugged, for as long as she had known her Carlotta had been a law unto herself. She loved her friend and mistress like a sister, but she worried about her. Carlotta was apt to be rashly spoken and not afraid of offending those who disagreed with her views.

'Will you wish to wear your amethyst earrings?' she said resignedly.

'Here endeth the lesson, eh?' Carlotta said, her eyes glittering with good humour. 'Yes, the amethysts and the ropes of pearls. Thank you Juanita. That is all.'

When Juanita had left the bed chamber, she poured herself some hippocras. Sipping from the chased-gold goblet she savoured the sweet mustiness of the spiced wine, tasting grapes and cinnamon and a trace of cloves. In a moment she reached across to an oak chest and picked up the letter which had arrived the previous day.

She was proud of her ability to read and Charles, whatever else his faults, had also been proud of his wife's accomplishments. Not many of his peers could boast a wife who had read the classics and was able to offer an opinion on the works of Orpheus. He had felt that her refinement reflected well on himself.

Unfolding the parchment Carlotta glanced at the ribbon and the heavy wax seal before running her eyes over Don Felipe's crabbed handwriting. The letter was short and gave no indication of the reason for his visit. It simply said that he would call on her at midday and that they had something urgent to discuss.

She had only a vague recollection of a tall, rather severe, dark-haired man. But, then, everyone seemed tall to a child. Don Felipe was a merchant who had made his fortune in wool. He visited the family home on occasion to discuss business with her father. He had seemed stiff and humourless, his manner formal and she had not liked him very much.

A chill ran down her back and she shivered. How odd, for the morning was bright and warm.

Draining the cup of wine, she poured herself another measure, then slid back down under the bedclothes. She wished that Juanita would hurry up and bring her bath water. It would be pleasant to lie in the perfumed water strewn with rose petals while Juanita washed her hair and rubbed it with orange-flower water.

Plumping up the pillows, she closed her eyes. The bedclothes smelt of Hernando and she smiled as she remembered their night of love. In a day or two she would send him a message.

Don Felipe Escada eased himself back in his saddle. He had been riding since the break of dawn and was anticipating taking advantage of Carlotta's hospitality.

He remembered Carlotta as a dainty thing, with large dark eyes, olive skin, and a great unruly mass of dark hair which struggled to escape from her headdress. The last time he had visited her father he had been struck by her poise and pert manner. She had been twelve or thirteen and her swelling hips and budding breasts had prompted an unexpected response in him.

Even at that age Carlotta had possessed many of the devilish wiles of a woman grown. His staff of Adam had stiffened and become an aching rod, pulsing with a life of its own. Remembering how he had hurried home and bathed in icy water and then kneeled naked on the cold floor of his private chapel, he flushed. It had taken hours of prayer before the image of the pretty child faded from his mind.

His well-shaped mouth curved in a grim smile. Unclean desires had never made him their master. Felipe understood that the answer to human weakness was the stringent mortification of the flesh. For no man was safe from the boundless desires of women who, as the weaker sex, were prisoners of the unbounded lusts of their privy parts.

Just thinking about such things made him hot and aroused evil humours in his blood. It was a good thing that he wore a hair shirt under his studded velvet doublet. The coarse fabric rubbed against the old welts and new scratches on his back, but he ignored the prickling discomfort. In an evil world, where the threat of Godlessness haunted him, Felipe was secure in the knowledge that he had himself under control.

As he passed through the village and urged his horse onto the road which led to the large house, he thought again of Carlotta. I have been too harsh, he reasoned, no doubt she has changed. Marriage schooled a woman, teaching her the virtues of modesty and forbearance. Also the practice of affording wifely duties to a husband tempered young passions.

By all accounts Charles Mendoza had been a hard man, ruling his household with a rod of iron. Felipe expected to find a quiet respectable widow, a woman who would give him little problem and be amenable to the offer he would put to her.

It was perhaps a pity that her circumstances would have to change so dramatically, but he gave that only a passing thought. Donna Carlotta Mendoza was merely a pawn in the game of her betters. As long as she gave him no trouble he would see to it that she was adequately provided for. There ought to be enough left from the sale of the estate to leave her with a generous dowry. Her best course would be to get married again.

He permitted himself a dry smile. Perhaps if she was personable and pliant enough he might consider marrying her himself. He had been thinking that it was time to take a wife. It would be pleasant to have a biddable woman to run his house and warm his bed on cold winter nights.

Ah, there was the house, the pale stone visible

through the avenue of poplar trees. The harsh cry of a peacock split the morning air. Felipe dug his spurs into his mount's side and trotted up the wide avenue which cut through a formal garden. Scents of rosemary, thyme, and lavender reached him from the stone urns which were placed amongst the trees.

He was early for their appointment, something which was quite deliberate. Carlotta would be taken by surprise and her reactions to him would be unguarded because of that.

Felipe dismounted and handed his horse to the groom. He smoothed down his doublet and straightened his hat, his mouth curving with good humour. He liked to have the advantage over people.

Chapter Two

Carlotta flicked her thick dark plait over one shoulder and concentrated on defending herself from the attack by Monsieur Draycot.

Her booted feet were planted solidly on the oak boards and she gave no ground as she thrust and parried, matching the fencing master stroke for stroke. A trickle of sweat ran down her neck and soaked into her chemise, but she paid it no heed.

Suddenly she locked swords with Draycot. There was the light of triumph in the master's eyes. Another second and he would be the victor. Shifting her weight and twisting her wrist in a movement of her own devising, she put all her strength into forcing his arm upwards.

'Touché, monsieur!' she cried, as his sword surged upwards into a spinning silver arc.

Draycot bowed from the waist, his good-humoured face splitting in a grin.

'It is no no dishonour to be bettered by you, Donna Mendoza. When the pupil bests the master, why – that is the best flattery of all!' He crossed the barn and retrieved his sword.

Carlotta stood, hands on hips, waiting for him to

13

continue with their lesson. Draycot's eyes slid past her shoulder as he straightened up and she turned to see what he was looking at.

A tall man, dressed in figured black velvet and wearing a short cloak, strode into the barn, accompanied by a flustered looking Juanita.

'Your pardon, mistress,' Juanita stammered. 'Don Felipe insisted that I bring him out to see you at once. I explained that you were not ready to receive visitors . . .'

'God give you good day,' Felipe said, doffing his hat and trying without success to hide his shock at her choice of clothes.

'Likewise to you, sir,' Carlotta said, glancing at the stern face of her visitor.

'I seem to have found you indisposed,' he said stiffly.

'Not at all, sir. I am dressed for the task in hand. Had you arrived at the time you stated you would have found me dressed fit to attend you.'

It amused her to see the flush creep into his pale cheeks as he took in the details of her loose shirt, leather breeches, and high leather boots. She knew that her stays were visible through the damp shirt and no doubt he could see the tops of her breasts bulging provocatively upwards towards the loose drawstring neckline.

She had not remembered details of Felipe Escada's face. Now she saw that he had high cheekbones and hooded dark eyes. His dark hair was only lightly streaked with grey and his mouth was firm and sensual. He would have been a handsome man if he had not worn an expression of extreme disapproval. He looks as if he is standing down-wind of the privy, she thought.

'Do . . . do you wish me to take Don Philipe into the presence chamber and serve him refreshment?' Juanita said, a slight tremor in her voice displaying her unease.

'That would be most pleasant. Will you not join me, Donna Carlotta?' Felipe's voice held an easy authority, as if it did not occur to him that she would refuse.

14

Juanita darted a nervous glance at him and Carlotta felt a flicker of anger. Who did Felipe think he was to come here upsetting her servants? He had come striding out to the barn uninvited and now he sought to order her about.

'No matter, Juanita,' she said coolly. 'If Don Felipe wishes to wait until I have finished my lesson I will be pleased to place myself entirely at his disposal.'

Felipe's dark eyes flashed with anger and Carlotta suppressed a laugh. You didn't expect that did you, she thought? She was amused to see Juanita's eyes widen in horror at her daring.

'As you wish,' Felipe said, recovering his poise.

He strolled across the barn, his spurs ringing on the oak floor. As he leaned against one of the brick pillars which supported the wooden buttresses, Juanita bobbed a curtsey and hurried thankfully out of the barn.

Carlotta turned her attention back to Draycot who had been waiting patiently. Assuming an 'on guard' position she prepared to continue her lesson.

'How now, Draycot,' she grinned.

For another ten minutes she concentrated on bettering her swordplay. Draycot gave her no quarter and by the time the lesson was over, her hair was sticking in damp strands to her forehead and her loose cambric shirt was plastered to her body outlining every dip and curve of her torso.

She was conscious that Felipe's eyes never left her tiny waist and swelling hips. His mouth was taut with disapproval as he took in every detail of her leather-clad buttocks and thighs, but his eyes burned with repressed lust. She felt a wicked urge to provoke him. He was even easier to shock than Hernando.

Monsieur Draycot took his leave and Carlotta bent forward to tug at the top of her boot, the action causing the loose neck of her shirt to gape open. Felipe was treated to a goodly portion of cleavage and a view all the way down to her corseted stomach. She heard the hiss of his indrawn breath.

Felipe had clenched both fists and seemed to be having great trouble in controlling himself. His mouth tightened into a thin line and his eyes darkened further with emotion. The tension in the air was almost palpable.

Suppressing a smile, she said evenly, 'Well, Don Felipe, shall we go into the house? I am ready for some refreshment now. And I confess that I am curious about the reason for your visit.'

Felipe bowed stiffly and followed her. He seemed to be having trouble swallowing. She noticed that he had drawn his short cloak over one shoulder, so that it covered his groin. She found the thought of his unwilling arousal stimulating and wondered what he looked like naked. His shoulders were broad and his waist slim. He had no slackness of the belly, unlike many others his age.

In the presence chamber Juanita served them with wine, then withdrew to the kitchen. Carlotta decided not to change into the gown which Juanita had laid out earlier. There seemed no point now in trying to impress Felipe with her charm and grace. Besides, she had the distinct impression that he was far more affected by her male apparel and she was not entirely displeased by the fact.

Sitting in a chair she waved Felipe to its twin which was opposite the hearth. She crossed her legs, swinging one booted foot, and took a deep swallow of the wine. Philipe sipped his wine slowly before he began speaking. He averted his eyes from her and she had the impression that he was gathering his dignity.

'I have some news which will come as a shock to you, Donna Carlotta, but I see no better way of stating my case than to be forthright.'

She smiled. 'Then please be so. I prefer straight talking.'

16

'Very well. I come here today to present you with these papers and to give you notice that you are to quit this house and grounds before four months have passed.'

Carlotta looked at him blankly. 'What words are these to come calling with? Surely you jest.'

Felipe shook his head. 'I assure you that I do not. Shall you ring for your scribe and have him read these papers to you?'

She held out her hand. 'I read and write very well, sir. And will judge the content of these papers for myself.'

His look of surprise would have been amusing in other circumstances. As he handed her the papers he said, 'I do not approve of such education for women. It breeds a wantonness of thought and a weakness of reasoning powers.'

Ignoring his comment, she scanned the pages. Her pulses quickened as she absorbed the message contained within the writing. The papers were legal documents, naming Felipe as the rightful owner of her house, land, and all properties.

'What trickery is this?' she said angrily. 'My husband left me everything. You can have no claim on anything that is mine.'

'You are mistaken. That document you are holding gives me the right to claim recompense for debts incurred by your father. As his only living relative you are responsible for paying those debts.'

Carlotta flung the papers at him. 'This cannot be lawful. I know nothing of my father's debts. You have a damned nerve, sire, if you think you can come here and order me off my own land! I'll see you in Hell before you relieve me of a single sod!'

Felipe stood up, a dark flush staining his cheeks.

'I shall be glad to relieve you of these lands. You are an immodest woman with an evil tongue and are not fit to own such properties! I have seen how you flaunt yourself. Instead of concerning yourself with household duties you wear men's clothes and fight with a sword.' He paused and when he continued his voice was hoarse. 'I know that you showed me your bubs with the hope of inflaming my passions, but I am armoured by my faith against such as you. God's blood woman, but you're no better than a common bawd!'

Carlotta's temper rose. She tossed her head.

'And you, sire, are a hypocrite! I saw the way you looked at me in the barn. You wanted nothing less than to tear off my garments and paw my breasts. It is ever the way of men to blame a woman for the thoughts which are bred by their own hearts!'

For a moment she thought he would choke.

'Enough of this,' he spat. 'Hold your vile tongue. You do not profit by berating me. It were better for you to beg me to show you mercy. I have no wish to turn you out and leave you destitute, but I will if you insist on acting this way.'

He took a step closer and she saw that he was breathing heavily. There was a sheen of sweat on his upper lip. 'There is a way for you to keep your position, but it will mean becoming modest in your thoughts and putting yourself under the guidance of a man in the way which God has ordained for women. If you will subject yourself to my care, you may yet be won back to a state of grace.'

Carlotta trembled with rage. Oh, Blood of Adam, he was talking about marriage. The self-righteous knave. Did he really think that he could blackmail her? Was this what he was about? She was convinced now that the documents *were* forgeries, a tawdry bauble to threaten her with.

'Well? What have you to say?' he asked.

She saw the anger and the lust warring on his face. His lips twisted with triumph as he saw the uncertainty on her face and she lost all control. There was a red mist before her eyes.

'This, is my answer!'

Picking up the jug of wine she threw it full at him.

Felipe spluttered and coughed as he wiped his face on his velvet sleeve.

'You will regret that,' he said coldly. 'Hell-cat woman, I would take a birch to your back if you were mine. I'll see you in court. I gave you a chance, but you spurned me. So be it. I'll strip you of everything, even your shift, and watch you walk bare-foot and bare-arsed through the village.'

'Get out! Get out now! Before I call my servants and have you thrown out.'

Felipe began moving towards the door, drops of wine running down his velvet hose. At the door he turned and smiled thinly.

'You do not believe that I can take everything you own. That is your mistake and a grave error of judgement. I have powerful friends and the law on my side. I'll be back with proof of my claim and men to remove you from this house! Think on this. I'm sure that you will see the wisdom of accepting my offer. I look forward to our next meeting. By Our Lady you'll be singing a different tune then.'

As soon as the door closed behind him Carlotta began to shake with reaction. Hardly able to believe that the conversation had taken place she sank back into the chair and sat staring at the piled logs in the hearth. She didn't hear Juanita come into the room.

'He cannot do it, can he?'

Carlotta reached for her maid's hand.

'No. He was just trying to frighten me into marrying him. What a hateful man.'

Juanita cast her a worried look. 'He is rich and powerful. Perhaps it were better to have treated him with more respect.'

Carlotta cursed softly.

'The day that I am frightened by one such as he, is the day that I enter a nunnery!'

The prospect was so unlikely that they both began to laugh. But although Carlotta laughed as loudly as Juanita, she could not quite banish the little shadow of fear that spread subtle fingers through her veins.

Felipe went directly to his bed-chamber and opened the door which led to his private chapel.

Stripping off his clothes he threw them into a heap on the cold flagstones. His hands were shaking as he removed his boots and hose. Facing the altar where two candles burnt, one either side of a wooden statue of the Virgin Mary, he fell to his knees.

The cold of the stone floor bit into his calves, but did nothing to quell his ardour. His erect penis stood up potently in front of him. The shaft was so engorged that it was painful, the glans as purple and shiny as a ripe plum. He had been erect since the first moment he saw her in the barn.

Her immodest clothes had shocked him deeply. He had never before seen a woman wearing leather hose. Her bottom was so provocative. It seemed to tremble as she walked. And the shape of her waist and breasts were visible through the thin man's shirt she wore. What breasts they were: full and round and crested with berry-red teats. He had glimpsed one of them when she bent over and displayed herself to him.

Oh, the wanton trull. He itched to carry out his threat. He imagined her white skin reddening under the birch, her lush young body twisting and writhing as his arm rose and fell. He saw the weals standing out on her slender back and felt them hot and delicious under his fingertips.

His cock twitched and pulsed as his lips moved in prayer. Hunching his shoulders, he clamped his hands to his raging groin where his two cods felt as tight as stones. His lips moved faster as he prayed, endeavouring to banish the image of Carlotta from his mind.

Her beauty was sinful – the beauty of the Devil. She

was the very image of original sin; was not woman born guilty of Eve's crime? Even in anger she was splendid, with her cheeks flushed and her black eyes spitting sparks. He did not blame himself for responding to her. He was only a man and the church taught that the flesh was weak.

If he had known that Carlotta was so beguiling he would have sent a messenger, but it was too late now. He was caught in her web. Perhaps she had slipped a love philtre into his wine, for there was nothing before him but her face, her eyes, her mouth.

Dear God, her mouth. So lush, yet soft and fresh like a flower.

On the altar there was a length of coarse rope, knotted at intervals. Crawling towards the altar on his belly he reached up and grasped the rope. As he began to strike the rigid staff of his manhood, he moaned. The pain seemed to vibrate right through him and he writhed as splinters of heat cramped in his belly.

His arm fell again and again and the agony was hot and throbbing. He cried out, calling out the names of martyred saints as he thrashed the rope against his throbbing red organ.

'God save me. Deliver me from temptation,' he moaned dropping the rope and falling onto his hands and knees as his semen spurted in creamy jets onto the flagstones.

As the last sensations of his climax faded he had an image of Carlotta walking through her village. Her shift was torn and stained and her hair hung down her back in a tangled dark mass. There were scratches on her legs and her feet were bare, so white and slender against the dust of the track. She looked like a penitent.

He stretched out his arms as if he would gather her up and press her against his breast.

'Carlotta,' he whispered. 'Marry me and be my salvation.'

Collapsing onto his side he began to sob.

Chapter Three

Carlotta stood looking out of the window of her bed-chamber. She had a clear view of the garden with its fore-court, bordered lawns, and tree-lined walks. At this time of year the air was heavy with the scents of pinks and gillyflowers.

Behind a screen of fruit trees was the kitchen garden and beyond that the vineyards which sloped down to the river. Her gaze travelled to the near distance where deer frolicked in the park. Through the trees she could just see the tops of the village houses and the tall building which was the mill.

Normally the sight of her well-kept grounds and productive holdings lifted her spirits, but today there was a knot of tension in her stomach. It was eight weeks since Don Felipe had presented her with the documents by which he laid claim to her house and lands and it seemed that his threats were not idle after all.

She crumpled up the letter she held and let it drop to the floor.

'He'll not rob me. I won't allow it,' she said, but her voice wavered, the small sound of it frightening her.

The letter had come from Diaz de Cerdagne, the man she had appointed as her agent. He regretted the fact that there was nothing more he could do. For the past weeks he had been investigating Don Felipe's claim. Carlotta had hoped that it would become obvious that Felipe was a man of bluster rather than substance. But her hopes had been dashed.

Diaz's letter made it clear that the claim had been upheld in the courts. He advised Carlotta to make arrangements to move to a small house on the estate.

'Don Felipe is inclined to be generous,' Diaz wrote. 'You may take what furniture you wish and whichever members of your household as are necessary for your comfort. A small yearly allowance is to be set aside. You will not be left destitute.'

Carlotta pressed her lips together, tears of anger prickling her eye-lids. So this is what it is to come to.

The house which Diaz mentioned was tiny. There would be room only for Juanita and herself. What was to become of her? She would have little hope of a future. As soon as her altered state became common knowledge she would be shunned by those whom she had counted as her friends. Either that or they would offer charity. She did not think she could bear their pitying glances.

The offer of the house and allowance was no real choice, as Don Felipe well knew. It was a gesture on his part only. If she wished to keep her place and position she must agree to become his wife. She shuddered, thinking of his hard cold eyes and his sensual mouth. No, it was impossible to put herself into the power of such a man. As her husband he would have the right to mould her to his will, make her into the sort of cowed milk-sop who hung onto any man's every word.

Her anger rose until she could taste it in the back of her throat. It was hot and sour, but she began to feel better. She always felt stronger when in a temper. It was time to shake off the fear. What she needed was a plan. It was no use to sit waiting for her fate to befall her.

Crossing the chamber she sat at her writing desk and reached for parchment. Dipping the quill into ink she began penning a letter to Diaz.

'It is most important that we meet. Will you come to my house exactly a week from receipt of this letter? And please to bring with you every document, every last scrap of information which concerns Don Felipe Escada. I wish to know my enemy and therefore must have an understanding of his business dealings, who his friends are, and which of the officials at court are in his pay. Also I have certain transactions for you to make for me . . .'

For a while she wrote rapidly, then gave a sigh of satisfaction. Sprinkling sand on the ink she shook the letter dry, then folded it before affixing her seal.

With luck she ought to be able to salvage something from this sorry mess. She hoped that she could trust Diaz. He was a man of integrity and she had always paid him well for past services, but she knew that he was just as likely to desert her – did not all the wolves come running when they scented their prey weakening.

'They are here, mistress. Don Felipe is riding at the head of a great band of men. What shall you do?'

Juanita wrung her hands as she peered through the leaded windows of the presence chamber. The sound of horses' hooves rang on the cobbled road outside.

Carlotta stood up and smoothed down her skirt. The moment had arrived.

'I must go out and face them,' she said with a confidence she did not feel.

She knew that she looked pale and drawn. She had not slept well since the court officials had served notice on her three days since. There was some security in knowing that her secret arrangements had been made,

24

but the thought of what she was about to do made her heart surge like a mill-race.

Juantia spun around and crossed the room in an instant. Her eyes were blurred with unshed tears.

'Oh mistress, please wait,' she said, gripping Carlotta's arm. 'All is not lost. Tell Felipe that you will agree to all his demands. He will be merciful and we could be happy living in that little house.'

Carlotta patted Juanita's hand and then removed it gently. She smiled fondly.

'And think you that he would ever let me alone? He means to have me, Juanita, by fair means or foul.'

'Then you are leaving? But where will you go . . . no matter. Wherever you go, I will come too. You are all the family I have.'

'Bless you for your loyalty. I fear that it might be tried to its limit when you know my intentions.'

'I care not. I'll never leave you,' Juanita sobbed, wiping her face on her over-skirt.

Carlotta was near to tears herself and that fact made her brusque. 'If you really mean that, stop blubbing and go and pack your belongings. Take only what you can carry.' She held up her hand when Juanita would have asked questions. 'You'll have to trust me. Saddle two horses and bring them to the front of the house. Will you do that?'

After a moment Juanita nodded and hurried out of the room.

Carlotta walked through the house steeling herself not to dwell on all the dear familiar things around her. This cannot be happening, she thought. It seemed like a dream, but the solid presence of Don Felipe, his retainers, and the court officials were testament to reality.

Taking a deep breath, she opened the front door and stood facing the gathered men. Don Felipe doffed his cap and stepped forward, a frown on his face. He was dressed in a garnet coloured doublet and breeches and his ruff was snowy white against his chin. *He is dressed for a celebration*, Carlotta thought tartly.

'I did not think to find you still in the main house, Donna Mendoza. Did you not receive my notice?'

She lifted her chin and met his gaze, her dark eyes challenging. 'I received it,' she said coolly. 'Until you step over this threshold the house is mine still.'

Don Felipe's eyes fell under her scrutiny. She saw with satisfaction that there were two high spots of colour along his cheekbones. He motioned to a man standing beside him. Carlotta had a glimpse of a thick-set fellow with long brown hair, before he pushed rudely past her and disappeared into the house. In a moment he re-appeared.

'Nothing has been touched, Felipe,' the man said. 'The furniture is all there. Seems to me that the trull is intent on staying on. Mayhap she's a fancy to play merry bedfellows with you!'

'I'd sooner roll in the mire with a pig!' Carlotta spat.

There was a ripple of laughter from the watchers, hastily suppressed when Felipe rounded on them.

'Be silent,' he said, flushing darkly.

'She's a spirited wench and comely too,' the brown-haired man commented.

Carlotta allowed her gaze to flicker over the man. From the detailed inventory supplied by Diaz she judged this to be Alberto, Felipe's associate and a man privy to all his secrets. Turning aside from the glowering Felipe for a moment she smiled at Alberto, lowering her eyelids provocatively.

Alberto's face lit up with interest and he lapsed into silence. She felt his eyes on her as Felipe began speaking.

'Can you not see that it is too late for stubborness. Collect your things, woman, and away to the house which has been set aside for you. Quickly now, before I change my mind about letting you live on the . . . on my estate.'

26

Carlotta faced him squarely, the corner of her mouth lifting with dislike. His arrogance was insufferable. She saw the longing in his eyes, though she guessed that he did not realise that he was so easy to read. It would take the refined tortures of the Inquisition to make a man such as he admit to having base desires.

In that instant she decided to give him a final lesson.

'I would not live near you if you were to promise me all the gold in the new worlds,' she said. 'But come to my chamber. I have one thing to show you before I leave.'

'Leave? But where will you go?'

She smiled. For a moment he looked as if he actually cared what happened to her. His dark eyebrows dipped into a frown and he seemed unaware of the titters and whispers of interest that were rippling around the assembly.

'Just come with me, if you please,' she said.

The brown-haired man, Alberto, stepped forward. 'You might need a witness, Felipe. This wench is as slippery as a bawd in her courses. I'll come too.'

Carlotta hid her distaste. Alberto was crude and foul-mouthed, but she would have need of him later. She smiled.

'Why not?' she said sweetly.

Felipe ran a finger around the inside of his ruff. The pleated lace was scratching at his hot skin.

Carlotta climbed the staircase ahead of him and he tried not to dwell on the fact that she looked even more beautiful than he remembered. Her gown of violet murry-cloth overlaid with silver lace was spread over a bell-shaped farthingale. The embroidered stomacher drew attention to her small waist and pressed the swell of her breasts upwards.

She looked every bit the proper lady this day, although the memory of her in leather hose and shirt had the power to dry his mouth with wanting. He felt a leashed excitement. Carlotta was such a challenge, still peddling her tricks even though the game was lost.

He was going to enjoy teaching her to be self-effacing and obedient. Soon she would be his to order as he wished. The thought of her body, so soft and lush, so white and fragrant, made the blood pound in his ears.

For she would consent to be his wife. What other choice had she? With victory in sight, he decided to humour her for a while longer.

Alberto stamped along beside him and Felipe contained his irritation. Alberto was a good friend, steadfast in his loyalty, but he would have preferred to be alone with Carlotta. Still, no matter. They would have years together.

'Come in, sires,' Carlotta said, entering the bedchamber and waving them to a seat.

Felipe looked around in awed fascination. This was where Carlotta slept, unclothed herself, brushed out her long black hair, washed her privy parts. The scent of her perfume, orange-water and cloves, filled the air.

'I have something to show you, Felipe,' Carlotta said, reaching for a large, square-shaped object draped in cloth which was propped against one wall. 'If you will be so kind as to help me,' she said indicating that she needed Alberto's assistance.

Between them they lifted up the object and placed it on the tester bed, where it leaned against the carved oak posts. Felipe stood up and faced the bed, frowning in puzzlement.

'What new trickery is this?'

With a flourish, Carlotta flipped up the cloth to reveal a painting. Felipe could not contain his gasp of scandalised horror. He was speechless, struck dumb by the enormity of what he saw before him.

Alberto chuckled. 'Well, well. El Greco must have felt a tickle or two in his loins when he painted this!'

Felipe stared at the painting. Carlotta was lying on a fur covered settle. She wore nothing but a pair of garnet earrings. Her hair was loose, spilling over her shoulders to mask one breast but leaving the other bare. One arm lay along her thigh. The fingers of one hand were curved over her pubis, drawing attention to that forbidden area even while it veiled it.

Felipe swallowed, his throat suddenly as dry as dust. Surely that was a shadow under her hand, a suggestion of the hair on her Venus mound. She had dared to have a famous artist – one who was known for his religious works – depict her womanly parts, the sinful vulva, the ever-hungry maw, by which men were corrupted.

Her wickedness thrilled and appalled him. He had not dreamed that she was capable of something such as this.

His cock stirred into life and he backed away from the painting and sat down hastily. He felt as if a hot stone had become lodged somewhere in his lower belly and the pressure was making his cods ache. The pounding of his blood made him feel light-headed.

'This is an outrage! It's filth! The grossest wickedness!' he cried.

Alberto chuckled. 'Surely it is. But I'd rather look on it than all the iconry in Christendom!'

Carlotta laughed too and the sound of it was rich and throaty. Something in Felipe's chest winced and then blossomed at the sound.

'Well said, sire,' she said. 'But it seems that your friend does not share your appreciation.'

Alberto addressed Felipe. 'Perhaps you would rather I chopped it up and burnt it?'

'No!' Felipe was horrified by the hoarse rasp of his voice. 'No. I would not destroy a work by such a master. But it shall be hidden away lest it corrupt the minds of simple folk or the ungodly.'

'Ho! Then it will be considered fine viewing for churchmen, eh?'

Felipe darted Alberto a venomous look. This was not

29

a matter for jest. 'Leave us. I would speak with Donna Carlotta alone.'

Alberto shrugged. He seemed about to offer another comment, but a glance at Felipe's face curtailed it. He slouched from the room, but not before he gave Carlotta a theatrical wink.

Felipe rose to his feet. He took a step towards Carlotta. It was an effort to keep his hands at his sides. Part of him wanted to strike her, to wipe the smile from her lovely face. But another part of him wanted to throw her backwards onto the bed and tear off her gown. He seemed to hear the sound of ripping seams and to see her white flesh through the rents in the fabric.

Suddenly he felt exhausted. His head was throbbing and there was a point of the most exquisite pain at one temple.

'Why did you show me the painting?' he said tiredly.

'Because I wanted you to see what you would never possess,' she said, her tilted dark eyes flashing. 'You have cheated me out of my home and lands and you thought to steal away my body and soul too.'

His jaw dropped. She hated him. He felt numbed by the knowledge.

'Cheated you?' he said stupidly. 'My cause was lawful.'

'In the eyes of whom? The corrupt officials who you paid to further your cause? Or my father who you allowed to get into debt so that you could take his lands? I know all about you, Felipe and I shall never forgive you for what you have done to me. One day there will be a reckoning. I am leaving now. Juanita has horses saddled and ready, but first . . . You threatened to strip me naked and have me walk through the village bare-foot. Then so be it. Let all who are not purblind see how Don Felipe Escada treats defenceless women.'

Reaching for a dagger which had lain unnoticed on a bedside coffer, she used it to slit the laces which fastened her gown. He watched open-mouthed as she threw the stomacher and then the violet bodice and sleeves onto the bed.

He wanted to tell her to stop, but he couldn't do it. Every nerve in his body was strung taut as a bow-string. It seemed as if the whole area of his skin actually ached with lust. And he saw by the contempt on her face that she knew this. The shame welled up in him, but it made no difference.

As she dropped her skirt to the floor, followed by the farthingale which collapsed into a circle around her, she turned her back. Released from her gaze, he shuddered and felt the sweat running down inside his cambric shirt. When she turned around she wore only her shift and corset.

He seemed to be trapped in a moment of time. He saw the tops of her breasts which bulged over the black-work at the neck of her chemise, the fancy leather corset which constricted her waist so cruelly – how lushly her hips flared out from under that corset. Carlotta cut through the laces and the pieces of the boned garment parted, and fell away.

Surely she would not disrobe completely. He held his breath, not sure of her purpose. Did she desire to dishonour or curse him? If so then she was succeeding, for he knew that he would never in his whole life forget this moment.

He seemed to be screaming silently – yes, yes, do it. Take off everything. Mother of God, she looked like an angel. But when he spoke he found himself croaking, 'No. Stop. Don't . . . please . . . Have mercy . . .'

She laughed, that same rich infectious treble, and reached for the hem of her chemise. He saw her slim ankles clothed in cream wool stockings, her knees, then her pretty calves and rounded thighs, and then – Oh, God in Heaven – there it was.

The secret place. The woman-flesh. Her vulva, which was his darkest obsession and most shameful desire.

31

Her coynte was covered with curling black hair. As she moved her legs apart he glimpsed the red folds of flesh; they looked moist and tender. He fancied that he could smell her secret musky odour. In his mind's eye the bitter taint of brimstone rose up in a cloud around him. She was the Devil's tempter.

With a groan he thrust himself forward onto his knees. Her rounded belly was exposed as she drew the shift slowly upwards. Clenching his fists he pressed them to his groin, trying to allay the fearful throbbing pressure. But it was no use, he felt his seed burst from him in hot shaming spurts as her cherry-tipped breasts came into view.

Carlotta gave him a pitying look as she stepped over the heap of garments.

'So, sire, I wish you scant joy of my empty house. Mayhap you will keep the painting, to remind you of what you have lost? And now, I give you good day.'

Laughing mockingly, she swept past him, her shift trailing after her and her costly leather shoes making a faint sound on the oak boards.

Felipe stayed as he was, his head bowed, until he heard her leave the room and descend the stairs. Then he walked slowly over to the window. The huge cheer from the men told him that Carlotta was about to leave the house.

Juanita sat on one horse and held the reins of a second. A packhorse was fastened to her saddle pommel. Carlotta, now wearing her shift, leapt onto her mount. He saw without surprise that she rode astride, like a man. Her voice floated up to the window and he shrank back.

'You see how your master treats me, sires. I leave my house and lands in nothing more than my shift. Somehow I must seek my fortune. Yet I am glad to go. I choose freedom over the chains which *he* offered me.'

Raising her arm, she pointed upwards and all eyes fastened upon the window. She rode away accompanied by cheers and shouts of good wishes. Alberto's voice could be heard above the others.

'God go with you. Fare you well, mistress! Fare you well!'

Groaning, Felipe slid down the wall until he sat on the floor. Never had he felt so wretched. The sense of shame and loss was crushing. He had acquired a beautiful house and rich lands, but they meant nothing to him. The taste of victory was like ashes.

Carlotta had taken away his respect and made him a laughing-stock. She had somehow cheated him, using nothing more than her pride and courage against all the power and wealth at his command. But he bore her no ill will. None of that mattered. Nothing mattered, save one thing.

She had branded him. He knew that now. The sight of her nakedness, white and black and with a narrow ribbon of red, was burned into his brain.

He would never be free of her.

Chapter Four

Carlotta rode away without a backward glance. There was no sense in dwelling on what had happened. Now she must look forward.

She felt a fierce satisfaction in having bettered Felipe. One day she would make good her promise to him, but it would be a long time before she was in a position of power again. Juanita rode silently at her side. She had hardly spoken since they left the estate, except to ask where they were going.

When Carlotta told her, her eyes widened.

'But what can you want with that man? Alberto is Felipe's right hand.'

'Exactly, and he has all the information I need. Diaz was only able to find out so much.'

'You think Alberto will help you? Will he not tell Felipe that you have been prying into his affairs?'

Carlotta smiled. 'Oh, I think not.'

Juanita flashed her a worried glance. 'I can see that you have a plan. And I have the feeling that I do not want to know too much about it.'

Carlotta spurred her horse on ahead. If her maid knew what she was planning she would flee back to Felipe and beg for his protection. The enormity of the task ahead was daunting, but she would take things one day at a time. That way anything seemed possible.

When she thought of all she had lost and of the man who had cheated her, her grief and anger threatened to choke her. Damn you to hell, Felipe, she thought. Her hatred for him would be the beacon she kept ahead of her throughout all the difficult times to come.

They spent the first night in the shelter of a wood, grateful for the fact that the weather was warm. The next day they kept moving and by nightfall found themselves following a line of carts, farm workers, and tradesmen along a track which led into the gateway of a walled town.

According to Diaz, Alberto had living quarters here above the shop of a cloth merchant. Carlotta found the narrow street without much difficulty. A mercer's sign hung above the doorway of a building which was shuttered for the night. Dismounting from her horse, Carlotta banged hard on the door.

Let him be here, she prayed. If Alberto had stayed with Felipe in her house she could have days to wait for his return. An upstairs window opened and a man stuck his head out. Recognising him at once, Carlotta whispered her thanks to whichever saint was watching over Juanita and herself.

'Donna Mendoza,' Alberto said. 'By God's bones I did not expect to lay eyes on you so soon. What service may I do you?'

Carlotta looked meaningfully at her friend. 'Leave this to me. Understand?' she hissed. Juanita nodded, looking relieved and scared at the same time.

'Why – is that Alberto? Oh sire, forgive me for disturbing you. We have called at every house asking for a night's lodging, with no success. My maid and I are travel weary and have need of food and a bed. Would you refuse us too?'

'Indeed I shall not! Hold there. I'll unbolt the door.'

Even in the fitful light of the lantern he held, Carlotta

saw the quick flare of lust on his face. This was going to be easy. The door creaked open and Alberto ushered them in, having sent a boy to see that their horses were stabled.

Alberto called for roast meats, rabbit pasties and wine. Carlotta ate heartily, conscious of his eyes flickering over the laced-up front of her gown and lingering on the swell of her breasts.

'How fortunate that you should seek lodgings at my door. For shame that a gentlewoman like yourself is forced to take to the road like a beggar. You must let me help you.'

You did not offer your help when Felipe turned me out, she thought bitterly, but held her tongue. Alberto's knee pressed against hers under the trestle table and she returned the pressure, smiling up at him with eyes full of gratitude and promise. She was quite sure that he did not believe that she had found his lodgings by accident, but his judgement was coloured by his lust and any other thoughts were set aside because of it.

Despite Juantia's worried glances, Carlotta sat close to Alberto on the joint-stool. His heavy muscled thigh rubbed against hers. She could feel the heat of it through her gown and petticoats. He drank great drafts of the red wine, but ate little. In a short time his roughly handsome face was flushed and his attentions grew bolder. She felt his hand on her leg, the thick fingers squeezing her knee and then sliding up her fabric-covered thigh.

When he slid his hand down to the inner curve of her thigh, she moved her legs apart so that he could brush his fingers over the slight bulge of her pubis. Alberto's eyes glittered and his breath came faster. His tongue snaked out to wet his lips, which were surprisingly sculptured and well-shaped.

Carlotta stood up.

'I fear that the journey and the loss of my property

has left me greatly weakened in spirit. If you would show me where I may rest my head . . .'

'To be sure. Come this way,' Alberto slurred. 'Your maid may sleep in the stable. The straw is clean.'

Carlotta followed Alberto into the side room which was dominated by a huge tester bed. The sheets looked none too clean, but the bedcover – a huge pelt made of a patchwork of fur – looked soft and inviting. Before she could say another word, Alberto pushed her back onto the bed, gathered her into his arms and began kissing her.

It was more pleasant than she had expected. His mouth was firm and the pressure insistent. When he slipped his tongue into her mouth, tasting her and exploring the soft inner flesh she found herself responding. Since Hernando she had not lain with a man. All her energies had been directed into worrying about her fate. Now here was Alberto, hers for the asking. He was young and strong and smelt of clean sweat and leather.

She was a woman who was used to bodily pleasure and she relished the taste and smell of a man. The wine fumes in her blood relaxed her and she felt her body stirring as all her senses became concentrated on the single pursuit of sexual release.

Alberto began plucking at the laces of her bodice and she moved to assist him. Under the skirt and bodice of plain fustian cloth she wore only a cambric chemise, petticoats, and stays.

His mouth moved over the tops of her breasts as they were revealed by the loose bodice. Pushing his tongue into her cleavage he lapped the salt from her skin and traced a warm wet path back up to her neck.

'You taste of musk and salt,' he murmured.

Carlotta arched towards him as he dragged down the neck of her chemise and lifted each firm, red-crested globe free. She sighed and twined her fingers in his thick brown hair as his mouth closed over one nipple and his teeth grazed gently against the rigid cone. As he began suckling her in earnest, little shards of pleasure spilled through her and she gave herself up to the hot, sweetly pulling sensation.

Alberto's big hard body pressed down onto her so that she felt she was sinking right into the fur bed cover. The buckles on his padded leather doublet dug into her belly, but she did not mind. His thighs were tensed and she could feel the stiffness of his erection pressing between her legs.

When he reached for her skirts, she helped him to pull them above her waist. The fur pelt tickled the backs of her thighs and exposed buttocks, the tactile sensation adding an extra dimension to her arousal. Alberto's palm was rough on the skin of her thighs as he eased her legs apart. She tensed, steeling herself for the expected onslaught of his swollen shaft, but he held himself back from penetrating her; less impatient than she had imagined he would be.

'Open up to me my pretty wench,' he grunted amiably. 'And let me see whether your coynte is any different from that of a common doxy.'

He was enjoying the novelty of laying with a lady of substance, she realised, and the fact amused her. She did as he asked spreading her legs wide and smiling into his eyes. Lifting her chin, she said, 'Well? Is it any different?'

Alberto's thick fingers stroked her pubis and rolled the silky black curls around his fingers. Trailing his hand over the slit of her sex, he pressed the fleshy lips apart seeking the moist membranes within. He rubbed at the firm little bud which throbbed and tingled beneath his touch, smoothing it back and forth with the pad of his thumb until Carlotta's breath grew ragged.

'It's a neat and well-formed pipkin you have, my lady,' he murmured. 'But I've need to test you further. You seem moist and willing enough, but this could be trickery. I'll not dip my pizzle in a dry well.' His dark eyes gleamed with drunken amusement.

As he pushed a thick finger into her molten heat Carlotta bucked and writhed, grinding herself onto his knuckles. He laughed as she strained towards him, biting at her lower lip.

'Well, well. What a hot little piece, you are. By God's teeth, were Don Felipe aware of what's been denied him he'd go into mourning for a full year!'

The mention of her enemy was like a draught of cold water. She stiffened against Alberto and would have pulled away, but he held her down easily with one hand and lifted her legs around his waist. As his cock-head pushed into her she fell back, able to think of nothing now but the hard man-flesh which was forging its way into her tight wet passage.

The pleasure of being filled by the thick phallus was something so basic, so primeval that she gave herself up to it completely. She felt weak and pliant. Nothing else mattered at this moment but Alberto surging within her, filling her, invading her willing body. She loved the way the swollen glans pushed her flesh aside as it entered her, then moved in and up to lodge against the neck of her womb.

He thrust into her strongly, drawing almost all the way out before slamming back into her and she met him, stroke for stroke. The almost hurting force of him was what she wanted. It meant that she didn't think – didn't grieve – didn't regret. They were just a man and woman, locked in the eternal battle of the flesh. Mind-less creatures of lust and counter-lust.

Alberto murmured endearments, using the language of the streets as he plundered her flesh, and the crude terms added a potent spice to her pleasure.

'That's it sweeting, sink down onto my pintle. Sheath yourself on me. You like a good bulling, eh? Then Alberto's your man. Let me rest for a moment now or I'll spill my seed and be no good to you.'

39

As she lay still, hardly moving, concentrating on the feel of his pulsing cock resting within her, she thought that it was his general crudity that had drawn her to him. There was no false refinement about Alberto, just a bluff but honest appreciation of women. She preferred his type to noble gentlemen who gave themselves airs, but were cold and calculating at heart. And he had a sense of humour. She recalled how he had baited Felipe about the painting.

As he began moving again, she closed her eyes and let the feelings take over. Alberto's lips were at her neck, his hands gripping her narrow waist as he worked away at her. Briefly, in the midst of her pleasure, she regretted the fact that it was necessary to trick him.

But the thought faded fast. There was only the moment and the sensations which were building within her. When her pleasure crested and broke, she moaned aloud and her womb convulsed. Alberto was brought to his climax by the squeezing of her muscles around his buried shaft. With a great cry he pulled out of her and showered her belly with creamy drops.

It was a few moments before Carlotta recovered her breath. Alberto had thrust himself to one side and lay flat on his back. He was snoring loudly, his hose around his knees and his flaccid member curved against one meaty thigh. She bent over and studied his limp cock.

Strange how such a proud weapon and instrument of pleasure could look so vulnerable. She stroked the soft veiny shaft and the purplish plum, all polished from her moisture, then reached up and kissed Alberto's cheek. His eyelids flickered but he did not stir. She guessed that he would sleep for many hours.

It was comfortable on the wide bed with the fur pelt gathered in folds around them both and she was tempted to lay her cheek against the soft pile and close her eyes. The thought of curving her body around Alberto and nestling against his broad chest was far preferable to the journey ahead. But she still had a task to perform and little time. After she had taken what she wanted she could not risk staying and being found out.

Besides, she must get used to being the mistress of her own fate. Alberto might protect her for a while before he lost interest in her, he might even agree to help her, but ultimately she knew that she must rely on her own integrity. In Catholic Spain men used women for their own ends, wives had little power, mistresses even less, and a woman without property or status was fair game for all.

After wiping her belly on her chemise and putting her clothes to rights, she rose from the bed and went quietly across the room to a huge, metal-bound coffer which stood under the shuttered window. It was not locked and she lifted the heavy lid with ease. After a few minutes of sorting through the assortment of papers and documents she found what she wanted.

Rolling them up she thrust them inside her bodice. She felt a twinge of regret as she glanced towards the sleeping figure of Alberto, then shrugged her shoulders. She would do whatever she must to survive. Necessity made for odd bedfellows and selective loyalty.

Stealthily she left the bed chamber and slipped through the shuttered house, leaving by the back door which opened onto a small stable yard. Juanita was curled up in the straw, a cloak pulled over her for warmth.

She shook her maid's shoulder. Juanita awoke with a start, her eyes wide with fright. Carlotta pressed her hand over the other woman's mouth.

'Make no sound. Hurry and saddle the horses. We're leaving. It's best that we start now. We have a long journey ahead.'

Juanita yawned and rubbed her eyes, but she pushed back the cloak and rose to her feet. Wisps of her light brown hair were sticking out of her cap. The imprint of strands of straw marked her pretty oval face.

'Where are we going now?' she said sleepily as she began gathering up their belongings.

Carlotta felt a surge of affection for her childhood friend. She was dog-tired and still confused by their altered circumstances, yet it did not occur to her to refuse to obey her mistress. Her trust and absolute faith in Carlotta's ability to make things right was flattering, but it was also a burden. Carlotta was well aware that she must continue to plan and think for the two of them.

She smiled grimly, thinking it best not to tell Juanita the reason for haste. There was no sense in both of them worrying.

'We're going to the nearest port and on to a new life,' she said, wishing that she was as certain of what they would find as she sounded.

The journey to Cartagena on the east coast took them two weeks of steady travelling. They joined a band of pilgrims who were heading south and were saved the danger of travelling the roads alone. At night they were given shelter at convents and monasteries. But at Úbeda, where the pilgrims were going to pray at the shrine of Saint Juan de la Cruz, they parted company and headed due east.

Perhaps Alberto had not yet discovered her theft, for they were not pursued. Carlotta tried to think only of the next turn in the road, the next village they approached, anything to keep her mind from dwelling on the beautiful home she had lost. She could not bear the thought of Felipe surveying the estate, looking proudly at the wheat ripening in the fields and the olives turning black on the trees.

They kept to what main roads there were, the dust of the journey penetrating their clothes and clogging in their hair. Carlotta had tucked her mass of black curls under a cap like Juanita's. She wore plain serviceable garments and kept her slim, white, lady's hands hidden as much as possible.

To outward appearances they were itinerants, working women, seeking employment. Only she knew about the last of her money, a fortune in gold pieces from the sale of her jewels, which was sewn into her underclothes. She wore a dagger in a sheath strapped to her ankle and her sword was buckled to a belt between her petticoats.

If anyone challenged them she was ready to fight for their lives. On any other occasion she would have enjoyed the journey, but she hardly noticed the beauty of hillsides and valleys which were veiled with heather and broom. In the distance the misty blue tops of mountains formed a backdrop to the distant fertile plains. Then, one day, on the wind came the smell of the sea.

The fortified sea port of Cartagena had been a naval base since ancient times. The beautifully sited harbour was guarded at the narrow entrance by a fort on either side.

Carlotta knew from the documents that many of Felipe's merchant ships were berthed in Cartagena. In her possession were details of Felipe's associates, of types and amounts of cargoes, route maps, destinations, trading stops. Such knowledge would be worth a great deal to the right person. She had planned to sell it to a privateer or perhaps to a business rival of Felipe's. Then she would book a passage on a ship and she and Juanita would go to the New World where fortunes could be made.

But standing on the wharf, looking around at the huge rigged ships that were rolling gently with the movement of the tide, she felt dispirited by the vagueness, the smallness of her reasoning. There would be little satisfaction in giving someone else the means to wound her enemy. She was landless and about to be set adrift in an alien world, while Felipe slept in *her* bed, enjoyed the produce of *her* estate.

Clenching her fists she gazed up at the sweeping lines of a cross-sailed merchant vessel and smiled grimly. She recalled the look on Felipe's face the last time she saw him. The agonized lust in his hooded dark eyes as he watched her disrobe; the way his sensual mouth worked as he clasped both hands to his groin; his amazement and self-disgust as he spilt his seed inside his hose.

How she had loved to see him suffer. But she wanted more. He must be humbled, brought as low as she was now. And she wanted him to know that she alone was responsible for his downfall.

'I'll teach you the majesty of suffering, Don Felipe,' she said. 'I swear that I'll make you crawl on your belly to me and when you beg me to grant you release, I'll laugh in your face.'

A breeze blew in from the sea, bringing the taint of rotten fish and salt and whipping strands of her long dark hair into her eyes. The fire went out of her and her shoulders slumped. Oh, but she was too tired to think anymore this day. She needed to rest and take stock. The journey had been gruelling and she was saddle sore and in dire need of a bath.

After securing lodgings for herself and Juantia, Carlotta collapsed onto her trestle bed, grateful for clean sheets and a pillow stuffed with straw.

A few days later, they took their places at table in the tap-room of the inn. The food was good, a spicy fish stew and new bread, and they both ate hungrily. The smoke from an enormous hearth filled the room adding to the gloom broken only by the light from guttering lanterns. Carlotta and Juanita were screened from the main room by a huge oak post which held up the ceiling. They attracted little attention from the huddle of sailors and merchant men who were eating or swilling grog.

For some time Carlotta had been listening intently to the conversations of these men. She pricked up her ears when the talk turned to piracy. Apparently the Spanish authorities were having difficulty flushing out groups of French Protestants who had holed up on the islands of the West Indies.

'They're calling themselves the "Brethren of the Coast",' said a bald headed man sporting one huge gold earring. 'By all accounts they've small cause to love the Spanish.'

His companion spat a stream of tobacco juice onto the floor boards. He was a hard-faced individual with a fearful scar that cut across his nose and pulled his mouth down at one corner.

'Buccaneers! Blasted Huguenots. They're nothin' but murderers and servants of the devil. They deserve what they get.'

'Seems like they only wanted to grow baccy or sugar cane on them little islands. A man's faith is his own and it's harsh to kill men for wantin' to make a livin'. And now they've turned to lootin' ships. Can't say as I rightly blame 'em.'

'Godless heretics. May they all burn in hell,' his friend grunted. 'And you'd best watch your tongue if you value it. That's not papist talk you're spouting and priests have big ears.'

The men moved away and Carlotta leaned back in her seat, the germ of an idea forming in her mind. She was beginning to see how she could have a direct hand in ruining Felipe.

The enormity of the idea took her breath away. It would be the most daring thing she had ever done. Her blood quickened as plans began forming in her mind. She needed to find the right man and she had a shrewd idea where she'd find him.

But first she must find a ship to transport her. It would be a difficult task, even foolhardy, but not impossible. And the rewards would be great. She glanced at Juanita who was regarding her warily and gave her a reassuring smile.

No. It was far too dangerous. She couldn't expect the other woman to agree to *that*. And yet . . .

Chapter Five

Manitas le Vasseur grunted as he thrust into the woman lying beneath him. He could hardly believe his good fortune. It was months since he'd had a woman.

And this woman was young and beautiful, but only just. On Hispaniola the life was hard and it demanded everything of those who lived there. The woman was of mixed blood. She had coarse frizzy hair and smooth light skin which he could only describe as like honey mixed with milk. Next to his own physical bulk – he stood six foot three in his stockinged feet – the woman seemed slight and fragile.

Manitas reached out his hands and placed them on the shoulders of the woman who was bent over in front of him – she hadn't told him her name and he hadn't asked it. Withdrawing almost all the way out of her he leaned back, flexing his thighs and using his big purplish glans to open her passage again before he rocked against her and buried his cock to the root.

Ah, Lord, but he loved the silky feel of a woman's coynte, the subtle ridged caress of the flesh which enclosed his staff. He had almost forgotten how good it felt to hold a woman, to smell her hair and stroke his hands over the dips and curves at waist and hip.

47

Manitas was a big man in every respect and the woman had looked at him with fear-filled eyes when she first saw the size of his organ. But she was eager for his caresses and hungry for the delicacies he carried in his pack too, anything more than commonplace food being scarce in her village. He had promised that she could share his meal of steak smoked over green wood – on one condition.

She had nodded and laid back, letting him caress her and mouth her skin, but she turned her head away when he would have kissed her. Using all his skill, he gentled her as if she was a nervous fawn. Spreading her smooth thighs he knelt before her and tongued her coynte, rolling the moist lips open with his fingers and savouring the musky, sea-rich flavour of her. He used his tongue on the swollen bead of her pleasure, then pushed the tip into her entrance, circling it until it grew wet and receptive.

Her breath came fast and shallow as her back arched and her hips began to work. He waited until her eyes turned up to show the whites and she gave a series of hoarse little cries, before he stopped pleasuring her with his tongue. By that time she was so wet and swollen, so ready to be penetrated, that she bent forward over the log gladly when he asked her to.

Now she was lifting her bottom towards him, writhing and moaning with pleasure and every last bit of his huge cock was buried inside her. He felt his glans nudge against the bump that was her womb, so snugly did he fit. Digging the toes of his pigskin boots into the ground, he tried to gain more purchase as the woman bucked and surged under him.

Grunting, she pressed back against him, her firm globes butting at the nest of wiry hair at his groin. Her backside was like a ripe fruit and he looked down, watching as his slick shaft plunged into the wet red heat of her. She flexed her back and her buttocks gaped giving him a view of her anal orifice.

What a tight opening; too tight to admit his cock, but it was tempting nonetheless. Licking his finger he smoothed the spittle across the puckered little mouth, circling it while it twitched and pushed out lewdly towards him. Gently he inserted his fingertip inside her. She was hot and snug around him, the band of muscle giving only scant license to the invasion.

'You like that? Yes?' the girl murmured, clenching both orifices around him and beginning to utter more of her exciting breathy little cries.

Manitas sank deeply into her as the ripples of her ultimate pleasure flowed up his shaft. With a few more jerks of his taut thighs he spent himself inside her.

'Ah . . . ah . . .' he grunted as the sperm left him in great tearing jerks.

Sweet Jesu. He was sure that he felt things more keenly than other men. He had seen his friends bulling a tavern wench, one after the other, and they each came with a sigh or a groan or a mere grimace of the face. But when he climaxed he almost passed out and the feeling seemed to tingle over every nerve end and reach right down to the ends of his fingers and toes.

For a moment longer he lay across her, supporting his weight on his outstretched arms, then, after withdrawing slowly he wiped himself on a piece of soft leather.

'Here wench. Clean yourself,' he said, handing her a piece of leather.

She smiled, impressed by his gentlemanly manners. That was something the other buccaneers teased him about, but Manitas saw no reason to behave like animals just because they were forced to live like them.

Like his friends, he had done questionable things, but he had kept true to himself. Doing what was necessary to survive or to make life bearable made sense to him and he did not believe in agonising over the past.

Pulling up his rawhide breeches Manitas tied the

thong at his waist, then slipped his coarse linen shirt over his head. The woman had cleaned herself and was sitting looking at him with an expression of fatalism. It made him sad to see that she expected nothing. He wondered what treatment she had endured in her short life.

Crossing to the *boucan* where the cooking meat was sending out delicious odours, he hacked off a generous piece with his hunting knife and then doused it in rich pepper sauce from the flask in his pack. Laying the hot meat on a plate of leaves he gave it to the woman.

'Here. Eat your fill.'

She grinned, showing uneven and stained teeth, then started to stuff meat into her mouth with a speed that amazed him. The poor wench was starving.

He carved off some meat for himself and began eating. When he looked up, she had gone, melting away through the trees like a wraith. He would have liked her to stay. Women were scarce outside the settlements on Hispaniola and he missed female company. Most men travelled and hunted in groups, accompanied by their dogs.

Many of the buccaneers, deprived of the company of women, turned to each other for sexual relief and formed close relationships. Manitas had baulked at their practices. He could not bring himself to use a man like a woman, but he was an earthy sensual man and occasionally – when the need became great – he allowed one of the younger men to suck him to a climax.

A flush crept into his cheeks as he remembered the warm, willing lips closing around his shaft – the unshaven jaw under his hands – the feeling of thrusting into a thick muscular throat. The memories shamed him, but he would not deny that it had happened. Pleasuring the woman had reminded him of the time before he came to Hispaniola.

On Saint Kitts he had lived with a woman, a fine and lusty wench who had loved to sit astride him and wrap her legs around his waist while he ploughed a furrow in her lush body. She had liked to play games too and he remembered the feel of her firm buttocks under his hand as he spanked her before pleasuring her.

As a landowner he had the chance of being somebody. He thought of getting married. Then the cursed Spanish came to the island, bringing with them their hatred of anything not Catholic, and put his tobacco fields to the torch. No woman looked at a man who had lost everything.

For the past few years on Hispaniola, Manitas had hunted with a dog at his side, selling cured meat, hides, and tallow to the crews of passing privateers. But he wearied of the life. And the ever more numerous incursions of the Spanish who were determined to wipe out every single 'heretic stronghold' as they perceived them, was making life ever more precarious.

Manitas had ideas about making life easier. A few days ago he had left his companions and made his way to the coast where a rough shanty town was springing up. Through the palm trees there was a stretch of white sand and beyond that the crash of breakers rolling into the shore.

Taking a bite of the spicy meat, he chewed as he gazed out to sea. In the far distance, the Spanish ships passed along the routes through the Windward Passage and along the coast of Cuba. Something in his blood reached out to them.

The arrogant bastards. They thought they owned the world. If he only had the means he'd teach them a lesson. What better way to re-dress the balance than by skimming off some of the Spanish gold? There were sailors, engineers and runaway slaves amongst the buccaneers on Hispaniola. Manitas knew that he could get a crew together.

He laughed wryly. Big ideas, for a big man. He had the will and the courage to fight. All he needed was a ship. And that would take a miracle. But he could begin to make a difference in a small way. At least then he would feel better about himself.

Juanita looked around with horror at the cluster of buildings, some of them little more than wooden shacks thatched with palm leaves.

The air was thick and close, scented with strange foreign odours. Rough-looking men wearing an assortment of garments made of hide or pigskin sat around outside the buildings, smoking or cleaning weapons. There were a lot of skinny dogs running about.

'Why have we come here?' she asked Carlotta. 'There can be nothing for us on this God-forsaken island! It's hot and it smells. And those men frighten me. They look as if they have not seen a woman in a year. They would eat us alive if we stood still long enough!'

Carlotta smiled, looking surprised by her asperity.

'I don't think it is eating they have in mind,' she grinned. 'Come now, Juanita. Straighten your back and look them in the eye.'

Juanita's cheeks grew hot. She kept her eyelids lowered as they passed a group of whistling shouting men. How could Carlotta joke about this? She was angry and fearful, but also filled with a grudging admiration for her mistress. Carlotta's head was high as she strode along, one hand on the sword at her waist. She seemed to be afraid of nothing. Once her mind was made up, she was off in pursuit of whatever goal she had set herself.

Which was why they were now making their way across the sandy soil of a street on Hispaniola to what seemed to be a tavern. Inside the shuttered room it was dark and cool. Carlotta walked across the room in her usual way and all eyes were drawn to her. As usual Carlotta did not notice the effect she had. Juanita gave the occupants of the room a haughty look, intending to discourage unwelcome advances.

She saw the man at once. He was huge, tall and

broad and with swept-back dark hair, caught at the nape by a leather thong. He was not handsome exactly, but she had never seen anyone so arresting.

As Carlotta found a table and called for wine and food, he watched her. Not with a capacious hunger like the men outside, but with a calm measuring gaze. Juanita glanced at him now and then, taking in every detail of this enigma. He wore a rough linen shirt under a slashed doublet of padded and studded leather. Around his waist was a thick belt, bristling with weapons. His long legs were covered by pigskin breeches and wide-topped boots reached to his knees.

After their food had arrived, he sauntered over.

'Have you any objection to my joining you?' he said.

Carlotta shrugged. 'Why not?' she said coolly. 'Your eyes have been boring a hole in my back since first we came in.'

He grinned showing unusually good teeth. 'So you noticed me too? I thought so. But then, I am hard to ignore.' It was said without a trace of false pride.

Carlotta laughed and Juanita saw the man respond to the infectious husky tone of it. Juanita flashed Carlotta a warning glance – which, as usual, she ignored. Under the table she wrung her hands, wishing that her mistress would not make so bold. This man frightened her.

He had a wild and rakish look to him. His face was tanned and as rugged as the parched landscape, but he had intelligent blue eyes. Holding out his hand to Carlotta, he said politely enough,

'Manitas le Vasseur. And whom do I have the pleasure of addressing?'

'Carlotta Mendoza,' Carlotta said. 'And this is Juanita.'

Juanita nodded stiffly. Manitas's blue eyes darkened with interest as he looked from one to the other.

'Spanish, eh? And high-born from your colouring and bearing. All of you have that haughty look.' He could not quite disguise the coldness in his voice.

Carlotta ignored his rudeness. She leaned her elbows on the table and smiled with equanimity.

'You have no love of my countrymen?'

'I have cause to hate them for their damned arrogance and for their absolute certainty that they are, by the grace of God, the rightful rulers of the world!'

Juanita drew in her breath. Manitas looked quite terrifying with his blue eyes flashing hatred. Not for the first time she wished she had adopted Carlotta's practice of wearing a knife strapped to her leg. She looked pleadingly at Carlotta. Surely now her mistress would berate him for his rudeness and ask him to leave their table.

'And yet you wear a Spanish doublet and that knife in your belt was made in Toledo,' Carlotta said calmly, undaunted either by the man's great size or his outspokenness.

Holding her gaze, Manitas said evenly. 'I had them both from the spoils of a Spanish ship.'

'Did you indeed? Then let me buy you a mug of rum, monsieur, and we shall talk more about your Spanish booty.'

Carlotta concealed her mounting excitement as Manitas told her about the ships which sailed out from Hispaniola attacking and looting passing vessels. He had been amongst the crew which swarmed onto the deck of a square-rigged barque and relieved it of its cargo of wine and military supplies.

As he perceived that she had a keen interest in his activities Manitas became more circumspect.

'Why are you so interested in piracy?' he asked, his mouth curving in a dangerous smile. 'No woman as beautiful as you comes here by accident. So what is your design, eh? Are you running away from something? Or could it be that you're a spy for the Spanish authorities?'

Carlotta threw back her head and laughed.

'Indeed I am not!'

'Then what are you?'

Dark eyes glinting, she leaned close. 'I'm an angel sent to help you,' she said. 'For I see a man of ambition before me. I can help you get what you desire, Manitas, and you can help me get what I want.'

His huge hand closed over her wrist and she tensed but did not remove it. Glancing down she saw how fragile her slim white hand looked against his wide palm. The blue veins on the back of his hand were visible through the dark-golden skin. She felt a tremor of fear. How delicious. This man could snap her neck with one hand if he wished. But of course that was not what he wanted. She smiled inwardly.

Oh, this battle was very much to her taste.

There were lines around Manitas's eyes and a certain set to his mouth which denoted suffering. She felt that he was in some way a kindred spirit. He had known loss, but his grief did not seem as new, as raw as her own. Somehow she knew that she could trust him. But she needed to be certain of that fact.

She did not resist when he lifted her hand, brought it to his face, and opened it so that it lay palm upwards. Pressing his lips to her palm, he kissed her gently and then brushed his mouth across her wrist. His tongue snaked out to taste her skin and she felt the warm wet tip pressing against her pulse.

A tremor of lust speared her belly and she knew that he felt it too, but his eyes with their lowered lids were cool and appraising.

'Will you help me?' she said, her voice unsteady.

'Don't seek to play me fast and loose, my lady,' he said. 'I'll not have it. Your words smack of bartering and I'm no milk-sop ninny or foppish courtier to be bought with sexual favours.'

Carlotta snatched her hand away. 'Nor would I use such methods against you. When I lie with a man it is because I desire to pleasure myself and for no other reason.'

She enjoyed watching the flare of heat along his wide cheekbones. He had not expected such candour. Then he smiled widely and she realised that he was an extraordinarily good-looking man.

'And how are you going to prove that you have more to bargain with than what's inside your gown?'

Carlotta rose from her chair, a hot excitement coiling in her belly. Manitas's sheer size was daunting. It would be a challenge to try to control such a man – if she was ever moved to try. All she could think of was the way he was looking at her and the answering throbbing between her thighs.

'We can dispense with your doubts at once. Have you a room in this establishment?'

Manitas's dark eyebrows rose. He nodded. She enjoyed seeing him so totally nonplussed.

'Then lead the way, monsieur. After we settle the demands of the flesh we can talk business.'

Facing him across the low ceilinged room, Carlotta knew a moment of doubt. He looked even bigger now that she was alone with him.

Holding eye contact with her, he stripped off his doublet and shirt to reveal a solidly muscled torso. His skin was smooth and tanned and had the slight sheen of perfect health. There was a sprinkling of dark hair on his chest which trailed down into a line over his belly before disappearing into the waistband of his breeches.

Manitas's lips curved in a smile as he saw her look of appreciation and Carlotta's doubt receded. His eyes spoke a language she understood. There was no need for words or reasoning when flesh spoke to flesh. Moving close, she lifted her hand and trailed her fingers gently across the expanse of his chest. Circling his tight male nipples, she grazed them with her fingernails, smiling with satisfaction as the sensitive copper skin gathered into tight beads.

Manitas cursed softly when she closed her lips over one nipple and bit down gently. His large hands gripped her shoulders and he put her from him.

'Wait. Not like this,' he said. 'Take off your clothes. I want to look at you. My eyes are starved of the sight of a woman without pockmarks and whose ribs aren't showing through her skin.'

Taking a step back, Carlotta raised her hands to the fustian bodice which she wore over a loose blouse. Manitas watched hungrily as her fingers moved over the lacing. She set the bodice aside, then the blouse. Running her spread fingers up the sides of her stays she cupped the underswell of her breasts. Holding them up and drawing them together as if offering them to him, she laughed softly.

'Do you like what you see?'

Manitas pretended to be considering his answer, although his eyes were fastened on the tempting valley of her cleavage and the cherry tips which peeped provocatively over the drawstring neck of her chemise.

'Show me the rest,' he said thickly. 'And you'll have my answer in kind.'

It was exhilarating to disrobe for this powerful, exciting man. Carlotta felt a concentration of sexual tension deep within her as she drew each garment free of her body and dropped it on the rough boards of the room. The skirt fell into folds around her calves, followed by her petticoats. Soon she wore only her chemise. That followed the other garments and then she was naked, except for woollen stockings fastened above her knees with embroidered ribbons.

Holding her arms out to her sides, she turned slowly. The sunlight streaming in through split bamboo blinds spread a dusty yellow light on her bare limbs. She knew that her skin was flawless and felt a sense of pride in the beauty of her body.

Manitas made a sound deep in his throat and reached for her. Wrapping her in his arms he crushed her against his bare chest. She shivered with pleasure as her breasts were flattened against slabs of hard muscle and his wiry chest hair grazed her nipples. As his big hands slid up her back she encircled his waist with her arms and tipped up her head for his kiss.

His mouth ground down on hers and she opened her lips to his tongue. He tasted of wine and tobacco and something fainter which was essentially his own. Bending from the waist he slipped a hand behind her knees and swept her into his arms.

Still kissing her, he carried her to the straw palliasse in the corner, which served him as a bed. The heat of his skin against her own and the thoroughness of his kiss – he seemed to want to absorb her very essence through her mouth – made her senses swim with wanting. Relinquishing her mouth for a moment, he lowered her to the bed and then knelt beside her.

She watched him unfasten his breeches, fascinated to see if the huge bulge in the fabric would fulfil its promise. When his cock sprang free, she stared in unashamed awe. Manitas had the biggest phallus she had ever seen. It reared up from the nest of curling black hair at his groin and lay almost flat against his stomach, reaching beyond his navel. His shaft was very thick and veiny and topped by a shiny red glans which was partly covered by his cock-skin. His scrotum was also large, but firm and potent looking.

The lust boiled in her belly as she caught the smell of him, salt, clean sweat, the peculiar, flatter odour of his arousal. Such pronounced maleness was almost over-whelming. Her mouth actually watered. How would it feel to have such a monster pushing into her?

'Mother of God,' she whispered. 'You are a big man in every respect!'

Manitas laughed. 'Many women are afraid when they

see my pintle for the first time, but you seem only eager. Are you not worried that I'll hurt you?'

She smiled up at him. 'That sort of hurt only adds to my pleasure.'

Reaching out her hand she encircled his shaft, savouring the feel of the silky skin and the underlying heat of the engorged flesh. Manitas watched her, enjoying her delight in him. His hands dropped to his sides and he arched his back pushing his hips towards her as she drew his cock towards her mouth.

There was a single drop of clear fluid escaping from the slitted mouth of his cock. Carlotta liked to see a man so ready for her. Pursing her lips she pushed the cockskin back from the glans and ran her tongue around the big purple tip. He tasted rich and gamey. Delicious. She drew more of him in, sucking and teasing him with rolling motions of her tongue. Manitas groaned deep in his throat as he gave himself up to the pleasure.

His big hands came up to cradle her head and his fingers moved in her hair. She took as much of him into her mouth as she could, but it was impossible to encompass his whole length. It did not matter. As she worked on him with her mouth she clasped the root of his shaft with her hand and began moving it back and forth.

After a while Manitas grunted and pulled away.

'Enough,' he said, frowning.

'What is it? Do you not like what I am doing?'

His fingers slid down her cheeks and caressed her jaw. 'Oh I like it well enough, my willing Señora. But there are things I like better.'

So saying, he pushed her backwards and then straddled her, one huge thigh either side of her hips. Grasping both wrists in one hand he held her arms above her head. Pinioned by the weight of him and helpless against his strength, she twisted under him.

'What are you doing?' she said, not so much alarmed as stimulated by the rough treatment.

He grinned. 'I like my women spread out before me, submissive and eager for my caresses.' Leaning forward he brushed her mouth with his lips. 'I suspect that you are rather too spoiled and wilful, but now I have you as I want you.'

Before she could think better of it, Carlotta bit him. Manitas jerked backwards, his eyes sparking with anger. There was a single bright bead of blood on his lower lip.

Carlotta chuckled throatily and raised her head to nurse the tiny wound with gentle kisses. Savouring the morsel of blood on her tongue, she murmured against his mouth.

'Just so you know that you have not won the whole battle. I might accept you as my master in bed, but when it comes to doing business, we'll be on equal terms.'

Manitas laughed. 'Do you say so indeed? We'll talk on that more. You are quite a woman. I wonder how many pretty boys you have bent to your will.'

'More than you can count . . .' she said, tailing off as his free hand began stroking her breasts.

'I don't doubt it,' Manitas said, his fingers pinching her nipples cruelly until she gasped and cried out. 'And have any of them claimed a forfeit for the wounds you have given them? As I am about to do.'

She shook her head, wincing under the onslaught of his fingers. 'No. They wouldn't dare! And neither shall you! Stop that at once . . . Oh . . .'

The tingles of pleasure-pain spread through her torso and she felt her face grow hot as he watched her every expression. She was actually blushing, something she had not done for many years. This huge handsome man was doing just what he wanted with her and she realised that she loved it. Perhaps she had, after all, been looking for a man who could match her capacity for pleasure: a man who would see past her strong will and who had the strength to best her on his own terms.

She moaned softly as he squeezed her breasts and then began slapping the under-swell of them – not hard, but just enough to make them bounce. The weight of them snapped against her stretched rib-cage as he let them fall after each gentle blow. Her nipples were rigid cones, each of them throbbing from the earlier pinching. She ached for him to suck them, to relieve the hot discomfort.

But she would not beg – not yet. Oh, it was deliciously humiliating to have him handle her in this way. She knew that her eyes were wide open and glazed with passion. The folds of her coynte were swollen and slippery. She could hardly wait for him to force open her legs with his knee and enter her. She arched her back and pushed her pubis towards him invitingly.

Her lips curved with a smile of confidence. None of her lovers had been able to resist her when she signalled her readiness to be penentrated.

But it seemed that Manitas could. She rotated her hips, grinding herself against him. He ignored her and kept his attention focused on her breasts. What was wrong with him? Surely he could read her signals. Her black brows dipped with frustration.

'You must wait, my sweet wanton, until I am ready to grant you release,' he grinned. 'I am more concerned with my pleasure than yours. And I'm no pretty boy to bend to your will.'

Carlotta was not used to being gainsaid. Her mouth tightened with anger. Just who did this barbarian think he was?

'Let me up!' she ordered. 'A pox on your gall! I've had enough of your games. I'm no tavern trull to have her skirts thrown over her head and bent over a trestle!'

'Now there's a pretty sight to conjure with!'

Before she knew what he meant to do, he pulled her upright, then flipped her over as easily as if she was a child. Dragging her to the edge of the straw mattress, he positioned her so that she was looking down at the wooden boards and her bottom was tipped up towards him. Retaining his hold on her wrists he shifted his weight and lay beside her, one heavy leg pressing across the back of her thighs to keep her pinioned.

'An inviting sight indeed,' he said, stroking her bottom with a calloused palm.

Carlotta struggled to get away, but her heart wasn't in it. Part of her was furious at him, but another part – as yet unexplored – was awakening, unfolding like ripples of dark-red velvet. Something inside her relished his roughness and called out to the mastery he was imposing on her.

She relaxed onto the straw mattress, expecting him at any moment to drag her legs apart and explore the damp furrow between her buttocks.

Her coynte felt so swollen it actually ached and she was aware of a liquid heat such as she had never known before. He is making my body weep with readiness, she thought, and felt a pang of lust so strong that she bit her lip to keep from groaning aloud. All she could think of was his huge cock and how it would feel when that big collared plum first pushed past the closure of her intimate flesh.

When his hand crashed down onto her bare buttocks, she cried out with shock. No one had ever spanked her and the indignity of it brought tears to her eyes. She jerked and writhed against his hand, trying to escape his pitiless work-hardened palm. He took his time, spanking first one buttock then the other, until her whole bottom felt as if it was on fire.

'Stop! Oh stop,' she wept. 'I'll kill you for this! By Our Lady I swear I'll run you through!'

'Such sweet words of love,' Manitas laughed, rubbing her abused flesh with his free hand, with gentle circular motions.

Incredibly, Carlotta felt the pain disappear and in its place there came a tingling warmth which spread out-

wards and downwards to centre in the throbbing wetness between her thighs. And now, at last, Manitas
nudged her thighs wide apart, exposing and opening
her coynte. She felt her wet folds part and her hungry
orifice gape.

Positioning himself between her legs he leaned forward, bracing himself to take his weight. The rigid pole
of his cock pressed up against the parting of her bottom,
but he did not thrust into her; he contented himself
instead using her crease as a source of friction.

She winced as her sore flesh met the ridged muscles
of his stomach. His breath came faster as he rubbed his
shaft up and down the damp crevice. She was horribly
aware of the inner surfaces of her buttocks as they
cradled his potent maleness. With each thrust she felt
his big glans brush against her anus and his shaft
exerted a referred pressure on the whole of her sex.

She drew in her breath, feeling dizzy with wanting
him so badly. Why did he deny her the ultimate
pleasure of penetration? What was he waiting for? Her
female orifice was ignored, bereft. Oh how shaming it
was to want him so much. The need to feel him pushing
into her grew and grew. She thought she might climax
just from the erotic tension of having her whole body
held open and waiting under him.

'Tell me what you want,' he whispered hoarsely. 'If
you want my cock in you, you must ask for it.'

She crimsoned. It was impossible. He was making
her do things that no other man ever had. Now he
wanted her to beg, but her pride would not allow him
that final victory. She shook her head, gripping her
bottom lip between her teeth.

'Damn you,' she hissed, the tears stinging her eyes.

'So be it, Señora,' he said amicably. 'But you *will* ask
me to pleasure you, I vow it. And until you do you
must content yourself with a stroking.'

Slipping his free hand between her thighs he began
rubbing her sex, smoothing the slippery folds back and

forth in a subtle rhythm. Her strongly erect little bud pulsed maddeningly and she was powerless to stop the pleasure building to a peak.

'No. Stop. I do not want it like this . . .' she agonised, almost beyond words as he expertly drew her towards her climax.

She had only to ask him, to beg him to penetrate her and he would do it, but the words wouldn't form themselves on her lips. Her hips worked beyond her control and, unconsciously, she provided the stimulus for Manitas to gain release. Grunting, he held her buttocks more firmly together, exerting pressure on her hips with his knees while plundering the tight and unwilling crease. Still he spurned her natural opening.

If he hadn't a hold on her wrists, she would have thrust her hand between her thighs and penetrated herself with her fingers. But he denied her that too. His expert fingers squeezed and rubbed and smoothed her intimate flesh. She felt his swollen glans slide once more up the length of her exterior crevice and then Manitas gave a great groan and his semen spurted onto her lower back.

Squeezing her eyes shut she climaxed, even though she fought against it to the last.

Her moans were loud in her ears. She felt ashamed of the noise she was making, but she could not help it. The release was so intense, so hard won. His fingers continued to press against her swollen sex as if absorbing every pulse and throb of her pleasure. He did not remove them until the last sliver of sensation had faded. Carlotta lacked the strength to push him away and was glad when he rolled onto his side.

Although free of his weight and his restraining grip, she didn't move. It was a moment before either of them recovered. Manitas got up first. She remained face-down, listening to the sounds he made as he moved around the room. For a large man he did not make much noise.

He did not walk, so much as prowl. This was probably a legacy of his way of life on Hispaniola. He moved like a hunter. She imagined that it would be unnerving to have him appear silently at your side. Manitas was someone you would not wish to make your enemy.

In a moment he was back. He sank onto the palliasse beside her and put two pottery cups on the floor. As he poured them each a cup of wine, he said cooly:

'And so my beautiful Señora, shall we talk business?'

Chapter Six

*T*he sound of the lash was loud in the stillness of the chapel.

Felipe knelt on the flagstones, facing the altar. He was naked and slightly hunched over. The smell of incense drifted on the air and hung over the altar in ragged skeins of bluish smoke. Two thick wax candles cast a fitful light over the small room and sent his shadow looming up the wall. He raised his eyes to the portrait which hung on the wall above the wooden statue of the Virgin.

Carlotta, so beautiful, so unattainable. Where was she now? But for him, she would still be living on her estate. There would be a chance for him to pay court to her.

As the lash bestowed her cruel kisses on his skin, he kept his eyes on the portrait, drinking in the pearly whiteness of her skin, her raven hair, the half-smile on her mouth. It was her mouth that he loved – hated – most. Her mouth reminded him of that other orifice. The brief glimpse of it nestling under the glossy pubic curls was burned into his brain. Moist red folds, fragrant, inviting.

He thought again of the way she had stripped off her

gown in her bed chamber, taunting him with her beauty, punishing him by displaying what was denied him. Oh God, how white and slender she was. Only the Devil could fashion such a fair disguise for so much wickedness.

She was Lilith, the Whore of Babylon, Jezebel. Rich with the sin of Eve.

And he, poor fool, was still enslaved by her. Even her absence had not freed him. She haunted his waking hours and his dreams. Only last night he had awoken in a sweat, certain that he had heard her voice in his ear. His blood was racing, his arms reaching out to enfold her, even as his eyelids fluttered open. But the room was empty. Only the night air blowing down the chimney, bringing with it the first taint of winter's chill, stirred the bed curtains.

It was months since she had left, but she was still incandescent in his thoughts. A constant presence wherever he was, whatever he did. Every morning he awoke with a huge erection and needed to abuse himself before he could concentrate on his business affairs.

He had lost weight and there were dark shadows under his eyes, hollows in his cheekbones. He knew that he could not go on like this. He had become wretched, a miserable, self-absorbed sinner who was driven to desperate acts in his quest for release.

The only way to get relief was to punish himself, to beat the evil humours out of his body.

The whistle of the lash jerked him back to the present. His lips whitened when the next blow fell, cutting across his shoulders and laying a weal across the old scars.

That one hurt, but not enough. Not nearly enough to exorcise her image. No matter what he did, no matter how much he fasted, purged himself, or prayed, he could not get Carlotta out of his mind. Pain was the only thing that made any impression on his senses.

'Harder, curse you! Harder,' he grunted.

The whore stifled a yawn and drew her arm back for another blow. The sound cut through the air and cracked onto his back. Felipe winced, his whole body tense, waiting for the moment when the pain would sink and the heat and pleasure bloom within him.

'Ah . . .' he groaned when the lash curled around his arm and the tip spread fire across one nipple.

It was almost time. His whole body was a throbbing mass of aches. Now he would do the penance which he had set himself. It had been an inspired punishment. Fight fire with fire. That was the way. Soon he would be free of her. He was convinced of it.

'Stop,' he said to the whore. 'Put down the lash. You know what to do.'

'Same as always?' She sounded uninterested, as if she couldn't wait to be paid and leave.

Sauntering over to the altar, she hitched up her skirts and planted her backside on the fine, white linen cloth. Felipe stood up and walked towards her, his erection bobbing in front of him. She threw him a pert look, her eyes glinting in the candle light.

'Why don't you let me see to that, señor? You look to be in sore need. It would be a pleasure to serve such a fine looking man as you. I'll not charge you extra.'

He glowered at her. 'Mind your business and set your eyes to alight on the holy cross. You are here to do God's work, wench, not to ply your filthy trade.'

She was young and, he supposed, comely in her way. Her round, good-natured face was topped by a mop of frizzy yellow hair and her bare arms and chest were white and firm, if none too clean.

'Well?' he said.

Casting her eyes heavenwards and making a sound of resignation, she lay back on the altar and stretched her arms out to the sides.

'Ready,' she said tonelessly, beginning to recite the prayers as he had instructed.

With trembling fingers Felipe lifted her skirts and petticoats and rolled them up to lie in a bundle around her waist. He kept his eyes averted from her rounded belly and thighs until he had taken a step back.

The whore was instructed not to look at him, but to tell her rosary beads whatever he did to her, and she seemed biddable enough. Her voice was toneless, without interest, but the beauty of the latin phrases imprinted themselves on his senses nonetheless.

The urge to close his fingers around his straining shaft was strong, but he resisted it. He would do nothing to bring on his climax. If he was granted release, then it would be by the grace of God. Raising his eyes he looked between the whore's thighs – to that place; the source of all his longing.

She had a thatch of coarse brown hair on her mound. Her legs were a little apart and the plum shape of her coynte was standing proud at the base of her belly. The fleshy lips were parted a little and he could see the sinful reddish folds within.

With a groan he fell to his knees and buried his face in her groin. She smelt of sweat, musk, and cheap perfume. Wonderful. Grasping her fat white thighs, he dug his fingers into the flesh as he pushed them apart. And there it was, uncovered to his gaze. How lewd it was, how tantalising.

He pressed his face into the warm well of her secret female flesh, covering his lips and nose. There was something soothing in the smell and texture of her coynte, something which gave him comfort. But he fought that sensation. It was a diabolical trick. This place was wholly wicked. It was the Devil who put the other thoughts into his head.

Trembling, he tasted her, making little animal sounds in his throat. He lapped at her, feeling the delicate conformation of the folds and the opening which led to her womb. How subtle was the design of the Devil's artistry. Under his tongue the rain-tasting flesh was slippery and delicious. His cock leapt and throbbed and he felt the tension inside him gathering and peaking.

Her voice droned on and the cadence of the prayers washed over him. Gripping her thighs harder, he rubbed his face over her sex, smearing her salty wetness over his cheeks, his chin, his lips. Her frowsty privy curls brushed against his nose and he arched his back, his hips pumping in a parody of the act of sexual union, as his semen jetted from him and splashed onto the side of the altar.

Oh Lord, deliver me from sin, he prayed inwardly as the spasms of pleasure faded and his body grew quiet. Make me clean and whole again. The whore's voice died away and he felt her waiting for him. She made a muffled sound and he flushed. Did she dare to laugh at him?

Shame washed over him in a drenching wave, but he felt better despite that. For a while he had been granted release. It would be some hours before he was plagued by lustful imaginings. And if he drank enough before climbing into his bed, he might even be able to sleep without dreaming.

He stood up, a trickle of sperm running down his thigh. It was cold and he dashed it away with his hand. Disgust twisting his mouth, he slapped the whore's thigh urging her to her feet.

'Your money is on the settle in my bed chamber. Take it and get out.'

She smiled, to reveal missing front teeth.

'To be sure, señor,' she said equably. 'And will I be coming back at the same time, seven days hence?'

Felipe let out a deep shuddering sigh. His shoulders drooped and he turned his back. Then he said, in a voice so low that she had to strain to hear it, 'Yes. God help me. Come back then. But for now just go.'

Carlotta rested her elbows on the trestle table and looked across at Manitas who was eating heartily of a stew of spiced pork and plantain.

He ate with single-minded relish, giving his whole attention to the meal. She suspected that he would approach any given task in the same way. Was he as thorough in all his dealings? She coloured. Certainly he was a consummate lover.

She spooned stew into her mouth. The food was good, hot and fragrant with the flavours of black pepper and chillis. Dipping a piece of black bread into her bowl, she mopped up the last of the gravy and then sat back.

Manitas looked up and caught her staring at him. He grinned and pushed the crock which held more stew across the table.

'You eat like a bird. Take some more. Have our recent exertions given you no great appetite? I, for one, am as hungry as a wolf.'

Carlotta met his gaze, aroused by the way he was looking at her. His blue eyes danced with humour and self-satisfaction, but there was a spark of lust and appreciation in their depths. She wanted him again already, but she concealed the fact behind a stony face. He was too sure of his own attraction. No doubt many women went weak at the knees when Manitas Le Vasseur strode into a room.

She did not intend to be counted amongst his vanquished. And the sooner he realsed that, the better; even if the image of his powerful naked body did loom large in her thoughts, she thought, with heavy irony. She still burned to feel him inside her, to taste the pleasures of his enormous cock – which he had, so far, denied her.

'Your name is French,' she said to fill the uncomfortable silence. 'Yet, Manitas, is a Spanish name.'

'My mother was French and my father an *hidalgo*. She never knew his name. He abandoned my mother and went off to the New World in search of riches. My mother gave me her name.'

Although his voice was cool and without passion, she had the feeling that he still nursed a bitterness towards the Spanish soldier of fortune who had fathered him. She did not comment, but reached out and poured herself a glass of wine. As she shifted position, the soreness of her spanked buttocks sent an erotic thrill straight to the base of her belly.

Manitas was watching her closely. Damn his eyes. She could see by his expression that he knew exactly what she was thinking. His firm mouth lifted at one corner and the fine lines around his blue eyes crinkled attractively.

She felt herself unbending and suddenly she smiled. It was impossible not to like this giant of a man. But that made no difference to her plans. She was determined not to be swayed from her course by simple lust. That had never happened in the past and it would not now. Not even with a man as charismatic and potent as Manitas.

'Have you thought about my proposition?' she asked him at length.

He nodded slowly. 'I'm still considering it. I think better on a full stomach.' He stroked his chin, and went on eating.

She felt a burst of impatience. How infuriating he could be. She had offered to put up the money for food and supplies enough for a long sea voyage. All he had to do was procure a ship. It was what he craved. Why was he holding back?

'Any man with half a mind can see what riches are to be had for the taking,' she said tartly.

'True enough,' he said, shrugging his shoulders.

'Then why are you not eager to accept my offer? Perhaps you do not believe that I have money.'

It was true that she did not look as if she possessed a great fortune. Her clothes were serviceable and of rough cloth and her thick dark hair, although clean and shining, was undressed, pulled back simply and clasped at the nape with a ribbon. She smiled inwardly. What a difference a few short weeks made. Her beauti-

ful clothes of figured velvets and brocade, fine under-
things of silk and lace, elaborate hair styles and her
jewellery of gold set with precious stones – all those
things seemed like a dream.

Manitas stopped eating finally and gave her his
undivided attention. Steepling his fingers, he leaned
towards her.

'Thus far, I have seen scant evidence of any wealth.
Oh, you have bold plans and a sharp enough tongue
for ten women, but the only jewels you have to give
weight to your words, are those rubies that crest your
breasts. Fine enough they are, they won't put food into
the mouth of a ship's crew.'

Narrowing her eyes, she glared at him.

'You still think I am trying to buy your help by letting
you into my bed? If I was a man you'd take me on
trust!'

He grinned. 'If you were a man, I'd have sent you on
your way. Aye, and with a bruised jaw for making my
ears ache with such tales. Come now, admit it, you
have no fortune to barter with.'

She was tempted to put a single gold piece on the
table, but her hoard was too precious to risk losing even
that. He would have to take her on trust or not at all.

'Perhaps I should find someone else to help me,' she
said coolly. 'Hispaniola must be bursting with men who
are eager to make their fortune.'

She stood up as if about to leave, fully expecting
Manitas to protest or even to order her to sit down –
any other man would have pleaded with her to stay –
but he did none of those things.

'As you wish,' he said evenly. 'The choice is yours.
But you would be making a mistake. And you know it.'

Carlotta pressed her lips together, biting back the
angry words which rose in her throat. He was right. It
was him she wanted. It was going to be difficult to
accept that she could not bend this man to her will, but
it was a lesson she had better learn – and quickly.

She sat down again, gathering her dignity around her. Manitas picked up an orange from the bowl which stood on the table and held it out to her. She schooled herself not to snatch the fruit from him. Closing her hand around the orange, she reached for the knife which was strapped to her thigh.

She was aware of him watching her movements, as she cut into the peel. The sharp sweet odour of citrus scented the room.

'With such soft white hands you should be embroidering altar cloths,' he said, grinning wolfishly when she glowered at him.

'I would sooner hold a sword than a needle!' she said heatedly. 'Think you that I have no stomach for the work I've set before you?'

'I jest only. Do not look so fierce. You do realise what you are asking?' It's nothing less than piracy.'

'I know it,' she said stiffly. 'Surely the concept does not shock you? What have you been doing these past months, but raiding passing ships? You are a thief already. Come now. Do not insult my intelligence. I see by your face that this is something you want – and badly so.'

'True enough. I want my own ship more than anything, but I'll not put myself in any woman's thrall. And of a certainty, not in ignorance. There is much you aren't telling me. Why do you want to take up such a life? A woman with your looks could make a good marriage, have lands, servants, children.'

She felt a pang at all she had lost. For a moment there was a bitterness in her throat.

'My reasons are my own,' she said, and her voice held a tremor. 'Is it not enough that I have money and the will to advance it?'

He shook his head. 'For some men, perhaps. Not for me. Not if we're going to be partners. I will have the truth of it. By God, but you've fire in your belly! So, tell me. Who has wronged you?' His voice gentled.

'Wounds have a way of going bad unless they're sealed with a hot iron. Best let out your demons, Carlotta. Tell me everything and then have done with it.'

For a moment longer she gaped at him, amazed at his perception. She felt ashamed that she had planned to use him, playing on his assumed greed and roughness of character. He had robbed, probably killed, and had been shaped by life into a man with few soft edges. But in his own way he was a sensitive and honourable man.

She found herself telling him everything, holding back no detail, however humiliating. She could hardly bare to look at him as she recounted how she had been cheated out of her inheritance. Manitas's eyes sparked with anger when she spoke about Don Felipe. She told him how she had discovered, through her agent, Diaz, that Felipe had bribed court officials. The only part she omitted was the scene in her bed chamber. She could not bring herself to relive those moments. The very thought of Don Felipe's face, bound by agonized lust as he spilt his seed into his breeches, caused her to shudder with revulsion.

Finally, she told Manitas how she would have lost everything, but for the help of Diaz in securing the sale of her jewels. 'So you see that I do have funds. The money is in a safe place.'

When she had finished, Manitas was silent for a while as if digesting it all. He stroked his jaw and she expected him to make some comment about her changed circumstances, perhaps to question her, but instead he said, shortly: 'I too have experience of men like Don Felipe.'

There was such bitterness in his voice that she looked at him with heightened interest. She expected him to enlarge on the subject, but she saw by his closed expression that he had nothing more to say for the present. So she had not been mistaken when she sensed that he had suffered some loss in his life.

Manitas dragged his fingers through his swept back hair and the fierceness slipped from his face.

'Very well,' he said in a more normal tone. 'Now I understand. You want revenge on Felipe and his kind and you have good cause. But how will raiding Spanish treasure ships at random affect him personally?'

Carlotta realised that she could hold nothing back now. She must gamble on his integrity. Hoping that her trust in him would not prove to be misplaced, she told him about the documents she had stolen from Alberto.

'The charts show the routes taken by Felipe's and his associates' merchant ships. I have lists of commodities and suppliers. Felipe has investments in spices, cloth, and New World treasures and I know where his ships take on cargo and where they are destined for.'

Manitas grinned widely. 'Do you, by God! What a surprising wench you are. I won't ask how you came by that information. I don't think I want to know. With this knowledge we can ruin your bloody stiff-necked Don and get rich into the bargain. A sweeter revenge was never dreamed of!'

'So you accept my offer?' she said, somewhat unnecessarily. He had said 'we' after all and his suntanned face was flushed with excitement, but she was trying to maintain her dignity and not to burst into delighted laughter.

'Aye. On the condition that the vessel shall be mine and I'll be master of her. Partners we may be, but I'll not take orders from any woman.'

She no longer cared to dispute over the fine details. He had accepted her offer and that was all that mattered. There would be time enough to assert herself later.

'You can have mastery of the ship and gladly,' she said. 'I want only the use of it until I have brought down my enemies. If you will help me in that task you can have anything you want.'

He threw back his head and laughed, showing his

strong brown throat. She saw the smooth golden skin through the opening of his loose shirt and quickened with desire. Her fingers itched to stroke his skin, to feel the silky hairs on his chest. Manitas saw her expression.

'Come here,' he said huskily.

She went to him and he pulled her onto his lap. His big hands were warm on her arms, the heat of him penetrating through the loose weave of her sleeves. He smelt of leather, clean hair, and healthy maleness. Encircling her waist he crushed her to his broad chest, his mouth buried in her hair.

'And shall you be keeping house for me, here on Hispaniola, whilst I rap the knuckles of your Don Felipe?' he teased.

Carlotta chuckled and felt him respond to the infectious notes of her laughter. She felt light with happiness.

'Indeed I shall not, sire! I'm no native girl to sweep your hearth and warm your bed. Never was I a woman to sit and wait for her man. I'm strong and healthy. I can work and I'm a better swordswoman than most men. I'm going with you. Juanita will come also.'

Manitas grinned. 'Ah, you seek to repay my jest about the altar cloths with a jest of your own. The very idea of women at sea, ha! It will be an inn for you then, until I return. One trip ought to be enough for a start. We'll have money enough to build a fine house and I'll bring you back silks and jewels enough to replace those you lost . . .' He tailed off, as she pulled away and stood up.

'What's amiss, sweeting? Have I said something wrong?'

'I'm serious, Manitas. I'm coming to sea with you. And nothing you say or do will stop me.'

His brows drew together and his face darkened.

'What foolishness is this? It's far too dangerous. The sea is a harsh mistress and leaves no space for battles of will. She demands everything of those who sail upon her. If I'm to be the master, I say who goes or stays. Besides, the men won't have it. It's bad luck to have women on board ship.

'Then you'll have to persuade them otherwise,' she said coolly. 'As you're the master, you tell them that I'm going to be aboard. Either I come with you or I find someone else to help me. I mean it, Manitas. Those are *my* terms.'

Manitas just looked at her, then slowly he began to smile.

'You are an impossible woman. I hardly know whether to kiss you or lock you up for your own safety!'

Eyes flashing, Carlotta glared at him, her hands on her hips.

'Don't even think of such a thing,' she said. 'Lest you favour notching of the ears and nostrils!'

Manitas reached for her. His voice thickened by desire, he said, 'Then I'll settle for kissing you. Bring the wine jug and let us repair to my room to discuss this matter further.'

Carlotta avoided him, stepping neatly to one side.

'I think not. You have work to do. Find me a ship and crew, monsieur. And then seek me out. You'll find me lodged at the inn.'

At the door she turned and blew him a kiss. Her heart was light as she walked down the street. The sound of tropical birdsong hung in the air and palm trees shaded the dusty road. Overhead the sun beat down, striking silver glints off the waves which broke on the shore.

She felt a mixture of fear and excitement. Soon she would begin to wreak her revenge on Don Felipe. Now all she had to do was persuade Juanita that it was necessary for them to throw in their lot with pirates.

Chapter Seven

Juanita shaded her eyes with her hand, looking down the sweep of the hill towards the shore on the northern part of the island. Visible between the trees was a battered three-masted rig, her masts moving gently with the movement of the wind and waves.

Stacks of supplies, barrels of fresh water, salted pork, piles of fruit, all stood ready on the shore. She could see men moving on board the ship and in the midst of them was Manitas Le Vasseur, unmistakable on account of his height and great size. Even from this distance she could see that he bristled with weapons.

She shuddered as she took in the long knives thrust into his waistband, the double-edged sword secured to a baldric which ran diagonally across his chest. In one hand he held his most prized possession, his French matchlock musket. It was an ugly weapon, with a spade-shaped stock and a four-foot barrel.

How could Carlotta bear to be associated with such a barbarian? That he desired her strongly was plain. And Carlotta seemed to welcome his rough advances. Juanita blushed as she recalled the occasion when she had returned to the inn unexpectedly and surprised Carlotta with her lover.

Even now the images were clear in her mind. She felt an echo of the excitement which had built within her that day, a feeling prompted by viewing something which was meant to be private.

Carlotta's dark hair had streamed over her bare shoulders, strands of it masking the bulge of her cleavage which jutted over the pulled-down neck of her bodice. Manitas's hands were at work on her breasts, his fingers drawing out her nipples into little tube shapes while his face was buried against her shoulder. The way he pinched and tweaked the tender flesh looked painful, but Carlotta's throaty moan held pleasure as well as eagerness.

But it was not her mistress's reactions which demanded Juanita's full attention. Her eyes were drawn to the enormous organ which reared up from the opening in Manitas's breeches. She stood transfixed, unable to look away from Carlotta's slender white fingers which encircled the thick reddened shaft and began to stroke it.

Neither Carlotta nor Manitas noticed her standing in the doorway and she held her breath, watching as the tight cock-skin was smoothed up and down and the moist bulb of the purplish glans came into view. How strong the cock looked; and the big haired ballocks looked tight and full of seed.

There was a weak feeling in her knees and a sort of tingling heat low down in the pit of her stomach. Pressing her hand against her open mouth, Juanita drank in the sight of her mistress pleasuring the buccaneer. When Manitas slid his hand up her leg, Carlotta gave one of her throaty chuckles and moved her thighs to accommodate him.

Juanita was shocked and fascinated. Her experience with men was limited to some brief fumbling with a stable lad and a few encounters with drunken noblemen. The latter had consisted of hot hands thrust under her skirts while wine-scented kisses were pressed to her mouth and bosom. Once a bold young man had taken hold of her coynte and stroked her until she was hot and shaking in his arms.

She had been ready to give herself to him there and then behind the tapestry with hunting scenes which screened the alcove, but she recovered her good sense in time. Pushing him away, she wriggled free before his caresses became even more insistent. But in the safety of her own bed, she had wondered what it would feel like to have a man lying between her thighs.

As she put her hands on the place he had touched, mirroring the movements he made, she had imagined the pleasure-pain of the moment when a man pushed himself into her. She stroked the swollen and slippery flesh until the tension built within her and became a sweet ache that was almost unbearable. Then something had crested, seeming to break, and wave after wave of exquisite sensation had swept over her. That was when she discovered that she could give pleasure to herself. And though she prayed for forgiveness, she could not stop herself committing that licentious act, time after time.

Manitas made a sound deep in his throat as Carlotta squeezed his cock-tip. Juanita pressed her thighs together, trying to quell the throbbing which was spreading between her legs. Manitas's cock twitched and pulsed as Carlotta stroked it. She had seen male organs before; even noblemen were not averse to uncovering themselves and pissing in the outside court-yards and gardens, too lazy to use the privy. But this was the first time she had seen an erect cock at such close quarters. It looked so enticing, so dangerous. She longed to touch it, to see if the skin which sheathed that impressive male hardness was as soft as it looked.

Lost in her own erotic imaginings, she started when Manitas looked up and saw her. The guilty colour flooded her cheeks. His eyes met hers and he smiled knowingly. Lifting one hand he crooked a finger and

81

beckoned to her to enter the room. Stammering an apology she fled, trying to shut out the sound of his mocking laughter.

Carlotta had not spoken of the incident, but it was there between them. Juanita knew that sometime the subject would arise. She half dreaded, half longed for Carlotta to speak to her about the pleasures of lying with a man.

Dragging her attention back to the present, she focused on the misery that was consuming her. The ship would be ready to sail in a few short hours and her life was about to take the most unexpected turn yet. Surely it was impossible that they were about to become pirates. Such scavengers of the seas could expect no quarter if they were captured.

Pirates were hanged or worse. She remembered seeing the mouldering bodies of thieves and cut-throats hanging on gibbets at a cross-roads. The fly-blown corpses were a common enough sight and a source of amusement to those who passed by, but suddenly the image had new meaning for her.

She would follow her mistress to the ends of the earth if she so desired, but on this occasion Juanita doubted the wisdom of Carlotta's actions. Perhaps she would refuse to go. She could make a life for herself on Hispaniola. There was work to be found in the large port city of Santo Domingo. If she could not find a position as a lady's maid, she would seek work in an ale house or scrub floors; anything would be preferable to raiding Spanish ships and risking life and limb.

But in her heart she knew that she could not bear to be parted from Carlotta. If only her mistress were not so headstrong. Carlotta hated Don Felipe with an abiding passion and would not rest until she brought him low. Juanita felt that it was better to accept their losses and look ahead. For what could two women do against a man as powerful as Felipe?

There came the sound of a footfall behind her and she turned, her eyes widening with surprise.

Carlotta was dressed ready for the life ahead. She wore leather stays, long and notched to fit low on the hips, over a loose blouse. Her coarse woollen skirt barely reached to her ankles and was looped up and secured to a belt at her waist. Underneath she wore a serviceable petticoat of red serge; striped stockings and stout buckled shoes were revealed below. Her hair was twisted into a plait and pinned crown-like around her head.

She looked like a pirate queen. All she needed was a kerchief at her neck and a pair of pistols. Behind her, in the doorway of the inn, stood a sea-trunk which held everything they would be taking with them.

At the look on Juanita's face, Carlotta laughed.

'Why so shocked by my dress? I did think of donning doublet and breeches, but 'twil be difficult enough for the crew to accept women on board. I don't wish to inflame their passions by offering them a view of well-filled hose!'

Juanita did not respond to Carlotta's tone. The last thing she felt like was jesting.

'So we really are going with them?' she said in a low voice.

'I told you so some weeks hence, did I not, you silly goose? Oh, Juanita do not look so whey-faced. Where's your spirit? It will be an adventure.'

Juanita grimaced. Somehow she had hoped that Carlotta would change her mind when the time came to make the choice, but she saw now that there never had been any hope of that.

'I was sick on the journey here,' she said desperately. 'And I'm terrified of storms. There'll be no privacy. I cannot swim –'

'Most sailors cannot swim. As for the rest, you'll get used to all that,' Carlotta interrupted in a voice that brooked no argument. 'We *have* to go. And that's an end to it. Do you think I should trust Manitas and his men to share out the plunder fairly? I need to be there to see what is taken. Besides I want to deal with Felipe's associates personally – should we be lucky enough to find any of them on board their merchant vessels. Come now. Hurry and change your clothes. They are laid out ready in our room.'

Juanita went into the inn, to the upstairs room which she had shared with Carlotta for the past month. She had grown used to sleeping in a single truckle bed. The straw mattress and sheets were well-worn and rough, but they were clean. The only other furniture, a table and chairs and a clothes press, shone from her regular attention. The floor was swept clean and the grass mats shaken free from dust.

The little chamber with its sharply sloping ceiling had begun to feel like home. Part of her had hoped that their travels were over. She was sad and fearful about exchanging the comfort of the inn for the unknown terrors of the seas.

As she undressed and pulled on the garments which Carlotta had laid out for her, her hands trembled. In any other circumstances she would have been amused by the fact that their roles, on this occasion, were reversed. It ought to have been *she* who prepared Carlotta's clothes, she who packed the trunk. But, sensing her reluctance to leave the island, Carlotta had taken charge and made all the arrangements.

With an air of fatality, Juanita pinned up her light brown curls and covered them with a square of cloth. There was no sense in fighting against destiny. When Carlotta set her mind on something there was no reasoning with her. Despite her fears she felt a surge of admiration for her mistress.

Somehow she doubted whether Manitas realised how stubborn and wilful Carlotta could be. He was probably blinded by her beauty and sensuous body; most of her lovers were. As Juanita left the room, she was smiling.

The prospect of watching Carlotta get the better of the huge buccaneer was an entertaining one.

Carlotta was aware of the hostile glances and low voiced complaints of the ship's crew, but she ignored them as she strode across the deck of the *Esmeralda*.

At her side Manitas gave her a look which said, 'What else did you expect?' but she ignored him too. She understood why the men did not want women aboard. In their view Juanita and herself were an unwelcome distraction. Some of the men would feel protective towards them and wary of engaging in battle when the time came, others would feel something more basic. But whatever their thoughts and desires, women meant trouble.

Carlotta hoped that they would accept her eventually. She expected no help from Manitas. He had made it plain that he did not approve of her decision to come with them. Well, she was prepared to prove herself when the time came, but for the present she was determined to keep calm and put on a brave face.

Glancing around she took in the details of the ship. The rig was old and had seen better days, perhaps her former owner was glad to be relieved of her. The crew had scrubbed the deck and repaired the sails. Two new longboats were secured next to the main hatch.

Seeing where her glance fell, Manitas said, 'You have noticed the pinnaces? They will be the means by which we board our first galleon.'

Carlotta made her way to the poop deck and the hatch which led below. There were a number of cabins on the lower deck. Manitas showed her into the largest and most well furnished of them, a confident smile on his face as he sat on the bed.

'Juanita and I shall share this cabin,' she said coolly. 'A smaller cabin should be sufficient for your needs.'

Manitas seemed about to protest. Obviously he had expected her to share his bed and his cabin. His lips tightened and she saw the effort it cost him not to comment. Finally, he shrugged.

'As you wish,' he said tonelessly. 'I will leave you to make yourself comfortable. If you need me, I'll be on deck. We sail on the next tide.'

Carlotta closed the door after him. She suspected that Manitas was used to having everything his own way where women were concerned. Having herself as a business partner must have seemed like a novelty to him, something to pay lip service to only. She wanted to impress on him the fact that she intended acting as she saw fit – whether he approved or not.

Juanita set about unpacking.

'It is better than I expected,' she said, exclaiming in delight over the bed which fitted neatly into an alcove. 'I had thought we might have to sleep on deck, bundled together with the crew. Those men frighten me. They are so rough looking. And their eyes seem filled with hate.'

'They fear us,' Carlotta said. 'Or perhaps it is that they fear the beast within themselves.' She saw how pale Juanita was and laughed to lighten the mood. 'With such comfortable quarters you need not go up on deck too often. And I can take care of myself. Nothing bad will happen to us. Trust me. Have I not always protected you?'

Juanita nodded, but she looked doubtful.

They set sail a few hours later and Juanita began to feel sick almost at once. Her skin taking on a greenish tinge, she crouched over a leather bucket.

'I . . . told you . . . this would . . . happen,' she gasped between bouts of sickness. 'Oh . . . I'm certain I'm dying . . .'

'It will pass. Let it take its course,' Carlotta said calmly, tending her until the retching became less violent.

She wiped Juanita's face with a cool cloth, smoothing back the tangled hair from her forehead. Finally Juanita

86

stopped retching and slumped against the bed, too weak even to sit. Carlotta spooned a little brandy and hot water between her lips and put her to bed.

'Sleep now,' she said. 'You'll awake refreshed. In a few days you'll have found your sea legs.'

Juanita groaned by way of a reply and allowed Carlotta to tuck the bed covers around her. In a few minutes she sank into an exhausted sleep. Carlotta felt a twinge of remorse. Juanita would not be ill if she had not insisted on them both going to sea.

The room smelt sour and musty and she sprinkled a few drops of lavender water onto the lip of the metal candle-holder. The fresh scent filled the room and reminded her of clean linen sheets. She saw again the enormous tester bed in her panelled bed chamber, the embroidered cover of rose-coloured brocade. Felipe slept in that bed now, if he had not already sold her house and lands. A pang of loss spread through her.

'I had no choice, Juanita,' she said softly. 'Felipe must be made to pay. I won't rest until I've ruined him.'

It was warm in the cabin and she unlaced her stays, slipped off her blouse and skirt, and changed into a loose robe of figured silk – one of the few things she had brought with her from her former life. It was strangely comforting to feel the caress of the familiar garment against her bare arms.

The cabin was filled with the sound of creaking timbers and the muted rumble of the waves. Juanita's deep breathing could barely be heard above the noise. Carlotta sat beside her, looking down at the white and pinched little face.

Like many people with good health and a strong body, she was impatient with those who were ailing, but she was more worried about Juanita than she cared to admit. She would have welcomed the solid, practical presence of Manitas, but did not expect him to seek her out just yet. No doubt he was nursing his bruised pride.

Juanita slept on and the hours dragged by. Carlotta

dozed for a while and awoke in a panic before she realised where she was. The presence of the sea, only feet away through the wooden hull, seemed like an angry beast. The pounding noise and the smell of salt in the air was exhilarating. She stretched and yawned. Inactivity always made her restless. It would be pleasant to lean over the ship's rail and feel the sea air on her face, but she resisted the urge to go on deck deciding that it was prudent to stay in her cabin for a while longer. That way the sailors would not be reminded of her presence.

She realised that she felt hungry. The motion of the waves and Juanita's sickness had done nothing to blunt her appetite. By the end of another hour she had decided to dress and go in search of the ship's kitchen, when Manitas tapped on the cabin door.

The smell of food which wafted into the cabin as he entered it made her mouth water.

'I thought you would both be hungry,' he said, placing the dish of roast pork and vegetables on the table.

'Juanita is sleeping. Best not wake her,' Carlotta said.

Manitas nodded. 'The little one suffers badly with "*le mal de mer*"? Shall you come to my cabin to eat? Our talking will not disturb her there and I have a good Rhenish wine we can share.'

'I thought sailors ate hard biscuits and washed the weevils down with brackish water,' she said.

Manitas grinned. 'They do, on long voyages. We should not be at sea for more than a few weeks at any time. Besides, it's always possible to stop off at one of the islands and hunt for fresh meat.'

It seemed that his good humour was quite restored. She was pleased that he did not simmer over supposed slights. It would have been tedious in the extreme, since they were obliged to live in close proximity for the next few weeks.

She returned his grin, registering that he was looking

with more than casual interest at the loose silk robe she wore. The thin fabric clung to her body, the soft outline making clear the fact that she wore no stays. His eyes lingered on the soft swell of her bosom.

Their eyes met and, holding her gaze, he put out a finger and slipped it inside the overlapping folds at the front of her robe. His touch on the inner curve of her breast made her skin tingle with wanting.

'And what else shall we share – besides the Rhenish?' she said, her voice low and husky.

As she followed him to his cabin, she was aware of a mounting excitement. The thought of his expert fingers on her body, his mouth covering hers, was intoxicating. Once inside the room, she schooled herself to be patient and eat first. She enjoyed anticipating the fleshly pleasures to come – especially this time. Manitas was about to get his second lesson of the day.

The stew was surprisingly good. The cook had flavoured it with bay and cardamom. There was fresh bread to accompany it, warm and fragrant and studded with ripe black olives. The wine was smooth on her tongue and imparted a satisfying glow as it slipped down her throat.

Conscious of Manitas's eyes on her, she looked up and smiled.

'Mmmm. That was wonderful. Thank you. I cannot eat another bite.'

He sipped his wine, regarding her over the rim of his wine goblet. His mouth curved in a wolfish grin.

'It is my pleasure to serve you,' he said gallantly.

Oh it will be, it will be, she thought.

'How long before we intercept one of the merchant ships on my list?' she said.

'One week, two, depending on the weather. Are you so eager to get your hands on Felipe's riches.?'

'I'd prefer to get my hands on his person. My fingers itch to close around his scrawny neck – but I'll settle for his goods for the present.'

'And speaking of the laying on of hands . . .' Manitas reached for her and drew her to her feet.

Carlotta let him lead her to his narrow bed. She remained standing in front of him when he sat down. His hands rested on her waist at the place where it met the curve of her hip. When he would have pulled her down to sit beside him, she resisted.

'Wait just a little,' she said in her most seductive voice.

'As you wish,' he said, loosening the belt of her robe.

The garment slipped from her shoulders and slid to the floor. Underneath she wore only a thin, knee-length chemise and her stockings and shoes. The red-brown cones of her nipples pushed against the chemise. She felt them hardening as Manitas's warm breath played over them.

She waited for him to press his lips to her breasts and mouth her nipples, or to gather the full globes in his big hands as he loved to do, but he did neither of those things. He slid his hands up the outside of her legs, his calloused palm catching on her woollen stockings. As he moved higher and encountered an obstruction, he looked up at her.

'Do you always wear a dagger strapped to your leg?'

'Always,' she said, smiling down at him. 'Women are so often at the mercy of men.'

'And are you not at my mercy now? I thought it was where you wished to be.'

Oh, he was very sure of himself and of his erotic hold over her senses. Even sitting, he topped her by a head and shoulders. His sheer size was daunting. The thought of making him do her will excited and aroused her.

'Perchance I am weaker than you,' she said lightly. 'But things can change quite unexpectedly.'

His hands continued their explorations and she let out her breath on a sigh when he reached the bare flesh above her garters. His touch on her thighs was soft and

90

knowing. She felt the desire gathering into a hot knot inside her. She should stop him now, she reasoned, if she was to put her plan into action, but her body wanted more.

Just a little longer then.

His fingers stroked the hair on her Venus mound and she swayed towards him. The folds of her coynte were growing swollen and heavy. A trickle of wetness seeped from the centre of her as Manitas parted the flesh-lips and pressed a fingertip to the hard little bud which was pulsing with a life of its own. He circled the protuberance, using the pad of his thumb which was slick with her moisture.

Enough is enough, Carlotta decided. In another moment she would not be able to think straight.

'Wait,' she whispered. 'I'm too hot for you. I'm ready to reach my peak now. I want to make this last. Let me ready *you* this time.'

Manitas grinned and removed his hand.

'As you wish. Play your games if you've a mind to,' he said indulgently, slipping the two fingers he had used to caress her into his mouth. He rolled his eyes with pleasure as he tasted her musky juices, then lay back and linked his arms behind his head.

Carlotta swept her eyes over his remarkable frame. He looked bigger than ever sprawled out like that. His shoulders filled the width of the bunk and he was forced to bend his legs a little so that his booted feet rested against the side of the alcove.

'You've hardly room to lie down. How will you sleep?' she asked him.

'With my knees folded into my chest and my dreams filled with you,' he said.

He could be so charming. Coming from another man such words would have been trite, but he made them sound fresh, as though he had never spoken them to another woman. She smiled down at him. Take care,

91

she warned herself. Do not fall under his spell. It would be a mistake to allow Manitas too much power over her.

There was about him, an over-powering maleness tempered by those flashes of unexpected subtlety. She desired Manitas more with each passing day. The erotic tension throbbed inside her like a live thing. As she changed position she became aware of the wet fullness of her coynte. She had never been so ready for a man.

'Close your eyes,' she whispered. 'Are you willing to play a game of trust?'

He nodded happily. His lips were slightly parted and there was a flush across his high cheekbones.

'Good,' she said. 'Then give your wrists to me,'

After only the slightest hesitation he held them out. Removing the belt from his waist, she bound his wrists together, then secured them to the lamp hook which was placed at the head of the bunk.

'How does that feel?' she asked him, keeping her voice light and playful.

'Somehow familiar,' he grinned. 'Did I not hold your hands just so, the first time we shared pleasure?'

He had done indeed. And she had not forgotten it. Neither had she forgotten how arrogant he had been in his treatment of her body, though it was true that he had given her pleasure.

She began moving her hands over his chest. Slipping them inside his jerkin, she stroked his skin. He felt warm and smooth. Good, he was relaxed, suspecting nothing more than a teasing game.

Stretching out his legs, he tensed his muscles and sighed with pleasure. She felt his chest tauten under her fingers and his nipples gathered into tiny firm teats. Her desire for him increased. She liked the thought of having such a powerful man at her mercy; as indeed he was, not that he realised the fact.

'Does this game please you?' he said huskily.

'Oh yes. And you like it too. I can tell by the tightness

of your breeches. You will like it even more. I vow it. Lie still while I undress you.'

Manitas moved his head on the pillow, settling his cheek more comfortably. He seemed content for her to have her way a while longer. His lips curved in a confident grin.

'When you let me up, woman, I'll give you something to remember,' he said, the desire sounding thick and dense in his voice. 'I know what it is you want from me and I am ready to cede you that now.'

Her blood leapt. Could he mean what she thought he did?

He had come to her room in the inn on a number of occasions during the past weeks. Each time they kissed, he stroked her body and brought her to her full pleasure with his fingers. For some reason he continued to deny her his cock, spending himself in her mouth or outside her body until she was nearly driven mad with frustration.

Once he grasped her breasts, squeezing them together to form a channel for his cock. She had arched her back in helpless frustration, as he thrust himself into her cleavage, riding the deep channel until his warm seed splashed against her chin.

For that humiliation, and for the other times, she intended to exact her revenge.

'Soon. Soon now,' she murmured to him as he moved impatiently under her hands. 'Lift your hips, so that I can unlace your breeches. That's the way.'

She peeled the fabric open and his erect cock sprang free. He moved his hips a little more and she pulled the fabric down to his thighs, revealing the curling hair at his groin and his scrotal sac. His balls looked tight as if he was ready to spurt at any moment.

'Mmmm,' she said. 'You're more than ready for me.'

She looked down at his big beautiful cock. It was thick and flushed. A drop of clear liquid trembled at the eye of his glans. Encircling the hot shaft she held it firmly and began moving the tight skin up and down.

Manitas groaned and surged towards her. In another moment he would ask her to stop. Already he was straining against the belt which held his wrists captive. The lamp hook creaked as he pulled on the leather. She saw the tendons on his wrists standing out whitely against the suntanned skin, but the sturdy belt held firm.

'Don't struggle,' she murmured. 'I'll ensure that you don't spend in my hands.'

Gauging his readiness, she eased the cock-skin down so that his purplish glans was laid bare. With the pad of her thumb she smoothed the moisture around the tiny slitted mouth. Manitas bucked against her.

'Enough of your teasing, wench,' he ground out. 'Let me up now and have done. I know you want me to turn you onto your belly and bury myself to the hilt inside your coynte.'

'Oh I think not,' she said, smiling sweetly. 'I've waited too long for you to grant me that pleasure. I'*m* going to have *you*. I'm mistress over you this night. And you cannot do anything about it.'

As she lifted her chemise and straddled him, his eyes flashed dangerously.

'The hell you are! I'll not have any woman swiving me! That's man's work!'

He thrust upwards from his hips and almost succeeded in throwing her off. In an instant she had her knife in her hand and was pressing the point of it under his chin. Gripping his naked hips with her thighs, she bent over him and stared him in the face.

'I would say that this makes us even. Wouldn't you? I'm no match for your strength, but see how I show my claws? Have a care now. I'll not hurt you if you do as I say.'

Manitas gave a roar of outrage, but he kept his chin stretched away from the knife point. He could have overpowered her easily enough if he had really wanted to. And they both knew it.

Carlotta lifted herself up and positioned herself over him. His cock lay hard and heavy against his belly. She felt his length pressing against her parted sex. If anything he was harder than before.

Manitas's breath left him in ragged gasps. His ribcage rose and fell and there was a sheen of sweat on his golden skin. Dipping her head, Carlotta mouthed the curls that frosted his chest. She darted out her tongue and licked his taut flesh. He tasted of soap and, more faintly, of salt.

'Delicious,' she said. 'What a feast for any woman.'

Behind the anger in his eyes, she saw curiosity and something else. In all the weeks she had known him she had never glimpsed such a raging lust in him. Sometimes she had marvelled at his control. Now she realised that it was himself he fought. For Manitas, power meant control – but some deeper, darker side of him reacted passionately to the lack of it.

The exultation rose up in her and her womb spasmed with eagerness. She could wait no longer. She ached to feel him inside her. Throwing her head back, so that her dark hair tumbled down her back and brushed his naked thighs, she took hold of his shaft. It was wet and slippery with their mixed juices.

Her own scent of arousal was strong in the closeness of the tiny room, and the pungent muskiness excited her further. Wiping her hand up the groove of her coynte, she reached out and smeared some of her seepage across his mouth. It was a parody of his action earlier and Manitas responded readily.

Groaning, he pushed out his tongue to lap at her slim white fingers, seeking out every creamy drop. When she thrust her fingers between his lips he writhed under her, savouring her taste and making little noises of pleasure deep in his throat.

The sounds found an echo inside her. An area in the

95

pit of her belly pulsed and throbbed. It gave her a feeling of immense power to be able to push him to such a pitch of arousal. How she gloried in acting as her true abandoned self.

'Oh, Manitas. This is new to you, I think,' she murmured. 'How does it feel to be bested by a woman?'

He wrenched his head away and glared at her. 'Tease me all you wish. But you'll not best me, wench.'

'Shall I not?' she teased. 'Then what am I doing now?'

She lowered herself onto him and collared the swollen plum with her flesh. His cock-head was hot and delicious against her opening. Slowly she eased herself down onto his shaft, loving the feeling of being stretched as he breached the closure of her flesh. He was so big that she thought he might tear her and the fear added an extra note to her pleasure.

'This is for me,' she said hoarsely. '*I'm* taking *you* Manitas.'

She paused, allowing herself to become accustomed to his size. His shaft twitched and pulsed inside her. Manitas arched his back and thrust at her, but she raised herself up so that only the tip of him remained inside her.

'Mother of God. Do it then,' he grunted, his voice rough with frustration. 'But be not gentle.'

Taking him at his word, she sank down and worked herself on him.

'Ah . . .' she murmured, as the whole delicious length of him slid into her.

God's bones, but he felt good. Better than she could have imagined. The long wait had been worth it. She had never been filled so completely. It was as if he was forging new pathways to pleasure inside her.

As she took her pleasure of him, Manitas chewed at his bottom lip. The knife slipped from Carlotta's grasp and fell onto the floor, but neither of them noticed. Splaying her fingers on his chest, she pushed herself up and down, riding him hard. The big glans knocked against her womb on each inward thrust and she cried out with the hurtful pleasure of it.

Manitas surged against her now, no longer keeping up his pretence at outrage. His face was bound by an expression of ecstasy. Black brows drawn together, his eyes screwed tight shut, he matched her thrust for thrust. As he arched into a bow shape, his hips lifting clear of the bunk, Carlotta leaned back and took her weight on her outstretched arms.

Slamming down onto the heated shaft, she felt it rubbing against the place of pleasure within her body. Few men had been able to stimulate her there, on the sensitive pad behind her pubis. Her climax built quickly and she did not try to hold it back. It felt as if some great beast were advancing towards her through a dark forest. The thud of its footprints was the beat of her heart, the surging of her blood.

'Oh, God,' she screamed as she came, the waves of pleasure bursting over her and radiating through her limbs.

Pressing the back of her hand to her mouth, she muffled the cries which she was helpless to control. The pleasure went on and on and for a moment blackness beckoned. She flopped forward dizzy and half conscious, Manitas's groans of release echoing in her ears.

His heartbeat was rapid against her cheek and she lay still, totally spent and incapable of movement. Her hair spilled across his chest, masking the upper part of his body with rich dark waves. When, in a moment, his arms came down to rest on her, she smiled. She had known that he could break free if he wanted to. His hands on her hair were gentle and she turned towards him so that he could stroke her cheek.

'You're quite a woman, Carlotta Mendoza,' he said and there was admiration and respect in his voice. 'I have a feeling that you always get what you want.'

'Always,' she said happily, a great contentment spreading through her.

She knew that Manitas accepted the reality of their bonding now. Their bed would always be a battlefield, a fight for sensual superiority, and the thought was stimulating to them both. But as a man and woman they were equals.

She sighed as she began to drift towards sleep. When the time came she could count on Manitas's unconditional support. The first step towards Felipe's downfall had been taken.

Chapter Eight

Carlotta stood beside Manitas as he poured over the chart spread out before him.

'We'll take the ship there,' he said, pointing to the line which marked out the ship's route. 'Those small islands will give us cover. We'll be on her before she knows it.'

The Spanish ship was owned by Antonio Alva, a banker and close associate of Felipe's. Carlotta knew that it would be a blow to Felipe's finances as well as his pride to lose one of Antonio's merchant ships.

'It'll be soon then? I'll go and ready myself,' she said to Manitas.

She was eager to board the ship and strike the first blow against Felipe. Besides, she had missed her fencing lessons with Monsieur Draycot and her sword arm needed exercising. The thought of boarding the treasure ship and besting the Spanish sailors was stimulating. It did not occur to her to be afraid.

Manitas shrugged.

'I suppose it is useless for me to remind you of the danger? I thought as much. Then I won't waste my time trying to persuade you to stay aboard the rig. You'll be in the first pinnace. It's safer for you there. Just promise me that you'll stay clear until the galleon is secured.'

'Why, Manitas, you sound as if you truly care for me,' she said, sparkling at him. 'and I thought it was just my body you enjoyed.'

'I'm just safeguarding the key to my coffers,' he said dryly. 'This is no matter for jesting, Carlotta. Your life is at stake. Have I your word that you'll obey me in this?'

'As you wish,' she said.

She lowered her eyes so that he could not see the glint of excitement. Of a certainty she had no intention of doing any such thing. His concern for her was touching, but misguided. She was no milk-sop weakling who would faint at the first sight of blood. But Manitas could not know that. He had never seen her use a sword. If he had, he would not have been worried about her safety.

Manitas was still studying her and she smiled to reassure him. The last thing she wanted was for him to have her forcibly restrained aboard the *Esmeralda*.

'Hmmm,' he grunted. 'Best change your clothes. You cannot climb in those skirts. Bind up your hair too. You're too striking in that garb. Every knave aboard the galleon will make you his target.'

Carlotta saw the sense of his words. She and Juanita had maintained a precarious balance between respect and superstitious fear from the crew. The fact that she was perceived as Manitas's woman meant that she was tolerated, but only just. She had grown used to the surly looks and muttered condemnations and had taken pains, up until now, to see that she did not provoke a stronger reaction.

She left Manitas to his chart and went to his cabin. Sorting through his chest of clothes she found a pair of leather breeches, a coarse linen shirt, and a studded leather doublet. They were all in a small size and she wondered where he had obtained them. He must have packed them away, ready for the moment when she would need them. His foresight surprised her.

Stripping off down to her stockings she slipped on the male garments. The breeches skimmed her thighs and hips and were too big on the waist. She belted them tightly over the shirt, then plaited her hair and stuffed it into a close-fitting cap. It was strange but liberating to feel the linen and leather against her naked skin. For most of her life she had worn stays, only leaving them off when there was no chance of discovery from maids or governesses.

It was considered shocking for a woman to be unrestrained by layers of petticoats and a stout boned corset. The church warned against the dangers of uncovering one's limbs. If the blood ran too freely, then evil humours would gather and lewdness would rise in one's thoughts, but Carlotta had never cared for convention nor the canting of priests. She did care, however, that her appearance might invite new censure from the crew. In view of that she buckled on her sword belt, wearing it outwardly for the first time.

The weight of it against her hip was reassuring. Her lips curved in a smile. No doubt the crew would find the sight of an armed woman doubly shocking. Well it was time she stopped sheltering behind Manitas and became herself.

Her suspicions were confirmed the moment she stepped on deck. Though she was concentrating on the smell of salt in the air and the clean spray which blew in with the wind, she could not help but hear the rumble of disapproval from two men who were swabbing the deck with buckets of sea water. She recognised the men as compatriots of Manitas. Both of them had been buccaneers on Hispaniola.

'Manitas must be addled in his wits,' one said loudly enough for her to hear. 'Bad enough that he tempts fate by bringing two women on board. But he has brought us a woman who thinks she is a man! Devil take it. There's nought so unnatural!'

The other laughed coarsely. He was a man of medium

height. His shoulders were narrow, as if stunted, but his body was corded with muscle. She recalled his name, Julio. Many times she had felt his eyes on her, but when she turned her head he slunk away.

Julio's small eyes glinted with lust as he raked her long legs and rounded hips. It was the first time he had faced her and she realised that this was some sort of test on his part. She stared him down and saw his mouth twist with contempt.

'Mayhap we should look inside those breeches,' he sneered. 'She has a woman's paps, but I'll wager there's a tiny pizzle hanging between those white thighs!'

'Nay! She has a sweet enough coynte to be sure. Manitas is no pederast.'

Carlotta did not respond to their crudity, although she felt her temper rising. She had once fought a duel over lesser insults. She lifted her chin. They were stupid and ignorant, she decided, and had no place in her life. Why should she heed them? She was about to move away, when Julio took a step towards her.

'A sweet coynte, say you so? I think I'll see for myself,' he said, his mouth cracking open to reveal broken and stained teeth. 'Come on, my pretty. Show us what you conceal inside your breeches. For the Brethren of the Coast share everything equally amongst them. Manitas has had you all to himself for too long.'

Both of them tittered, exchanging conspiratorial glances. Hearing the exchange, others began to gather around. Julio laid aside his bucket and took another step closer to her. Carlotta felt the tension gathering and resigned herself to dealing with Julio. It seemed that she must make an example of him. Something like this had been bound to happen. The men wouldn't have dared to speak that way if Manitas had been there, but he was below deck absorbed in the charts.

She felt her anger burning in her throat and fought to control it. The words of Monsieur Draycot echoed in her ears. 'Anger is your enemy. A cool head is your friend. Let not passion deflect your sword arm.'

His instructions, so long repeated that they were as second nature to her, came to her aid now. Though her heartbeat drubbed in her ears, her mind was calm. Flexing her fingers, she laid them on the pommel of her sword, unconsciously shifting her weight onto the balls of her feet.

Julio caught the movement and, for a moment, looked less sure of himself. She smiled and beckoned to him.

'Come then. Take my breeches from me – if you can. I might be short of a scrap of dangling flesh, but mayhap you'll find that I'm a better man than you.'

The other sailors whooped with laughter.

'The wench has spirit!' someone called out.

'Aye, too much for a decent woman. Teach her a lesson, Julio,' someone else said.

Carlotta drew her sword and held it point down. The sun glinted on the wickedly sharp point of the rapier. Julio's smile wavered, but he seemed unwilling to back down. The others called out encouragement. He turned to them, a worried look on his face.

'And what of that pigsticker she's holding? I don't favour a bloodletting.'

'Not when it's your own blood, eh! You're not usually so slow to take up a challenge,' another of the men called out and threw him a cutlass. 'Here. Tickle her with that. But have a care. Manitas won't look favourably on having his property damaged.'

Julio caught the cutlass deftly. Passing the solid-looking weapon from hand to hand he advanced on her. When he was a few paces away he stopped. His small eyes narrowed until they were slits. They were the colour of muddy water.

'Now then, wench,' he said softly. 'No need to get excited. I've no wish to mark that smooth skin of yours. Drop those breeches and show me what I want and I'll not harm a hair on your head.'

'A pox on you, you scurvy cove!' Carlotta moved in to the attack, the narrow silver blade flashing into action. 'I'll teach you some manners! It'll please me to lop off your ears and feed them to the sharks.'

Caught unawares by the ferocity of her response, Julio staggered backwards. His arm came up to defend himself, but the heavy cutlass was unwieldy; a weapon more suited to slashing at an opponent than engaging in swordplay. Clumsily he deflected her blows, the sweat breaking out on his forehead.

Carlotta, perfectly balanced, thrust and parried, her movements too rapid to follow. It was soon apparent that Julio was no match for her. She decided not to spare him, but to press home her advantage. There must be no mistake. The crew would be forced to respect her as one of their own from now on.

The men watched, spellbound by her grace and artistry.

'God's teeth. The wench fights like a hell-wain demon,' a sailor muttered in a low awe-filled voice.

Julio slashed and chopped with the cutlass, but the blade met with the air. Before he knew what was happening, Carlotta had slipped in under his guard and placed two slashes across the front of his doublet. A flap of leather peeled away and flopped forward to hang down over his breeches.

'Had enough?' she said coolly, standing back.

She was not even breathing hard. Julio, on the other hand, panting hard, lowered his sword and looked down at himself in amazement. He stroked his chest, then looked at his fingers as if expecting to see blood. His face was puce and his thin mouth worked furiously.

'I'll kill you for that. Wench or no,' he spat, beginning to circle her.

Carlotta watched him, anticipating the manner of his next attack. Julio's face was twisted and there were flecks of foam on his lips. She did not doubt that he intended to carry out his threat, but she was not afraid. She felt perfectly in control of the situation.

The sailors had fallen silent. They waited, some with evident enjoyment, others more warily. She knew what they were thinking. What if Julio killed her? Manitas would hang him or worse. And he would exact a heavy price from all of them.

Julio gave a cry of rage and launched himself at her, his cutlass raised high. She side-stepped him easily and, as he passed, gave a deft flick of her wrist. The point of her rapier sliced through the belt at Julio's waist and his loose breeches slid down to tangle around his ankles. Unable to check his speed, he fell sprawling across the deck, striking his chin on the newly swabbed boards.

The crew exploded into laughter as Julio's skinny buttocks were revealed. One of them called out to Carlotta.

'Well done, wench! That's finished him.'

'Never seen a woman who could fight like that.'

'Aye, Julio. Let that be an end to it. She's more than a match for you.'

Julio turned over slowly, a cut on his chin seeping blood. Grasping his breeches he pulled them up to cover himself, but not before Carlotta had seen his limp penis. It was the smallest male member she had ever seen, no bigger than that of a child. A few pubic hairs were clustered around the base of it and his balls were as small as grapes.

Her eyes sparked with pitying laughter. No wonder Julio felt such a need to prove his manhood. Julio read her expression. His small eyes hardened and became as flat as jet.

'A curse on you, *putana*,' he said softly, for her ears alone. 'I'll get you for this. Be certain that you watch your back from now on.'

A chill ran down her spine. She wanted to laugh away his threat, but knew that she had just made an implacable enemy. He would never forget the humiliation she had forced on him.

One of the sailors came forward and offered his hand to Julio. Julio slapped it away and rose clumsily to his feet. His cutlass lay a few feet away. Picking up the weapon he threw it back to its owner and strode away across the deck.

'Is there another amongst you who would prove his manhood?' Carlotta said, her voice ringing with authority. 'Come now. Surely someone is brave enough to best a mere woman.'

One or two of the men shuffled their feet, but no one made a move towards her.

'Not me, señora.'

'Nor I.'

She sheathed her rapier. 'Then I suggest you all get back to work. Manitas may be master of this ship, but I am his equal partner. From now on you will afford me the same respect you show him. Is that clear?'

There were mutters of assent and a few of them made awkward bows. The crew began to disperse, talking amongst themselves. The glances they threw at her were mixed with admiration and awe. At least now they knew that she would not be a useless burden during a fight.

At that moment Manitas appeared on deck. He took in the situation with one glance.

'What mischief is this?' he demanded.

Carlotta smiled sweetly at him. 'It's all over now. No harm's done.'

Manitas's mouth tightened. 'If someone has threatened you, they'll have me to reckon with.'

One of the crew laughed. 'You did not tell us that we have a wild-cat in our midst. It is *we* who need protection!'

Chuckling, the men went back to their posts. Manitas threw her a puzzled glance.

'What did he mean?'

'Just that I showed my claws a little,' she smiled up at him, the corners of her eyes lifting provocatively. 'It seems that I need to do that on occasion to prove a point. I'll not have any man dismissing me as a useless piece of frippery!'

Manitas threw back his craggy head and laughed. 'As I know to my cost!' His voice roughened and she saw his eyes quicken with interest. 'But I'll wager that they did not enjoy finding that out as much as I did.'

Slipping his arm around her waist he escorted her below deck.

Manitas crouched in the front of the pinnace which was bearing down on the galleon.

The little craft pitched alarmingly as her bow cleaved through the angry waves. It seemed that at any moment they would be swallowed up by a wall of water, but somehow the long-boat rode each glassy slope and trough, bobbing like a cork in a millpond.

Despite her brave words on board the *Esmeralda*, Carlotta's face was white to the lips and the taste of bile was on her tongue. The surging grey-green water, the stinging spray which soaked her to the skin, and the advancing bow of the huge galleon all combined to freeze her with mortal terror.

Manitas was too absorbed in the task at hand to notice Carlotta. She was left to master her fear as best she could.

'Strike the sail,' Manitas called out, as they approached their target.

Almost invisible to the galleon, the pinnace slipped in under the formidable guns. The tiered and gilded sterncastle towered overhead, so close that Carlotta could see the ship's lantern and the carved balcony which led off from the master cabin. The galleon blocked out the sun and dwarfed the pinnace.

Carlotta swallowed her fear, gripping the sides of the boat so hard that her knuckles showed through her skin. Beside her, Manitas took aim and fired his musket with deadly accuracy at the Spanish steersman. Others of the crew fired at the men handling the sails while the rest aimed shots at the portholes, keeping the curious seamen from peering out.

'Steady now,' Manitas said. 'Wait until our other boat wedges itself against the Spaniard's rudder.'

When the ship and helmsman were both disabled, Manitas gave the order to board. Grappling irons were thrown over the rail and the buccaneers swarmed up the attached ropes.

'Stay here,' he ordered Carlotta over his shoulder. 'I'll send a man for you when it's safe.'

She nodded, waiting until he had climbed hand over hand, before making a move. It was far more terrifying to stay in the pinnace. Water was slopping over the sides at such a rate that it seemed to her that it might sink at any moment. The galleon at least looked solid and stable. She feared the prospect of a battle far less than a watery grave.

Before any of the men could protest she launched herself at the nearest rope and began to climb. The ship's timbers were dank and slimy and left greenish marks on her clothes as she brushed against them. Gritting her teeth she pulled herself up, trying to ignore the cold in her cramped hands and her protesting muscles. She was breathing heavily by the time she reached the ship's rail. The rounded bar dug into her belly as she hauled herself up and threw her leg over it.

Despite her trembling limbs, she drew her sword in a single smooth movement and launched herself onto the deck and into the midst of the fighting. A Spanish officer bore down on her, his pistol cocked. Side-stepping, she ducked and a shot whined past her ear.

Before the officer could re-load, she stretched out with her rapier and pierced his upper arm: a clean cut which bisected his muscles. Swiftly she incapacitated his other arm and left him sagging against the main mast. There was hardly time to recover her balance, before a brawny sailor closed with her. He too was dealt with swiftly, as was the next man after that. In a moment Manitas was at her side.

'Damn you. Don't you ever follow orders?' he grated.

She flashed him a grin, knowing that her eyes were wild with elation.

'Never!' she said. 'Don't you know that yet?'

Turning on the balls of her feet, she tackled a man brandishing a cutlass. The fighting was thick and fast. Carlotta fought skilfully, exhilarated by the shouts and screams of pain, the smells of sweat and blood. It was as if her blood fizzed in her veins.

It was over with quickly; the Spanish sailors had been thrown into confusion by the speed of the attack. Many of them jumped overboard and struck out towards the nearest island. Breathing hard and wiping the sweat from her brow, Carlotta lowered her sword. The deck was slippery with blood and she set one of the captured Spaniards to swabbing it down.

'You there, Guido! Get to the whipstaff,' Manitas ordered. 'Steer her towards the island where the *Esmeralda* is moored.'

'Aye, master.'

The other buccaneers took up their positions. Carlotta moved towards the main hatch, intending to go below to investigate their haul. Manitas closed his hand on her arm.

'Wait. No sense in taking risks,' he said. 'Get behind me. And this time, obey me.'

She followed him down the steps, knowing when it was unwise to argue. His musket was cocked in case of resistance, but the remaining sailors had lost the will to fight. Those officers who had not taken part in the fighting were crowded together in the master's cabin. They surrendered at once.

Cowering behind the officers was a portly man with a florid face. The deep lines running from nose to mouth and the slack flesh under his chin spoke of dissipation. He wore a suit of figured, blue brocade; the doublet pouched forward into the fashionable peascod shape. His shirt of cambric was visible, topped by a split ruff of fine lace. The man's sturdy legs were clothed in matching blue stockings, also much embroidered.

The fine clothes looked ridiculous on the individual who was very short as well as over-weight. Carlotta recognised him as once. The paper she had stolen from Alberto, Felipe's confidente, had been extremely detailed even down to intimate descriptions of all Felipe's associates. She smiled inwardly, wondering what Antonio Alva would have made of the entry concerning himself. It read:

'Antonio Alva. Banker. A man over-fond of food and physical pleasures. He is as stout as an ox and with a countenance to match. His eyes are close-set and his ears would grace the sides of a jug.'

She gave a mocking bow and doffed her cap so that her hair tumbled down her back in midnight waves.

'Delighted to make your acquaintance, Señor Alva,' she said. 'What a surprise and pleasure it is to find you aboard.'

Antonio Alva seemed unable to voice a reply. His mouth sagged open and his chins wobbled with alarm.

'God's bones, a woman!' he managed finally. 'I'll be damned. Who . . . who are you? What do . . . you want with me?'

Carlotta did not answer. Let him try to reason that out for himself. She turned her attention to Manitas, who was conversing with the officers.

'For the love of God, do not harm us, señor,' the Captain was pleading. 'We have wives and children. You may demand a heavy ransom for us. It will be paid.'

'Your ship and all its goods will suffice,' Manitas told

110

them. 'I have no argument with you. You may all quit *my* ship if you please.'

'Before you do,' Carlotta said, approaching the captain and handing him a roll of parchment secured with a wax seal, 'take this. Carry it back to Spain for me. Hand it to one Don Felipe Escada who owns the Mendoza lands and estate. I wish him to know who is robbing his associate and stealing his money.'

'Don Felipe!' Antonio burst out. 'What do you know of him?'

'Silence!' Carlotta said. 'You are not in a position to ask questions. Better that you plead for mercy.'

Antonio's face took on a purple tinge. 'Insolent wench! You . . . you immodest wretch! You dare to order me? By what right do you rise above the station which God had appointed to women? The authorities shall hear of your hand in this. I'll see you clamped in the stocks and flogged until your skin hangs in rags. By God, just wait until I return to Spain, I'll – '

'Hold your blather, man. You are staying here,' Carlotta cut in. 'I have a special fate reserved for you.'

'Oh . . .' Antonio sank into a bench, his chins wobbling with alarm. He glanced up at Manitas, an appeal in his blood-shot eyes. 'What say you, señor? Does this woman speak for you?'

'She does,' Manitas answered mildly. 'And I advise you to show her a jot more respect. Your future is in her slim white hands. Having delivered such a rich prize to me, I am disposed to deny her nothing.'

'Then I may do as I wish with this fat banker?' Carlotta said. 'You have no objections?'

'None. Boil him in oil for all I care. Only let me watch.' He winked at her to show that he was baiting Antonio, and she grinned.

'I have something much more colourful planned.'

Antonio's mouth sagged open. Drops of sweat ran down his full cheeks and dripped onto his lace collar. He sank to his knees, his hands raised in supplication.

'I beseech you, señor. Let me go. I am a rich man. Name your price.'

Manitas gave a bored sigh. He gestured to one of his men.

'Throw this popinjay into the brig. We'll deal with him later. And now, Carlotta, shall we see what's in the treasure room? And there's the small matter of your disobedience to address.'

The treasure room was on the orlop deck, immediately below the gun deck. The ceiling was low and the little room was dim, lit only by a single flickering lantern.

Manitas opened a sealed chest and Carlotta exclaimed in delight at the shower of gold which spilled onto the floor. As they broke open more of the chests, the glow of gold filled the room.

'There'll be more goods in the hold,' Manitas said. 'Casks of sugar, rare hardwoods, liquid amber, tobacco. Maybe even prized llama wool. We'll not go hungry for many a long day.'

Carlotta picked up a necklace, fashioned into a design of feathers set with turquoises. There were earrings, ornate collars, rings; all of gold set with precious stones. In another chest were silks, velvets, and figured brocades. The heavy scent of rare spices, cinnamon, nutmeg, pepper, pervaded the room as Manitas continued to examine their treasures.

Carlotta had not realised until this moment how starved her eyes had been for the sight of luxuries. Something within her responded to the tactile beauty of the rich fabrics. Losing herself to sheer indulgence she draped herself in lengths of violet, primrose, and emerald silk, strewing the rough boards with a waterfall of rich colour.

The tangle of velvet and crumpled brocade, some of it shot through with threads of gold, lay like an exotic carpet over the ship's boards. In another casket she found flagons of painted glass, one of them stoppered by a single carved ruby. Breaking the seal, she applied perfume to her throat and wrists, dabbing some between her breasts.

The perfume was like nothing she had ever smelt. It was rich and dark. A scent of the New World; strong and musky-sweet, but with undertones of something indefinable and lingering. Whatever it was it worked a potent spell on her. Closing her eyes she breathed deeply of the sensual aroma which blossomed on contact with her skin. And now the fragrance was somehow familiar, evoking a deeply erotic response within her, coupled with an odd sense of . . . loss?

It seemed then that the air thickened and shadows moved towards her. She felt dizzy, her head was swimming. The sweet smell was cloying in her nostrils. Something – a memory – was just out of reach. There was a sense of a woman close by, waiting. The image was insubstantial, like a movement seen from the tail of one's eye.

Carlotta turned quickly and for a second the figure solidified. She realised that she was seeing herself, her image like a reflection in a looking-glass; but her face was darker-skinned, and her hair looked different. It was straight and glossy. She felt a dart of fear and the sweat broke out on her skin. What was happening to her?

It must be the perfume. She could almost feel the deep, dark notes of the fragrance spreading through her, warming her blood and expanding her mind. Perhaps a high priest of the heathen races had put a hex on the flagon. The New World savages were known to worship idols and eat human flesh – no doubt they practised witchcraft too. She gave a little cry of alarm and threw the flagon back into the chest.

'What ails you, sweeting?' Manitas said. 'You're very pale.'

Shaken by the odd experience, Carlotta sought for an answer.

'It's nothing. I felt strange for a moment. It's probably because I'm cold. My clothing is soaked.'

She opened the drawstring neckline of her shirt. The movement dispersed the heavy fragrance somewhat and her head cleared. She took a deep steadying breath and turned her head, searching for the shadowy image of the woman. There was nothing. Apart from herself and Manitas, the cabin was empty. Gradually her heartbeat returned to normal. Had she imagined the whole thing?

Running her fingertips over her chest, she realised how chilled and clammy her skin felt. Perhaps her soaking *had* brought on a fever. The sooner she took off her wet clothes, the better. They stank of wet leather and sea water.

She became aware that Manitas was watching her closely, a questioning look in his dark eyes. He came up and moved around behind her. His arms encircled her waist and he drew her back against the hard wall of his abdominal muscles. His warmth and solidity was comforting, rooted in reality. She almost laughed aloud at herself for having such strange fancies. It was not like her at all.

Manitas seemed to fill the small cabin with his presence. She absorbed his strength and potent maleness. And now there was no room for anything else but him in her mind.

The hardness of his erection pressed into her as he rotated his hips. Immediately she pictured his cock, strongly erect and powerful. How she loved to feel it inside her, stretching her sensitised membranes. Its very bigness excited her senses.

Under the sodden linen shirt her nipples prickled with anticipation. She shivered, imagining Manitas stripping her naked, exposing her long white limbs and laying her down on the carpet of cloth, then plunging into her without waiting for her to signal her readiness.

She arched against him and he laughed huskily.

'So eager for pleasure, sweeting? We have a matter to settle, remember? How am I to punish you for putting yourself at risk?'

'Why not claim a forfeit?' she said, making her voice light.

'I intend to,' he said, and there was a steely glint in his eye.

His arms around her were like a vice. Behind his playfulness, she detected the resolve he had shown on other occasions. Sometimes he was prepared to let her take the lead, but this was not one of those times. She was acutely aware of his enormous strength and the size of him in relation to herself. It would be a brave woman who refused him in this mood. But she had no intention of resisting him. The hint of danger aroused her even more.

He allowed her to move out of his embrace and she turned to face him.

'What is the forfeit,' she said, smiling with promise. 'I am at your command.'

He made a small sound in his throat, something between eagerness and impatience. She seemed to feel the echo of it between her thighs, where her coynte was softening and swelling, the fleshy lips growing thick and moist.

'Take off those wet clothes. All of them. I want you naked and on your knees before me.'

Trembling slightly, she pulled off her boots and let them fall to the floor. Her padded doublet followed. As she pulled the wet shirt over her head, the warm air of the cabin caressed her skin. She rubbed at her chilled arms until the gooseflesh subsided.

Manitas watched as she took off her other clothes. Soon she stood naked. Holding eye contact with him, she sank down until she was kneeling amidst the tangle of rich fabrics. She had been naked before him on other occasions, but never had he seemed so intent on enjoying the evidence of her vulnerability.

Emotions chased across his face. She could almost see his thoughts. What would he ask her to do? Something humiliating; something which would make her shake with mortification? Oh, yes – please.

A blush spread over her skin and she knew that her neck, shoulders and breasts were glowing a soft rosy pink. It was difficult to resist the urge to put her hands over her Venus mound. Manitas was looking at her with such passion and intensity, his gaze seeming to penetrate beyond her skin, that she felt the need to shield part of herself from him.

As a child, she had loved a story about a giant who ate naughty children. That story came to mind now and she felt an erotic thrill that penetrated deep within her. Behind the closed lips of her sex, her body's moisture gathered. She could feel the hot slickness, waiting to seep forth at the touch of his hand.

Manitas reached out and ran his hands through the thick dark waves of her hair, fanning it out over her shoulders. The dark strands tickled her breasts. He smoothed his calloused palms over her shoulders and upper arms, the roughness catching at her skin and causing her to sigh inwardly.

'Such skin. Rich and pale, like a pearl,' he murmured. 'You need no more adornment than the curling black fleece which graces your coynte, but I shall indulge my senses. You are so beguiling when you are compliant.'

'I am what you wish me to be, master,' she said huskily, drinking in the flare of lust in his deep-set eyes.

'Then you will do as I say, at once. Without comment. That strong will of yours must be curbed, for I shall punish you if you show rebellion. Do you understand?'

She nodded, recalling the tingling heat of her spanked buttocks on that first occasion. The way he had thrust into the silky crease of her buttocks, pleasuring himself while denying her lusting coynte its respite. She had felt the echo of his touch on her flesh, in the smarting of her outer crevice, and on the tightly puckered mouth of her anus for hours after she had left his room.

How delightfully cruel he could be. And how part of her responded to the darkness of his passion. The willing submission flooded her body as the desire seemed to centre within her, unfurling like a moist red flower whose petals pulsed and swelled.

Manitas, in this mood, made her afraid. But he was compelling too; unpredictable. A mixture that acted on her senses like hot spiced wine. A tremor passed over her skin as he walked around her, his eyes assessing, measuring. Waiting for him to speak, to tell her what he was going to do, filled her with anticipation. He stood to one side of her now. She could not see his face. As she started to turn towards him, he spoke.

'Did I order you to move? You are to stay as you are,' he said sternly. 'Straighten your back, square your shoulders, and thrust out your breasts. Display yourself for me.'

She did as he asked, her nipples tightening and the surrounding flesh quivering with anticipation. Her coynte was hot and heavy, eager for his touch. She waited with bated breath for his next words.

'Part your knees,' he said, standing directly in front of her now. 'I want you to open your body to me.'

She did so, slowly, feeling his eyes on her pubis, his gaze moving lower as her sex hung down a little between her open thighs. The pressure inside was such that she felt like bearing down, pushing out the rosy folds so that they pouted wantonly towards him.

'Delightful,' he said, reaching out to stroke her belly and pull gently at the glossy curls on her coynte.

Her acquiescence seemed to fascinate him. No doubt he had expected some resistance on her part – she had always fought against his dominance in the past – but she remained submissive, eager for whatever he would do.

117

'Such docility earns its own reward,' he said.

He moved out of her line of sight and she heard him walk across the cabin. Unable to see what he was doing, she quivered inwardly. The erotic tension within her was almost unbearable. Manitas seemed to be searching for something. There came the sound of a casket opening and the chink of metal on metals.

He did not trouble to hurry himself. The arrogant bastard. He knew what this waiting was doing to her. With her heart full of dread, she waited for his return.

This time, he had something special in mind.

Chapter Nine

Manitas dipped his hands into the small jewel chest, which was constructed from some dark wood and lined with iridescent shell. He brought out fistfuls of gold chains and ropes of pearls set with gold shapes which glinted with rough-cut gems.

'Ah, the very thing,' he said, bringing the chest across the room and setting it down beside Carlotta.

She remained still as he looped the necklaces over her head and settled them tightly around her breasts. Lifting the heavy underswell of flesh, he arranged the ropes and chains of gold so that the full globes were supported and forced to jut out seductively through the jewellery.

The gold was cool and thrilling against her skin. It seemed that he intended to cover her with jewels like some barbarous princess from the New World. She liked the image that presented itself and imagined herself in a tropical forest, sunlight slanting down upon her through the trees, as she knelt before an idol carved in stone.

Now what had prompted her to think of that image?

'What is that perfume you are wearing?' Manitas asked, kneeling before her and tweaking her nipple until it grew erect.

'It . . . it was in one of the flagons . . .' she began, her breath catching in her throat as he put spittle on the little nub of flesh and began forcing it through a link in one of the chains.

When the chain had closed around her nipple, he rubbed his palms over and around her breasts, capturing the sweet odour of them. Cupping his hands, he raised them to his face and inhaled.

'Such a strange and beguiling fragrance,' he said. 'It might have been made for you.'

Her imprisoned nipple throbbed and burned and a warm cloud of the spicy perfume rose around her. It flowed outwards from Manitas's hands as he placed more jewellery around her neck. As before, her heartbeat quickened and in the hollow of her throat a pulse throbbed so deeply that she thought Manitas must be able to see the movement of it against her skin.

How heavy the perfume was and how strangely penetrating. The light in the cabin grew dimmer. Surely the air had a thick and grainy quality. She closed her eyes for a moment, confused by the many different sensations that were crowding in on her.

Manitas was pinching her other nipple now, wetting it and easing it through another link of chain. The pleasure throbbed dully in her lower belly as the circle of metal enclosed her jutting flesh. Manitas murmured to her, but she did not hear what he said. His voice sounded faint as the strange, light-headed sensation came over her for the second time.

Somehow, she was not afraid now. Her head swam, but it was a pleasant feeling, mixed as it was with the sexual heat coursing through her. She was enjoying the pinching pleasure-pain in her nipples, and the coldness of the jewellery against her skin – she had the feeling that she had been decorated like this before.

And the jewellery itself – so fabulous and barbaric in design – was familiar. How could that be?

The pictures in her mind grew clearer. She saw again

the woman; the woman who looked so like her, but was not her. As if a thread connected them, their senses flowed together and they became one. And the image wavered, then steadied. She seemed to be moving outwards from a point in the centre of her forehead.

Whilst still acutely aware of her body's arousal and the concentrated heat at the core of her femininity, her mind registered the sound of drums, the clashing of metal instruments . . .

And now, around her shoulders was a cloak made of countless tiny birds' feathers; hundreds of them over-lapping, each of them glimmering with silvery tones of blue and green. The carapaces of rare beetles were sewn around the top of the cloak, forming a glittering collar. In her ear-lobes were round plugs of smooth blood-stone, burnished with flecks of gold.

The tropical mist seeped upwards from the moist forest floor and scents of vanilla and fern and rich fruity soil perfumed the air around her. The grass was soft under her knees and the representation of Quetzalcoatl, the Father God, looked down on her benevolently.

There was a circle of polished metal in the idol's hands. In the depths of the reflection she saw that her hair was thick and straight, a jet waterfall under the diadem of leaves formed of beaten gold.

Looking down at herself, she saw also that her skin was dark-gold in colour and her nipples were large and a purplish-brown. Around her waist was a girdle, made of the plaited fibres of a sacred plant. Her hand-maidens' voices were raised in song as they celebrated her fleshly sacrifice to her new master who stood nearby.

She was to be a gift to him, for he was a god from across the great sea. He had come from out of the East, as was foretold by the prophets, and brought good fortune for the Aztec people. His white skin and the stick he carried, which spoke with a thunderous voice, marked him out. She was eager to pleasure him.

121

Her hand-maidens' clever fingers plucked at her breasts and stroked her thighs. They covered her with chains of gold, pinching her nipples into dusky peaks, readying her for the white god's pleasure. Little shocks of arousal flickered over her dark skin. Her new master's face was sharp and cruel, hook-nosed and thin-lipped, but her blood responded to the darkness within him.

Under the polished helm with its curved-up brim, her master had high cheekbones and a neatly trimmed beard. His body armour, of strange design, flashed in the sun and his padded hose was embroidered with silver thread. High leather boots clothed his legs.

The vision was beginning to fade. Carlotta let it go. She ought to be afraid, and wondered at the fact that she was so accepting of this strange happening. A priest would say that such visions were sent by the Devil, but she had always been too strong-minded to be frightened by the warnings of fools and bigots.

These memories had no power to harm her. It was only the peculiar scent of the perfume, the cold kiss of the heathen metal, which had conjured them. The air shimmered around her and the cabin came sharply into focus.

A soft moan broke from her lips as Manitas settled a girdle of beaten gold around her hips. Carlotta raised heavy eyelids to him. She felt drugged, as if she had supped a hot posset laced liberally with hippocras.

'God, but you're beautiful,' Manitas said, his voice low and husky. 'Your eyes are like dark fire. Barbarity suits you. You make a most handsome heathen.'

Carlotta's lips curved in a secret smile. She wanted to know if the princess had enjoyed her conqueror lover, but perhaps she would have no more glimpses into that shadowy past. No matter. The actuality of Manitas in the present, his touch on her skin, was as knowing as that of the the hand-maidens in her vision. And his strong features were no less arresting than those of the princess's conquistador.

'Ah . . .' she breathed, when Manitas's hand brushed across her pubis and rifled the silky dark curls.

The backs of his fingers moved up the parted groove of her coynte dragging against her moist and swollen flesh. Her pleasure bud was hot and hard and seemed to flutter under his touch.

Carlotta trembled with the strength of her passions. It was as if the vision had added a new element to her arousal. Something was coiled within her, something that pulsed and pulsed, demanding to be sated.

Oh God, let Manitas give her release soon. But he seemed unaware of her desperate need, or if he was aware of it, he cared not.

Taking his time, Manitas fitted her pierced ear lobes with earrings, their twin weight pulling against the delicate skin. He fastened more of the chains around her waist, securing them tightly, arranging them so that medallions formed of carved gems hung down to mask her pubis.

As he slipped heavy bangles onto her wrist she moaned softly and arched her back, thrusting her hips forward so that the coolness of the medallions swayed and brushed against her swollen sex-lips. Even that slight contact sent a shiver of pleasure through her folds and caused her erect bud to harden into a little nut which throbbed like a tiny heart.

'Oh, please . . .' she whispered.

'You are impatient,' Manitas said in an admonishing tone. 'There will be no release for you until I give it. Any more of that and you know what will happen. What have you to say?'

'Forgive me,' she murmured, chewing at her bottom lip.

It was hard to voice those words. She hardly dared to move for fear of what he might do. But her greatest fear was that he would do nothing. It was quite possible that he would leave her there to burn with unsatisfied desire.

Manitas bade Carlotta change position and lift each ankle in turn so that he could put more gold around them. Even her toes were not ignored. He slipped a tiny gold ring onto each of them. As Manitas's fingers brushed against her imprisoned nipples during his leisurely decoration of her person, she tried desperately to disguise her eagerness. But it was impossible. Her nipples were pushed out towards him, two wanton, red-brown tubes, collared by the glimmer of gold.

Finally Manitas seemed satisfied. He sat back to survey the result. The unfamiliar weight on the different areas of her body caused Carlotta to concentrate her attention away from the fullness of her aching coynte.

Strangely the effect of that was to make her even more hungry for Manitas's touch. Every area of her body seemed to tingle and lust for him, but she had hardly time to absorb that new fact, because he was speaking.

'Forgive me. I did not hear you . . .' she said, her eyes widening with shock. In fact she had heard him, but was unable to believe his request.

'I said, lie down on your back, grip your thighs and tip your buttocks up towards me,' he repeated, in the tone she recognised as brooking no refusal. 'I wish to gaze on that jewel between your thighs.'

Haltingly, she arranged herself on her back. The velvet and silks moved under her as she placed her hands behind her thighs. She closed her eyes as she lifted her legs towards her chest, knowing that her sex was now fully exposed to his gaze. The chains and medallions slipped to either side of the bulge of her coynte.

'Oh no,' she moaned, as the thing she had feared happened. A trickle of creamy moisture slid out of her and trailed down towards the crease of her bottom.

'Open yourself wider,' Manitas ordered, scooping up

the wetness and massaging it into her pleasure bud. 'I want to see your readiness to obey me. Ah, you are wet already, but I'll make you wetter yet.'

Burning with mortification, she did as he said. She could not control the eager bucking of her hips as he swirled his fingers over her pushed-out flesh, circling the most sensitive heart of her until she thought she might scream with the pleasure of it.

Oh, Mary Mother of God, what if someone was to come into the little room and see her in such a humiliating position? One of the buccaneers might easily come to check that the expected treasure was intact. As if he read her thoughts, Manitas said:

'Do not fear. I have posted a guard outside. We'll not be disturbed, though your moans of pleasure will be a torture to the hapless cove! But neither will you be rescued. You'll stay as you are until I've had my pleasure of you.'

He knelt beside her and she felt the cool caress of a heavy gold chain as he trailed it against her inner thighs. As she moved slightly, her thighs brushed against her breasts and her sore nipples awoke again, tingling and throbbing, eager for his touch.

'And now you'll make a gift of yourself to me,' he said. 'I want to watch you dissolve and feel the echo of it deep within your flesh.'

'I can't . . .' she moaned. What she meant to say was, 'I can't stop this happening. I'm going to break – soon, oh, soon.'

But she was beyond words. The world had narrowed into sensation, her very soul seemed concentrated on Manitas, the instrument of her pleasure and shame. He laid one of the gold chains on each of the outer, haired lips of her coynte, adjusting them so that they tightened. Their weight served to open her further, the moist inner surfaces of her sex-lips were peeled back to lay almost flat against her inner thighs.

The heat rushed into her cheeks as she imagined what he could see.

Her tender inner folds were laid utterly bare and the opening to her body was revealed, forced to gape a little by the weight of the chains. Tears of shame trickled from the corners of her eyes and dripped into the tumbled waves of her hair. Oh it was terrible to be exposed and made helpless in this way, but it was chastening indeed to realise that she could not help responding to such harsh stimulus.

As Manitas pinched the hard, rosy pearl of flesh at the apex of her coynte, she trembled on the verge of her crisis, then climaxed deep and hard. Before the inner pulsings died away, she felt a new and shocking sensation. Her hips thrashed and she grunted and moaned as her pleasure ebbed and changed.

What was he doing to her? Something cool and round was being inserted into her central opening, followed by another and another, and then, before she had time to encompass that fact, one of the objects was brushing against the tighter orifice between her spread buttocks.

She tried to pull away, alarmed at the new instrusion, but Manitas's warm fingers scooped up more of her syrupy juices and anointed her anus, stroking it until the ring of muscle relaxed. Then she felt the smooth coolness slide into her as he worked the final pearl past the tight closure of her flesh.

'Oh don't . . . No more . . .' she gasped, overcome by the ticklish movements inside her.

It was almost too much to bear. The humiliation of having the jewels pushed into her body brought more tears to her eyes. She sobbed and wept, the pleasure and shame so mixed that she could not tell where each ended and the other began. How could he treat her like this? And how could she be enjoying it?

When Manitas thrust his big, warm fingers into her and began stroking her softened inner walls, playing the pearls between his fingers and rubbing them against each other, she cried out and came again.

'Oh . . . Manitas . . . oh . . .'

The pulsings were as deep and hard as the first time, driving the breath from her body and causing her to screw her face into a rictus of anguished pleasure.

Digging her fingers into her thighs she dragged them in more tightly to her chest. Lifting and pushing out her sex, straining against the chains which dug into her sex-flesh and held her open to him, she thrust her bottom upwards, her anus spasming helplessly.

The pearls rolled together wetly, divided only by a thin membrane inside her. She reached a climax again and again, the awful, thrilling sensations brought forth by the fingers rotating so sweetly inside her. Manitas bent over her and claimed her mouth as he slid his thumb into her anus and brought it together with the fingers inside her.

That final, gentle violation drove her wild. As Manitas curved his fingers and rubbed the tips of them together with his thumb, he captured the pearls and vibrated them against her sensitised membranes. She sobbed and wept, tasting her own tears in his mouth, not caring whether anyone could hear.

It was finally too much and she let go of her legs and lowered them to the cabin floor. Her skin quivered with little after-shocks of pleasure and her coynte and lower belly felt hot and heavy. She could not believe she would ever experience anything else like that. Then she realised that Manitas had moved away and was opening his breeches. His enormous, crested cock bobbed free.

'My turn now,' he said, flipping her onto her side and lifting one of her legs.

He did not trouble to remove the chains that held her sex apart and she made a sound of protest as they tightened, pinching the delicate skin. Manitas paid no heed, thrusting straight into her, filling her with the rigid cudgel of his maleness.

She bucked and groaned and bit at her hand as he pounded her flesh, his heavy balls knocking against the inner edges of her buttocks. His fingers had made the silken juices run from her body and she heard the soft, wet sucking sounds as he slid in and out of her wet folds. The big cock-head pushed against her inner walls on each inward thrust as he took his pleasure.

Carlotta arched her back, easing the pressure of the chains which held her open. She wanted to bring her legs together and close her body, to enfold him in the tightness of her pouting coynte, but the chains prevented that. One of his hands was holding her thigh up and the weight of his body kept the other in place. He surged against her, taking her at will. She had nothing left, no modesty, no way to shield anything of herself from him.

Her wetness flowed down the stiffened shaft and streaked her inner thighs. As Manitas continued to plunge into her, the sucking sounds became louder, cruder, mixing with her breathy groans.

'Stop . . . No more. Please . . .' she whimpered, shamed beyond measure by the vocal evidence of her body's wantonness.

But Manitas laughed and bit gently at her nape. Reaching under her, he ran his fingers up her parted groove and pinched the nub of flesh which was as rigid as a tiny cock. Pulling on the tiny flesh hood, he urged her to an almost painful peak.

'But yes, sweeting,' he said, removing one finger and tapping the sore tip of her nub with the other. 'I love your shame. It is what I crave. Once more now. Reach for your crest. Give yourself to me. Can you not hear how your coynte begs for its pleasure?'

'I can't. Please. Oh, God . . .'

Incredibly she came again; and this time the pulsing was more prolonged and somehow sweeter. Manitas moaned softly and meshed his fingers in the waves of her hair as her coynte closed around his shaft, milking him.

'Ah, sweeting. You wring me out,' he said, grunting and thrusting so deeply into her that she cried out with the almost-pain of his assault.

Manitas pulled out of her, his seed jetting hotly onto her spread sex. She felt his fingers tighten in her hair and the warmth of his palm against her skull. His belly pressed against her buttocks, the slabs of hard muscle flexing and releasing. It was some time before he stopped jerking against her.

In a while Manitas drew her back against his chest. His touch was tender now. She reached for his arms and fitted them around her waist. They lay entwined, both breathing hard.

Carlotta was barely conscious of anything but his nearness, the smell of him, and the sensation of his skin against hers. Mixed faintly with the smell of sweat and sex was the spice of the exotic perfume.

She let her mind drift. Somewhere just out of reach was the image of the pagan princess. She smiled in contentment, wondering if the conquistador had been as consummate a lover as Manitas.

After a while Manitas moved. He nuzzled her hair and his lips were warm against her ear.

'My sweet wanton. You're such a mixture of strength and compliance. There's no one like you. I'll build you an island stronghold and we'll rule together, you and I. You can torment your Spanish captives at your leisure. Do what you will. I care not . . . only . . .'

He paused and his voice grew softer. She thought she heard him say.

'Only never leave me.'

Later she was to wonder if she had heard him correctly. That last sentence seemed so outlandish.

Surely Manitas could not be falling in love with her.

* * *

Antonio Alva strained to see through the chink in the wooden wall. God's teeth, what was the pirate doing to his doxy? She was wailing like a cat in heat.

He grunted with frustration. When the woman had disrobed and then knelt so humbly before the man, she'd been in Antonio's line of vision. But, since they had sunk to the cabin floor Antonio had not been able to see what she was doing.

It was most frustrating. By the sound of it, the pirate was swiving her, good and hard. Antonio's hand trailed down to his breeches, where his stubby cock leapt and twitched. Slipping his hand into his breeches he took his cock out and began to stroke himself lovingly.

Christ, how he'd like to get his hands on that raven-haired beauty. She had the body of an angel and the bearing and manner of a warrior. He had never seen a woman dressed that way before, nor had he ever expected to see a woman brandishing a sword which ran with blood. He had assumed that she was an unnatural being, someone who wished to be a man. She looked fair of face to be sure, but no doubt her doublet and hose hid a skinny body, flat dugs, mishapen limbs.

It had been a shock to put his eye to the chink in the wall; he had seen her lush curves and rounded limbs, and observed how she made herself subservient to that over-sized pirate.

Somehow Antonio had not expected that either. He was confused. What manner of creature was she? She had spoken to him – a wealthy and powerful man – as though he were not fit to wipe cow dung from her shoe. And the pirate had approved, God rot him. Now it all came clear. The pirate felt moved to indulge his mistress's whims, so he allowed her to run around wearing men's clothing. But she was no real threat to his or anyone else's manhood.

Antonio's already florid cheeks darkened. He itched to show that forward wench a thing or two. He would soon teach her some manners. He considered that the pirate gave her too much freedom. A few strokes of the lash is what she needed, then she'd be as soft, as charming, as sweet-tongued, as he liked his women. Every real man knew that a woman should not be allowed to speak out of turn; her place was carrying out the wishes of her betters.

As Antonio stroked himself, his breath quickened. He squeezed his shaft, working the loose skin up and over his flaring glans. And, thinking of punishment, he recalled the servant he had chastised in the coastal town of Veracruz. While he and his friends waited for the mule train to arrive which was carrying the bullion, they had taken their ease in a tavern.

The stupid wench had spilt wine on the sleeve of his new doublet. Springing up from the table, he had dragged her by her hair into the back room. There, urged on by his friends, he had ripped off her single garment and laid about her with a stick.

Antonio's breath came faster, keeping pace with the moans of pleasure from the next cabin. A single drop of lubricant seeped from the eye of his cock and he rubbed it around his glans with the palm of his hand.

The servant girl had wept and writhed as he held her across the wooden table and beat her thighs and buttocks. She had been well-fleshed and her breasts jiggled enticingly as she tried to escape the blows. He loved the way the golden-brown skin of the native women took on a deep flush when they were chastised.

He had paused and stroked the hot and trembling buttocks, his passions rising as the musky scent of her filled his nostrils. He grinned, remembering how the wench rose fear-filled eyes to him when he mounted her, but she stopped wailing. No doubt she expected to be paid when he'd finished with her.

Ah, what delight it had been to thrust between those buttocks, to pull apart the rich globes and sink into the hot red centre of the woman. Afterwards he had pushed

131

her away and ordered her to get dressed. Her face was sullen when she pushed past him and went back into the tap-room. Ungrateful wretch. She ought to have been grateful that he left any skin on her back. Another man might have ordered her flogged to within an inch of her life or let his friends take turns at her.

His cock was hard and throbbing now. The pleasure mounted within his fat body, prickling within his reddened glans. He worked his hand back and forth along the shaft as the moans from the next cabin reached fever pitch.

In his imagination he substituted the dark-haired pirate's doxy for the native woman. The simmering buttocks he held apart were full and white and the pouting, wet coynte was surrounded by lush dark curls. Leaning into her, he rode her hard.

His balls tightened and the jism boiled upwards. With a groan Antonio spent himself, his semen dripping onto the floor of the brig. In the cabin next door, the pirate was still pleasuring his woman. The man has some stamina, Antonio thought with reluctant admiration.

He adjusted his clothing and went back to sit on the barrel which was the only item in the room, apart from a pile of dirty sacks.

He felt reassured by the sounds from next door. The woman was sobbing with pleasure, begging her lover to grant her release. When she had threatened him, on deck, he had been outraged and not sure how to react. But it seemed that the huge pirate was master of his woman after all. He was sure that he would be able to reason with a man. Women were weak-minded, good for one thing only, and not to be trusted. In Antonio's mind, his fate was by no means as precarious as he had feared it might be.

Chapter Ten

*J*uanita stood on the white-sand beach and peered out past the waves which were breaking over the reef. The *Esmeralda* was anchored in the deep waters of the bay. As she watched, the Spanish galleon sailed into view, drawing alongside the *Esmeralda* and dwarfing the smaller vessel.

She let out a sigh of relief. God be praised, the treasure ship had been captured, but she wished that she could be certain that Carlotta was safe. She had been half out of her mind with worry these past few hours.

Nothing she had said would persuade Carlotta to let Manitas take the galleon alone but, on this occasion at least, Carlotta had not insisted that Juanita go along as well.

'It's far too dangerous. You wait for me on the island,' Carlotta had said. 'A number of the crew are going ashore to fetch fresh water and hunt. You'll be safer amongst them. Watch out for Julio, he bears you and I no goodwill, and Manitas does not want him along. But Bartholomew Stow is a sound man. Stay close to him.'

Juanita was not too sure about being safer on the island, but she was glad that she need take no part in attacking the galleon. She was not brave; nor was she an accomplished swordswoman like her mistress. And now she was doubly glad that she had stayed on the island – otherwise she would not have had occasion to be alone with Bartholomew Stow, a man whose good looks and quiet manner had already impressed themselves on her.

Two others of the crew besides Julio, Stow, and herself, had rowed towards the nearest island. Juanita clung fearfully to the sides of the boat as the men navigated the shallow waters around the reef. Ahead was a stretch of white sand, where the breakers rolled in with a deafening crashing and boiling of white foam. White-faced she cowered in the boat as the men jumped over the side and hauled it to the shore.

It had been Stow who swept her up in his arms and carried her to dry land, the breakers rolling around his strong thighs. Juanita blushed to the roots of her hair at his proximity. His hands on her waist and under her knees were firm and warm. She could smell his strong male scent. It was a smell at once comforting and exciting, made up of clean sweat, tobacco, and tar-soaked leather.

The other three men exchanged ribald comments and Juanita's blush deepened.

'Caught yourself a mermaid, Stow?' one of them said.

'Nay, something better. A woman's no use to a man lest she be clefted, eh, Stow?' said another.

'Best use her then throw her back,' Julio muttered, slanting her a venomous look. 'She's bound to be trouble, same as her witch of a mistress.'

'Hold your tongue, Julio,' Stow said evenly.

'Best watch the wench well, Stow,' Julio said. 'Wouldn't want her to have an accident. It can easily happen on a wild place such as this be.'

'I told you to shut your yap,' Stow said, his voice hardening. 'Lest you want to answer to me.'

Julio grunted and was silent.

Juanita recoiled from the malice in Julio's voice. His mud-coloured eyes were hard and pitiless. Since Carlotta had bested him in the swordfight, Julio had sought every opportunity to bait either Carlotta or herself. She suspected that his spite extended to all women.

Pressing closely to Stow, her arms around his neck, she turned her face in towards him. He was solid and well-built and it was a disappointment when he set her down on the wet sand. She had felt safe with him.

After a brief investigation of the beach, the men struck out for the tangle of red birch, thatch palm, and logwood, which trailed down onto the white sand. Juanita looped up her skirts and began to follow them, but Stow put a hand on her arm.

'Nay, señora. The jungle's no place for a gentlewoman. You and me'll stay here.'

He grinned and her stomach gave an odd little lurch. Confused by her reaction to him she looked down at her shoes. While she was glad that he was her self-appointed protector, she was nervous of being alone with him. He was so strong and vital and far too good-looking.

'I need help to build a fire pit,' Stow continued, unaware of her growing discomfort. 'We'll feast on roast pig this night, if the men have good fortune.'

She collected driftwood while he dug a pit in the sand. It was warm work and she returned from one foray to find that he had stripped off his shirt and doublet and wore only leather breeches and boots.

Averting her eyes, she dropped the bundle of bleached and twisted wood onto the sand, then began sorting out some small twigs for kindling. When he wasn't looking she studied him. The crew often worked bare-chested, but none of them had affected her like Stow was doing at this moment.

He had broad shoulders and a deep, muscular chest. His hair, light-brown with paler, sun-bleached strands at the front, brushed against his shoulders. Her mouth

135

dried as she looked at his flat belly and narrow hips. A line of fair hairs trailed down from his navel and disappeared inside the waistband of his breeches.

She hardly dared linger at his groin where the leather covered a substantial bulge, outlining rather than concealing what lay underneath. Dragging her eyes downwards, she saw that his legs were long and well-formed. There was no spare fat anywhere on his body.

Juanita realised with a surprise that he was quite beautiful. Not in the showy or swaggering way of most sailors, but in a brooding, self-contained sort of way. As he dug out the pit, he pressed his lips together, his fair brows drawn together in concentration.

She liked the way his muscles moved under his sun-tanned skin. There was a slight sheen to his skin and she wondered how it would feel under her fingers. Like hot silk, perhaps. Stow looked up at that moment and caught her watching him. It was too late to look away, so she smiled tremulously. He grinned back at her. Oh, Lord, he looked as if he knew what she was thinking.

They worked side by side and Juanita's heart kicked against her ribs every time Stow spoke to her or fixed her with his calm blue eyes. The weather too was affecting her strangely. The heat pricked under her arms and down her spine. There was even a throbbing warmth between her thighs and a moist slickness within the folds of her coynte, which became more apparent to her with each movement.

She plucked irritably at the heavy folds of her garments as they chafed against her skin. Sweat-darkened patches were visible under her arms and around her neckline.

'Why not take off your bodice?' Stow said. 'Your blouse will preserve your modesty.'

What he said made sense. The boning of her stout leather bodice was digging painfully into her ribs, but it was surely immodest to remove it. Underneath it she wore only her blouse, having left off her stays because

136

of the heat. She had never before been partially clothed in the company of a young man.

Oh, but it was like a furnace next to her skin. The area around her lower belly felt hot and swollen. She could hardly breathe. Perhaps it would do no harm to take off some of her outer garments. She would put them back on before the others came back.

She glanced sidelong at Stow, who was concentrating on his digging. Making up her mind, she unfastened the bodice, laid it aside, then rolled up the loose sleeves of her blouse. Her breasts lolled forward against the thin, damp fabric. She hoped that her nipples were not visible. Freed from constrictions they were gathering into hard peaks, tenting the cloth.

I don't care if he can see, she thought boldly, shocked at herself. Stow's gaze flickered briefly towards her and she saw his eyes darken with interest. So he found her attractive. She was pleased by the fact and thrust out her chest. Let him look if he had a mind to.

Sitting down, she unbuckled her shoes. She felt Stow's eyes on her as she rolled down her stockings and peeled them off. Digging her toes into the hot sand she wriggled them, closing her eyes with enjoyment. When she opened them Stow was looking at her.

'We need some stones for the bottom of the pit,' he said, eyeing her bare calves and slim ankles with evident enjoyment.

His voice sounded a little horse, she thought with satisfaction. A sense of her own power settled over her. Under his scrutiny she felt like more of a woman. For the first time *she* was the centre of attention. So often it was Carlotta who drew all eyes. Juanita did not think ill of her for that; that was just the way of things. Carlotta was like the sun, blinding in her beauty and vivacity. It took a special kind of man to see the simmering warmth behind her own lesser prettiness.

'I'll fetch the stones,' she said, a burst of pure happiness coming over her.

The hot sand seeped between her toes as she struck out along the beach. Her hips swayed as she walked and she knew that Stow was watching her. When she had gone a few yards, she turned and saw that he had climbed out of the pit and was advancing towards the forest. As she watched, he shinned up the nearest palm and chopped away at the crown. A number of coconuts in their outer casings bounced on the floor.

When she returned with an armful of stones, he was sitting propped up on one elbow. He had chopped a hole in one of the big, greenish ovals and was drinking the coconut milk. The smooth column of his throat moved as he drank. Watching him, Juanita realised how thirsty she was.

'Here. I've opened one for you,' he said.

She drank greedily, the sweet milk flowing down her chin and soaking the front of her blouse. They both laughed at the waste and Stow opened another nut for her. She crossed her arms to cover herself, trying to ignore the fact that her blouse was plastered wetly to her breasts and the cambric was almost transparent. Stow must be able to see her erect, pinkish-brown tips.

'Thirsty work, is it not?' Stow said evenly, although his eyes spoke of other more earthy things.

She nodded happily, arching her back and lifting her face up to the sun. The warmth would bring out her freckles but she cared not a jot. She and Stow might have been the only people in the world. The two ships in the bay were as small as toys. There was nothing to mar the beauty of the stretch of white sand, the blue sky, or the sea breeze stirring amongst the fronds of the coconut palms.

Birds wheeled overhead, soaring upwards on the currents of warm air. When she asked what they were, Stow told her that they were terns and frigate birds.

He spoke little and did not make idle conversation yet she felt easy in his company. To her mind, most men said too much anyway and the larger part of it was not worth listening to. She took another sip of coconut milk, then wiped her mouth on the back of her hand.

'How came you to be abroad the *Esmeralda*, Stow?' she said.

He shrugged. 'I heard that Manitas was after getting together a crew. I met him on the Isle of St Kitts, where I worked on a tobacco plantation – before the damned Spanish burned us out. I knew he would be a fair man to work for.'

'But you're not the sort of man I would expect to find amongst a ship's crew. Most of the others are so rough and crude of speech. And they smell worse than a privy at the height of summer . . .' She broke off, hoping that she had not spoken out of turn. After all, Stow probably had friends amongst the crew.

'Forgive me. I did not mean . . . It's not that I think I am any better than those men. I'm just a maidservant myself . . . But you're different, gentler than the others.'

He gave her a searching look, then laughed. He had strong white teeth with no gaps. Again she felt that odd little flutter in her chest. Lord, his eyes were so clear and blue. She had to look away.

'I'm glad that I meet with your approval,' Stow said and dipped his chin in a mock bow. When he straightened up, his face wore an expression she had not seen before. 'In fact, I'm very glad indeed,' he said softly.

Juanita coloured. 'Oh . . .' was all she could manage to get out.

Stow put down the coconut he was holding. Deliberately he moved closer until he was kneeling next to her. Something about his manner alarmed her, but she did not want him to think that she was afraid of him. It took an effort of will not to move away and put a safe distance between them.

He was not as big as Manitas, few men were, but he was still a man of imposing size. She trembled with suppressed excitement as he reached for her hands and

139

drew her to her knees. Facing him, her head was level with his shoulders. The silence stretched between them. She did not know how to fill it. Carlotta would have known what to say. She doubted whether her mistress had ever been lost for words.

'Stow . . . I . . .' she began. 'Please. I've never . . .'

He put a finger to his lips in a gesture for silence. She swallowed audibly. Reaching out, he grasped her shoulders and drew her towards him. She gave a little cry of alarm, which was cut off at once by the pressure of his mouth against hers.

For a moment longer she resisted him, pushing her hands against his chest, but it was more a reaction of surprise. This was what she had wanted from the moment he scooped her out of the boat. She gave a shudder and opened her lips under his. His tongue slid into her mouth, strong and demanding.

As he tasted and explored her, she felt her legs go limp and swayed forward against him. Her breasts swelled and tightened against his naked chest. His skin was firm and warm. She smelt salt and sunshine and the deeper, heady musk of male arousal.

His hands moved up over the curve of her waist as his kiss deepened. She felt his thumbs scrape across her nipples and a jolt of heat went directly to the soft place between her thighs. A little sound of wanting rose in her throat and Stow stopped kissing her and drew away a little. She looked up at him, her eyes unfocused, feeling the need for him spreading throughout her body.

She wanted him to lay her on the sand, raise her skirts and take her – now, this very minute. Before this moment, she had never known what true desire was. Her response to the inept fumblings of drunken noblemen did not count. Their slobbering kisses and careless probing fingers, had left her unmoved. Yet, Stow had hardly touched her and her body had awoken.

She was ready and eager to surrender the burden of

140

her virginity. Surely he could tell that she was willing. Why did he not kiss her again? He was smiling down at her as if amused by the torrent he had unleashed in her.

Linking her arms around his neck, she pressed her breasts against him, loving the way he drew his breath in through his teeth. Ah, so he was as aroused as she.

With a soft groan he bent his head and mouthed the full curves of her cleavage. Pushing the loose neckline of her blouse over her shoulders, he released her breasts. They sat like an offering on top of the folds which supported them. Holding her close, his palms flat against her shoulder blades, he leaned down to suckle her.

When he closed his mouth on her nipples, she sighed with pleasure. The sweet, pulling sensation was exquisite. His teeth nipped gently at her engorged flesh and white-hot flashes of lust speared her loins. She closed her eyes and gave herself up to sensation. Stow released the first nipple and turned his attention to the other. Raising his hand he pinched and rolled one nipple, while nuzzling the other. His lips were soft and relaxed, while his tongue flicked back and forth in a maddening rhythm.

'Oh, Stow . . .' she murmured, her fingers meshing in his hair. The strands of it slipped over her fingers, sun-warmed and shining with health.

She arched her back and pushed her pubis towards him. The hardness of his cock pressed into her belly. Grinding against him she felt the hot shaft twitch and stir. Her insides seemed to be melting, drawing down and becoming a receptive liquid mass. The dew from her sex streaked her inner thighs.

Her coynte was so swollen and aching that it was verging on being painful. And the hard little bud, which was enclosed by the thickened purse of her sex, throbbed and throbbed.

Behind her closed eyelids, she saw a golden haze.

141

She felt entranced, a thing of helpless, quivering pleasure. Dear God in Heaven, she had never wanted anyone like this.

All of a sudden Stow drew back. She felt him stiffen, then he put her from him. She made a sound of protest and reached for him.

'Cover yourself,' he said thickly.

'But . . . why? Why did you stop?' she said, horrified to hear the note of pleading in her voice.

For answer he nodded towards the trees which bordered the sand. She saw three figures emerging from a clump of ironwood. They were dragging a litter made of sticks lashed together, on top of which was the carcass of a wild pig. Seeing Stow and Juanita so close together, they called out and made crude gestures.

'If it's time to take turns, I be next!' Julio called out.

'Then me. I like a woman who's oiled and ready.'

The others laughed, grasping at their crotches and leering.

'Don't put those teats away yet wench! There's men here to give suck to.'

Juanita scrambled to adjust her blouse. She was overcome with revulsion. The beautiful experience was sullied by the crudity of Julio and the others. They must think her no better than a common trull. And Stow probably thought that too. What had she been thinking of, letting him touch her like that?

She was overcome by shame and felt perilously close to tears. As she tied the drawstring neck of her blouse, she kept her head bowed so that Stow would not see her expression.

His hand closed on her wrist as he helped her to her feet, then he bent and picked up her leather bodice. Her fingers trembled as she put it on. She was shaking so much that she could not manage the lacing and he had to do it for her.

'Look at me,' Stow said softly. 'Pay the others no heed.'

142

Slowly she raised her chin and met his eyes. He has eyes a woman could drown in, she thought, overcome by misery. Then she absorbed the look on his face. It shocked her deeply. He did not trouble to disguise the naked need which was written there so clearly. He cared for her, he truly did.

'Will you be my woman?' he said softly.

She gave a little cry of joy and laid her cheek to his chest. His heartbeat was steady and strong.

'Oh, yes. Yes,' she murmured, not caring what the others thought.

As Julio came abreast of them, he sneered, 'Well. Well. How touching. Stow seems mightily taken with the wench. Mayhap he's her pimp now. What price for your whore then?'

Stow put Juanita from him and advanced on Julio. Before the other man knew what was happening, Stow had felled him with a single blow. Julio lay at his feet, blinking dazedly. Stow, fists bunched, glared at the others who were backing away.

'Anyone else got something to say?'

They shook their heads. Julio got to his feet, nursing a split lip. His eyes glared hatred at Juanita.

'Women,' he said, spitting a bloody gob into the sand. 'Women's always blessed trouble. You'll see Stow. You mark my words. Her and the other one'll bring us bad luck. You see if they don't.'

When Stow moved towards him brandishing a menacing fist, Julio scuttled off. For once Juanita was not affected by Julio's waspishness. As she helped prepare the fire pit she could think of nothing but the unassuaged need inside her.

When, she wondered, would she and Stow get the chance to be alone together?

When the key sounded in the lock Antonio stood up and brushed himself down.

'Confound these damned pirates,' he muttered under

143

his breath as he swept the dirty straw from his fine clothes.

He was thoroughly out of temper, having been left in the dark and malodorous space for some hours. Did these people not realise that he was a man of some importance? How dare they treat him like a common cutpurse?

Ah, here was the pirate chief, come to discuss terms. Antonio felt confident that he would soon be released – despite the interference of the black-haired beauty. Any man's greed, and especially a pirate's, was bound to get the better of his judgement.

But it was not Manitas who entered the brig. Antonio's mouth drooped with dismay as Carlotta strode into the small room. She wore dry clothes now; a set of black velvet hose and a doublet of padded red leather. The ruff at her throat was crisp and white. Her hair was plaited and pinned over her crown. There was a freshly-scrubbed wholesomeness about her.

Antonio felt a stirring in his groin. Her appearance was in sharp contrast to the picture of wantonness she had presented a short time ago. This new demure look was incredibly arousing in a subtler, but no less powerful, way. Was this really the same woman who had thrust her cherry-tipped breasts towards her lover and pleaded with him to pleasure her, her tangle of midnight curls tumbling down her naked back?

'How now, banker?' she said. 'Somewhat subdued I'll wager. Time for you and I to have a talk.'

Antonio bristled. So the wench hadn't changed her tune. After what he had seen in the next cabin he was not disposed to listen to any more of her insolence.

'Go fetch your master,' he said haughtily. 'I make my bargains with the trainer, not the performing bitch! Though I grant that you performed – certain privy tasks – well enough if my eyes and ears did not deceive me. There was a most convenient crack in the wall.'

Carlotta's eyes narrowed dangerously.

144

'So you stooped to spy on us? I'm surprised that you do not hide the fact.'

He laughed shortly. 'You did not trouble yourself to be discreet. Half the ship must have heard your moans. God's truth wench, but you're comely enough in the flesh, I'll give you that. Even more so when you're playing the part that God meant for you. The pirate has the measure of you and no mistake. Such a swiving he gave you, eh? Now, run along like a good little wench and stop playing at being a man. The jest is wearing thin.'

'I'm glad you enjoyed watching us,' Carlotta said with heavy sarcasm. 'But you are mistaken about my role on this ship. Manitas *is* my lover, but he is also my business partner. I have no master except myself.'

Antonio grimaced and made a lewd gesture. 'A man is always master over a woman. God has decreed it.'

Two high spots of colour appeared on Carlotta's cheeks.

'Say you so? It seems then, that I must give you a lesson. Besides, I've a score to settle. Without your help Don Felipe Escada would not have cheated me of my property.'

'Don Felipe cheated you? Then mayhap you deserved the lesson he dealt you! I do not regret helping him.'

'You pompous little man,' Carlotta said through slitted teeth as she drew her sword.

The light from the single lantern glinted off the razor sharp blade. She assumed a fencing position and twirled the sword, slicing at the air with an expert wrist movement.

Antonio flinched. 'Here now! What are you doing? Your pirate lover won't thank you for killing me! I'm worth a great deal to him alive.'

'I have no intention of killing you. I've something far more interesting in mind. You are in no danger, but you are about to learn what it means to be mastered.

Let's see how *you* like playing the servant. Mayhap you'll learn some manners.'

Lunging forward, she slit the front lacing of his doublet and then sliced his belt through.

Antonio gave a shriek of outrage and clutched at the parted cloth. Carlotta laughed as she used the sword tip to slash at the waist of his elaborate, padded trunk hose. Tufts of horse-hair spilled out of the cuts she made.

'My garments! These cost a king's ransom,' Antonio wailed, trying desperately to cover himself.

'You've had the sight of me naked, banker. Now you'll afford me the same! Be quick and disrobe, before my hand slips and I prick that over-fleshed belly of yours.'

'You would not dare!' Antonio staggered back, trying to avoid the flashing sword.

He tore off his clothes and threw them to the floor. Soon he was clad only in a loose shirt and woollen drawers.

Under the over-hang of his belly, his stubby cock pushed out the front of his drawers. Why he's half erect already, Carlotta thought, smiling as Antonio struggled to hide his arousal. She swept him with a withering glance and Antonio cursed under his breath and brought his hands up to cover his groin.

'Well, señor. It seems that you are more than willing to play at being my slave.'

'The devil I am!' Antonio said with spirit, but his voice lacked conviction. 'Hell will freeze over before I follow a woman's orders!'

'You have no choice but to obey me,' Carlotta said softly. 'But I'm moved to be generous. You decide. What's it to be? You can pleasure me or suffer a lashing.'

Antonio's eyes sank even further into their pouches of flesh as they narrowed with lust. His hands fell away from his groin and she saw that he was strongly erect now. Drawing himself up fully he puffed out his chest

146

and adopted a pose. Carlotta barely contained her mirth. He reminded her of a graceless, rotund peacock.

'I'll pleasure you – if I must,' he said, the gleam in his eyes and the slackness of his mouth belying his reticence. 'Not one of my many mistresses have been disappointed by my prowess as a lover.'

Carlotta smiled grimly. She felt certain that Antonio was as brutish a lover as he was a man. No doubt his lovers had not dared to complain. It delighted her to take her revenge on the horrible little object. Antonio, encouraged by her silence, took a step closer. His hand was at work on himself, stroking and squeezing. She could see the shape of his cock through the cambric of his drawers. The fat shaft and flaring ridge around the cock-head was clearly delineated.

She supressed a shudder. Everything about him revolted her. Did he really think that she desired him? She had noticed in the past that many ugly men had a high opinion of themselves and considered that they were irresistable to women. Well, Antonio was soon to discover that he was sadly mistaken.

Antonio's thick lips parted in a grin, showing broken and stained teeth.

'Nothing to say now, my beauty? Stunned by my potency, are you? I've something good ready for you,' he crooned. 'I'll make you moan and cry out, just as you did when that giant of a pirate was swiving you.'

Carlotta stood with her feet apart and one hand on her hip. She stabbed the point of her sword in the wooden boards and let go of the pommel. It swayed upright within easy reach of her hand. Slowly she unfastened her belt and drew down her breeches.

Antonio's tongue came out to moisten his lips as her lower belly and thighs came into view. His eyes bulged as she flexed her knees and thrust her pubis towards him.

'On your back then,' he said hoarsely, rubbing more

vigorously at himself. 'And open up those milk-white thighs. God's bones, but I'm eager to part your maiden hair and mount you.'

'You are presumptuous, señor,' she said in a voice that dripped ice. 'Do you think that I'd afford you the privilege of entering my body? On your knees, damn you! And do homage to your mistress.'

Taken by surprise Antonio gaped at her. For a moment it seemed that he might refuse. She was about to reach out for her sword, when he began to sink down to the floor, his eyes never leaving the cluster of silky pubic curls. As his knees pressed into the wooden boards, he winced.

'That's better. Now, bow your head, get your fat rump in the air and crawl over here.'

Antonio swallowed audibly. He was trembling all over. She expected to have to force him to obey her, but he assumed the position and began slowly to crawl across the tiny room. It was immensely satisfying to watch his ungainly progress. She had to suppress her laughter.

As he drew close, she leaned back against the wall and parted her thighs. Still on his knees, he paused in front of her, his head level with her waist. Meshing her fingers in his hair, she drew his head towards her groin and rubbed her pubic curls against his chin.

Antonio's hands hung limply at his sides. He made a sound halfway between a moan of outrage and a grunt of eagerness.

'Not that. Please I've never . . . It's not seemly . . .' he said. 'Oh, Lord . . .'

'Silence!' she rapped. 'I have other work for your mouth. Now, do homage to my womanly parts. Put your tongue to good use.'

She mashed his face into her pubis, grinding the musky flesh against his nose and mouth. Antonio gave a sob and, stretching out his tongue, took a first tentative lick.

'You can do better than that,' Carlotta said. 'Must I take the flat of my sword to you?'

Antonio gave a muffled grunt and began to lick and suck her coynte. Carlotta's knees grew weak as the pleasurable sensations spread through her belly. After the initial reticence Antonio bent to his task with a will. His hot tongue explored her wet folds, searching out the hardening nub of flesh at the apex of her sex.

Her breath came faster as he flicked the tip of his tongue up and down her pleasure bud, the movement easing back the tiny hood of flesh to expose the exquisitely sensitive core. Lipping each of her outer folds in turn, he nuzzled the tender flesh. After a time he pressed his head more deeply between her thighs, searching out the puckered orifice between her buttocks.

Carlotta sank down onto his face as his tongue tip played across the tight hole. The delicious heat and wetness of his mouth was drawing her towards a climax.

When his hands came up and took hold of her thighs, she did not protest. His fingers stroked her gently, reverently, and a smile of satisfaction curved her mouth. Antonio was learning that there was pleasure to be had in submitting oneself to the will of another. Perhaps his future lovers would benefit from these forced attentions.

'That's it. Pleasure your mistress soundly. If you acquit yourself well, I'll allow you your own release.'

Antonio murmured softly as he closed his mouth over her coynte and moved his lips over her thickened folds in an intensely erotic kiss. Carlotta ground herself down onto him, her hips working in a circle as she used him simply as an instrument to fan her lust. The creamy juices flowed out of her, bedewing Antonio's lips and chin.

She found the experience of wreaking a fleshly revenge a heady thing indeed. The haughty banker had become a willing supplicant to her every need. Without being instructed, he began giving her coynte long loving licks. She shuddered against his mouth, the tension gathering inside her.

As he centred his attention again on her pleasure bud, lolling his tongue against it and pressing gently, she was tipped over into a wave of pulsing sensation. She moaned aloud as her womb contracted and the sweet, rhythmic squeezing spread though her belly. Throwing back her head to expose her throat, she allowed her mouth to sag open as her climax crested, reached a plateau, then faded.

'Enough,' she said, her voice gentler now. 'Stay as you are.'

She pushed Antonio away and he remained kneeling, looking up at at her with an expression of arrogant pride. What a lover I am, his expression said. And she had to admit that he had been thorough and willing, especially since she was certain that it was the first time he had used his mouth on a woman's sex. It seemed almost a shame to abuse him further, but she forced herself. He had not yet received a complete lesson.

Pulling up her breeches, she fastened the belt at her waist. Antonio looked at her with dismay as she walked around him. His erect cock still jutted against his woollen drawers and there was a small wet patch where the tiny mouth had wept a few drops of slippery fluid.

'But . . . you said I could have you . . .' he began, his puffy face crestfallen.

'I said that you would be allowed your own release,' she corrected him. 'So take it. And I'll watch you.'

A deep flush stained his cheeks as he absorbed the meaning of her words.

'You wish to watch, whilst I commit the sin of Onan? I've never heard of such a thing. What kind of woman are you?'

His face hardened and his mouth thinned with outrage. He shook his head and began to get to his feet.

Carlotta placed her hands on his meaty shoulders and pressed him back down.

'I'm my own kind of woman, the kind I wish to be,' she said stoutly. 'And that was not a request. You'll do as I say. Remain kneeling and take down your drawers.'

For a moment longer he resisted, his mouth working with impotent fury, then his hands went to his waist and he unlaced his garment. The loose drawers slipped down his thighs and pooled around him. Jutting out from between his mottled thighs was his stiffly erect organ.

Antonio flinched visibly as Carlotta fixed her eyes on his cock. It was short and thick and twitched under her gaze.

'Take hold of your pizzle,' Carlotta said. 'Let me see how you coax yourself to pleasure in the privacy of your bed chamber.'

He shook his head, his teeth clenched. 'I'll not do it. It's a sin.'

Carlotta threw back her head and laughed. 'There are far greater sins in the world than pleasuring your own flesh. Do it. Or must I offer you some encouragement?'

When he remained still, his hands at his sides and his erection starting to dwindle, she reached for her sword. Antonio's eyes widened with alarm and he yelped when she used the flat of the blade to deliver two sharp blows to his fleshy buttocks. Red marks appeared immediately on the soft flesh and she placed the next two blows at an angle to them.

Antonio's cock leapt and quivered and suddenly he was even more firmly erect than before. His bottom grew redder as she struck him two more blows and he arched his back, crying out with the smarting pain. His breath quickened and he shuddered as she laid into him, the sound of the blade hitting flesh loud in the small room.

His next words surprised her.

151

'Don't please . . . Please. I beg you . . .' he moaned. 'Don't stop hitting me.'

His lips began to work and now he clasped his cock-shaft with eager fingers. He rubbed up and down, smoothing the skin back over the hardness within. The skin of his phallus was flushed and dark and the glans, partly uncovered now by the foreskin, was a deep purplish-red. As he stroked himself he began to groan, the sounds forced from between his tightly stretched lips.

Antonio's movements became more frenzied as he pulled at himself. The now fully exposed glans was moist and engorged. Droplets of silver fluid oozed from the slitted cock-mouth and hung there in threads until it was scooped up by his moving fingers.

Carlotta stopped beating him with the sword, but he begged her to continue, squeezing and releasing his fiery buttocks as he stroked himself into a frenzy. She beat him a few more times, but more gently now. He bent forward slightly offering up the hot red flesh of his bottom for punishment.

She found that she enjoyed having him at her mercy and had to make a conscious effort to stay her arm. Antonio urged her to beat him harder. He seemed bent on her causing him some actual injury. Taking care to vary her blows, she beat him on the backs of his thighs.

Antonio moaned loudly as his unmarked flesh began to turn crimson. His sweat-soaked shirt clung to the great bowl of his belly and he held the garment up with one hand while with the other he continued to stroke and jerk at himself.

'Blessed Virgin. Mother of God,' he cursed softly as his face screwed into a mask of pleasure.

Suddenly he stiffened and jets of semen spurted from him, the creamy drops spattering the floor. Carlotta gave him one final stroke of the blade while he hung his head, his hand clamped to his cock as he milked the final drops from it.

Moments later he sat back on his haunches, shoulders slumped with exhaustion. Carlotta glanced dismissively at him, then strode to the door.

'Well, señor Antonio. Your lesson in humility is complete. You are free to go. No ransom is required. Perhaps you will be a better man from this moment on, but I doubt it. I give you good day. Be sure to tell Don Felipe about your "special instruction" when next you meet with him.'

Antonio turned towards her, his heavy face was tear-streaked and ravaged by emotion. His skin shone with sweat and he kept touching his mouth where, no doubt, the last traces of her musky female scent lingered.

'No woman ever treated me that way,' he began. 'I just wanted to say . . . to say . . .'

Carlotta raised her eyebrows and glared fiercely at him. She expected a threat or an insult and was prepared to trade crude words with him.

'Yes?'

'Thank you,' he murmured, his voice low and filled with passion. 'Thank you from the bottom of my heart. And I will convey your good wishes to Don Felipe.

Carlotta looked at him in astonishment. He really had enjoyed everything she made him do. Perhaps the punishment had been ill chosen. No matter. She had enjoyed herself and she would choose more wisely next time.

'You do that,' she said. 'I want Don Felipe to know that I'm doing all of this for his sake. Tell him that I shall enjoy selling the fruits of this treasure ship. And tell him also that I am not finished yet.'

As she left the room, the absurdity of the situation struck her and she began to laugh.

Chapter Eleven

*F*elipe was sipping a goblet of hippocras and going through some business papers, when the servant delivered the letter to him on a silver salver.

Breaking the wax seal, he unrolled the parchment. Ah, this was a missive from his banker. No doubt it was an inventory of his share of the profits from the sale of goods on the treasure ship, recently arrived at Seville.

But no, this was no neat list. It was a personal letter. He recognised the flowing hand of Antonio Alva's personal scribe at once.

As he scanned the page his eyes widened in disbelief. The banker had lost the treasure ship to pirates off the coast of Honduras and Carlotta had been amongst their company? Impossible, surely. Alva must have been mistaken, for what would Carlotta be doing half-way across the world?

The fact that he had lost a great deal of money on his investment was not uppermost in his mind. Instead, he found himself thinking about Carlotta. It was some months now since she stormed out of her house and turned her back on him, spurning his offer of protection.

He felt sure that she and Juanita had found work in a

town nearby. Although it was true that he could not imagine Carlotta's unruly black curls covered by the white linen kerchief favoured by shopkeepers and their workers. So far he had not been able to find Carlotta, despite paying an agent to make enquiries about her.

But pirates, indeed! The idea was preposterous.

Further down the letter he found more evidence that it had indeed been Carlotta whom Alva had seen. The banker had spoken with her and spent time in her company. There was no more doubt in Felipe's mind, but he felt sure that Alva was missing out certain details of that meeting.

There was a certain quality to that part of the letter, an odd sort of . . . reverence? as Alva spoke of her. Another man might have missed it, but Felipe was attuned to anything regarding Carlotta. He knew only too well how captivating were her charms. He grasped the parchment hungrily as if he could absorb some of Carlotta's essence through the fabric.

What else had Alva to say about her? He sensed that she had somehow managed to bewitch the poor sot. Surely she had not given the banker that which she had denied Felipe? His hands shook. The image of Carlotta lying on her back, covered by Antonio Alva's slug-white body, made him want to retch.

He forced himself to read further, although he felt afraid of what he would find. Ah, here was the part he had half-expected, half-longed for. The purpose of this letter, apart from notifying him of Alva's financial losses and therefore his own also, was to convey a message from Carlotta to himself.

'Carlotta wished me to tell you that she would enjoy selling the fruits of your treasure ship,' he read. 'And she says that she had not finished with you yet. I fear that she intends to wreak a heavy revenge on you. Whatever you did to her, she will never forgive you. She wants to ruin you, my friend. And, from what I

155

have seen of her, she is capable of doing your finances great harm.'

The letters with their complicated loops and curlicues swam before Felipe's eyes. He could almost hear Carlotta saying those words. By God the wench was throwing out a challenge to him!

Felipe sank onto a wooden settle. He did not for a single moment doubt that Carlotta intended to carry out her threats. She wanted to bring financial ruin upon him. It was a laughable thought. One woman could not have so much power. But he had never felt less like laughing in his life. How she would take her revenge, he could not imagine, but she would do it. She was the strongest, most wayward, most perversely determined woman he had ever met.

And her hatred for him was what drove her onwards.

It saddened him that she felt that way. If only she had agreed to live in the little cottage on the estate. She would have learned that he was merciful, able to forgive her for her harsh words, immodest thoughts, and lewd actions. A few weeks of carefully orchestrated chastisement and she would have been as biddable a wife as ever a man wished for.

He closed his eyes against the vision that rose in his mind; Carlotta kneeling beside the bed they shared, her palms clasped together in an attitude of prayer. The filmy white bed-gown was loose over her shoulders and her hair was twisted into a night plait. The scratches from her most recent birching were visible across her shoulders and the slopes of her full breasts. Her erect nipples made rosy peaks in the fabric.

'Thank you for my punishment. May I take my rest now, my lord?' she asked meekly, her soft mouth curving in a smile. 'Or is it your wish that I receive your staff of Adam into my body?'

Her oval face was gentle and the dark eyes she turned up to him, were wide and adoring.

Felipe let out a ragged sigh as the image faded. There

was a raging heat at his groin. He could amost feel the cool smoothness of her limbs, the hot wet centre of her body. Things could have been so different. Yet, she had chosen to spurn his advances and seek her fortune. God only knew what would happen to her in the company of pirates. If that was her choice, so be it. He knew that he had nothing to reproach himself for.

After a few moments he stood up and laid the letter on his oak writing desk. There was a strange sensation in his belly, a mixture of dread and excitement. If the battle lines were drawn up, did it not mean that he might meet her again?

Perhaps it was time that he accepted the fact that she had branded him with her beauty and sensuality. Not a single hour passed when he did not think of her. His dreams were coloured by images of her, his thoughts returned again and again to their final meetings when she had taunted him with her nakedness.

'I won't let her have dominion over me,' he burst out, his hands clenching into fists. 'I can rise above this. She is only a woman and as flawed and weak as all her sex are.'

He could not allow himself to give in to his most base desires. If he once accepted that he would never forget her, he would go mad. But the physical ache, the mental longing, these things were real and he could not avoid the knowledge that they were his cross to bear.

Carlotta was the Devil's creature – she was Lilith, Jezebel, Delilah, and therefore, as a weak and sinful man, he could not be blamed for responding to her. No priest would condemn him. His only course was to continue to fight to be free of her influence over him.

As he crossed his chamber and opened the door to his private chapel he wrung his hands. Always, before he laid eyes on the painting, he experienced a surge of exquisite joy. He delayed the moment when he would look up and see Carlotta staring down at him – as vibrant and beautiful as she was in the flesh – her lush black hair tumbling over her shoulders to cover one breast and leave the other bare.

Without being conscious of the fact, he sank down before the altar until he was kneeling on the flagstones. The light from the two beeswax candles threw long shadows across the floor behind him. The altar cloth was as white as her skin. A faint peppery smell of incense overlaid the darker scent of damp stone.

Slowly, unable to stop himself, he lifted his chin and looked at the painting. The fine dark eyes seemed to bore into him, her mouth to lift in a sardonic smile.

'Oh, why am I so weak,' he moaned, aware that his body was responding just as it always did.

He reached out his hand towards the painting, horrified to see how badly he trembled. The sight of the full round breast and the berry-red nipple sent a dart of lust to the end of his cock. Oh, God, there was her slim white hand curved over her Venus mound with the shadowy suggestion of hair beneath the fingers. He had seen her coynte in the flesh, the shape and smell of it seemed burned into his brain.

How sweet were the pursed lips of damnation, how tender the moist red folds of ruin, how penetrating the musky odour of his downfall.

'Deliver me Lord from temptation,' he whispered.

There was the familiar heat in his groin and his cock swelled until it stood up to lie almost flat against his stomach. His cods ached and burned. There was only one way he could gain relief. With a ragged sigh, he reached for the fastening of his padded doublet and began to disrobe. The figured velvet parted and he pulled the garment free and threw it to the stone floor.

His fine pleated shirt followed the doublet. Underneath he was naked. Picking up the flail which he kept nearby, he began to flick it across his shoulders. He winced at the smarting pain as the knotted leather thongs bit into the old wounds across his shoulder blades.

Loosening his belt, he slipped his free hand into his breeches and sought the slit in his under-drawers. He would not take out his cock. Perhaps that would make his sin less onerous. Closing his fingers around his straining shaft he began to stroke himself in time with the lashes of the flail.

'Grant me deliverance,' he whispered, his voice shaking and the tears gathering in his eyes. 'What must I do to be free of her? Dear God, why does she haunt me so?'

The chapel mocked him with its silence. The only sounds were his guttural groans and the slap of knotted leather hitting flesh. As Felipe's hand moved faster and faster his cock leapt and twitched, the agonised desire boiling in his loins.

Then, in the midst of his mental torment, he found a quiet place. And it seemed to him that the answer to his prayers rushed in to fill the void.

He would make a pilgrimage and donate a sum to the church. Perhaps he would purchase a new reliquary for the Cathedral at Santiago de Compostela, the destination of many thousands of pilgrims. Yes, that was the answer. He would visit the shrines of Saint Theodore and Saint Athanasius also, and do pennance there. Surely then he would be free of his bodily lust, his unclean obsession. The succubus, Carlotta, would not prevail against the might of the holy saints.

As relief flooded his tortured mind, his lips curved in a beatific smile. Something seemed to uncoil inside him and the cadence of his suffering changed. His hand pumped energetically at his phallus and his cods tightened and drew close to his body. The jism burst from him and he cried out at the singular pleasure as the hot, cleansing spurts left his body.

The revulsion came over him swiftly, but it was not as bad as it usually was. He would seek help from the mother church. She would provide an answer. Soon, he would no longer need to indulge in the sin of Onan, nor to mortify his flesh.

Dropping the flail to the stone floor, he sank back onto his haunches, his shoulders drooping and his chin sagging forward onto his chest.

How wretched and flawed a thing is man, he thought, as he rose to his feet. For he knew that, despite all of his good intentions – and he *would* make that pilgrimage – he would still be desperate for the easement provided by the yellow-haired whore when she called on her regular visit, a few days hence.

'Think you that we have found our island paradise?' Manitas said, looking down at the slopes of the thickly-wooded valley.

Off to one side Carlotta could see the bright green of seagrape trees and beyond that the sinister black mangroves which marched down towards the shore. In the far distance, where the curve of the bay was visible, the sea was as still as a mill-pond.

Here, on higher land, was everything they needed; good soil, fresh water, and abundant wood for building and fuel.

Carlotta linked arms with Manitas and smiled up at him.

'There can be no more beautiful place on this earth,' she said happily.

The sound of chopping wood was loud against the sounds of running water and the cries of birds. Some distance away the settlement was taking shape. Already the main buildings and stockade were marked out, their dark shapes wreathed in the mist which covered the mountain tops and gave presage of each dawn.

The tiny island was situated to the north west of Hispaniola and was perfect for their purpose. Manitas intended to build a fort, which would give protection to the buccaneers when they were not at sea.

Carlotta watched as he took measurements, made

drawings, and then gave orders to cut timber. She was impressed by his expertise and his knowledge of building. Bartholomew Stow, who had known Manitas for some years, provided the pieces of the puzzle.

'Why did you not tell me that you were a military engineer?' she asked Manitas now.

He glanced down at her, his handsome craggy face alight with good humour. Lifting one eyebrow and propping a hand on his hip, he affected a posture of displeasure.

'So you've been asking questions? Must I tell you everything, woman? A man must keep some mysteries, lest his lover grow tired of him!'

She dug him playfully in the ribs.

'Oh, you!'

It was just like him to tease her with the sort of quips women used when speaking to their men. That was one of the things she liked best about him. He was so secure in his own maleness, that he could afford to joke about it. His great height and physical bulk, which he carried with easy grace, made him a natural leader of men.

Other men despised the softness inside themselves, but Manitas displayed his gentleness as often as his strength.

She remembered their loving the night before and felt her stomach tauten with desire for him. The exchange of power between them had become an exciting part of their love-play and Manitas now enjoyed being submissive by turns as much as she.

For a moment longer she studied the workers, smiling when she saw Juanita take a leather water-bottle across to Stow. Juantia gave him a pert smile as she turned away and he slapped her bottom, causing the others to laugh and call out. Juanita blushed scarlet, but looked pleased enough.

Carlotta liked Stow. He was a strong, fine-looking young man who knew his own mind and was not afraid to voice an opinion. She was pleased that he and Juanita had found each other.

'You look thoughtful,' Manitas said. 'Something on your mind?'

As she leaned against him, she became aware of the pleasant soreness between her thighs. The night's loving had left a subtle impression on her body. No doubt Manitas too had marks to remember her by. He had strained against the chains which held him as she rode him hard, grinding her bottom against his flat muscled belly.

'I was wondering . . .' she said innocently. 'Are your wrists sore, this morn?'

'A little,' he said, with a grin. 'But not as much as your rump is about to be!'

'So you would play turn-about? You'll have to catch me first!'

She pulled her arm free of his and tore away up the side of a limestone hill. Since they took the treasure ship she had worn men's apparel. Without kirtle and under-skirts to hamper her movements she put a fair distance between them before Manitas took up the pursuit. Stretching out her long legs she ran like the wind.

Long grasses and tree ferns brushed against her boots. The clear morning air was sweet in her lungs and the sheer joy of being alive lent wings to her feet. Manitas would soon catch her, his longer legs and greater strength giving him a distinct advantage, but she ran on regardless.

She felt again the wild excitement of a child playing 'chase' who dreads being caught, but who longs for the moment when she is captured. Her hair pulled loose from the thong she had bound it with and the salt-scented breeze moved amongst the strands.

As she pounded down a hill towards the shelter of a pine wood, hundreds of golden swallows flew into the clear sky. Manitas caught her before she entered the trees. Grasping her around the waist he bore her to the ground. Together they rolled down the hill and came to rest in the long grass.

He pinned her with the weight of his body. She giggled and struggled against him, but he held her fast.

'Your turn to be mastered, I think,' he said, his eyes gleaming with desire.

'Take me then. If you can,' she said, sparkling at him.

Determined not to make it an easy conquest she wrestled with him, the green smell of bruised grass rising around their locked bodies. It was exciting to feel the hardness of his muscles against her chest and the ease with which he held her wrists imprisoned in one hand.

While she fought and spat, he used his free hand to take off her belt and drag down her leather breeches. She wore no under-drawers and the cool morning air met her bare flesh. He stroked the full globes of her buttocks, his breath coming fast.

She moaned softly as his fingers grew bolder, pressing her thighs apart and slipping between the cheeks to take hold of her coynte. Before she realised what he was about, he had parted the outer lips of her sex and thrust two fingers deeply inside her. The suddenness and lewdness of his action made her cry out.

'You cozening knave! I'm not ready.'

'But I am. And I'm master of this game. Besides, you gave me no quarter when you had me helpless this night past.'

As he curved his fingers and began to move them back and forth, the forced pleasure blossomed within her. She arched her back and sank down onto his hand. His thumb pressed onto her anus, circling and coaxing the tight orifice into submission.

She had expected him to spank her, but this was even better. His thumb slid a little way into her anus, while his fingers continued to explore and stroke her inner flesh-walls. Still she struggled against him, the hot

163

colour streaking her cheeks as she moaned and writhed, surging against the hand which impaled her both fore and aft.

'Well, little cat,' Manitas said softly. 'Have you been punished enough?'

'No . . . Oh, no . . .' she managed to say.

Chuckling, he removed his hand from between her thighs and lifted her, placing her belly-down across his knees. He removed her belt and wound it around her hands. With her wrists secured at the small of her back, she struggled to get free, her buttocks bobbing up and down enticingly. The drawn-down breeches were jammed tightly against the underswell of flesh, lifting up her bottom and offering it to Manitas.

'Oh . . .' she gasped, as he replaced his hand and entered her again with fingers and thumb.

She was wetter now and more ready for penetration, but the crudeness of his handling made her catch her breath. The thumb in her anus probed deeply and her flesh rippled at the intrusion as he propelled her unwillingly towards a spiked pleasure.

Leaving her impaled, he began to lightly spank one buttock. Carlotta's pleasure bud was strongly erect and she squeezed her thighs together, trying to give ease to the throbbing morsel. But Manitas's hand prevented her putting pressure on the spot where she craved it most.

He knew that she longed to stroke herself, but her secured wrists prevented her from touching herself in any way. The fingers and thumb inside her served to heighten the torture of being kept teetering, wanting, thirsting. She did not know if she could climax without rubbing her pleasure bud and Manitas knew that too. He deliberately gave her just enough stimulation to drive her to the brink of a climax, but not enough to tip her over.

'How cruel you are!' she grunted, tossing her head to

clear the hair from falling into her eyes. 'You deny me the solace I wish for.'

'That's your punishment,' he said hoarsely. 'I reserve the right to choose the manner of it. You must take what pleasure you can from – this. And this.'

So saying, he thrust his fingers rapidly in and out of her, his thumb plundering her tight nether-hole even more soundly. She bucked against him, her legs jerking wildly, as he penetrated her to the hilt. He spanked her more determinedly now, his palm crashing down onto the same place each time.

The tears gathered in her eyes and she choked back a sob, knowing that her abused buttock was reddening, while the other was pale as milk.

As if he had read her thoughts, Manitas said, 'What a delightful contrast. A blushing wanton and a pallid virgin.'

The fingers inside her were maddening and far too knowing. He stroked the sensitive pad behind her pubis and ticklish strands of pleasure suffused her entire lower belly.

'No more . . . Please. Let me come . . .' she moaned.

'As you wish, since you beg so prettily,' he said. 'You only have to reach out and take solace for yourself.'

'Stroke me . . . there. And I will dissolve. Manitas, please. Pinch my tiny woman's cock,' she whispered, her cheeks burning with mortification.

She could not believe she had said that. He had punished her past the place any other man had taken her to. Surely now he would not resist her plea.

But Manitas was unmoved. Laughing, he shook his head, and his fingers churned inside the warm well of her hungry orifice. Her silky juices flowed freely around his hand and her coynte puffed out lustfully. Despite her neglected and spurned pleasure bud, she felt her climax approaching.

The hot smarting pain of her spanked buttock drew an answering response from inside her. There too she was hot and sensitised. Her bowels churned and she chewed at her lip, almost afraid to give free rein to the awful sensations of pleasure-pain radiating from within her bottom.

The rigid cudgel of his cock pressed into her belly and she gave a great surge forward until his erection was level with her pubis. As she came, she ground herself onto his tumescence, taking for herself the easement she craved and which he denied her.

There, I've bested him, she thought.

Manitas increased the pressure of the spanking and she cried out as the pleasure and pain mixed together, then fragmented and became lost in the overwhelming rush of her climax. Her guttural moans were loud in the stillness, but she cared not.

Manitas swooped down and kissed the back of her neck, murming against her hot skin.

'That was bad of you. You dared to defy me? More punishment is in order I think.'

She quivered with eagerness as he freed his cock. Surely he would remove her breeches now, so that she could part her thighs. But he thrust straight into her tight wet passage, compressed as it was by the closure of her buttocks. It was always a shock to feel his bigness and to realise that she was able to encompass so much man-flesh inside her tight coynte.

The sense of being stretched, invaded, was delicious and thrilling indeed.

'You're so hot and tight, lovedy,' he groaned, thrusting powerfully and butting against her eager womb with each inward movement.

She came again and again, writhing under him while he plundered her willing flesh. When he pulled out of her and spilt his creamy seed between her buttocks, she subsided on the grass with a sigh. Turning over she stretched out her arms to him and he rested his head on the pillow of her breasts.

The grass was soft against her naked bottom. She

wondered idly at the different sensations of soreness and ticklishness in each buttock. How soundly he had spanked her. She would be aware of his hands on her for days. It was a secret she would be proud to carry.

She brushed his hair with her lips. Manitas was a robust and pitiless lover – a perfect match for her. She had never felt such pleasure in a man nor felt so free to be herself.

She felt a pang of perfect happiness. I could stay here forever like this, she thought, and make a home for us both in the settlement – if I had not a task to complete.

Manitas stirred against her and she snuggled contentedly into his embrace. Bodily pleasure, while wonderful and eminently satisfying, was fleeting after all. Part of her longed to give up her quest for revenge and spend every free moment exploring all the ways to make erotic encounters more memorable.

But she knew that, until she had her revenge, she could not settle. Her hatred for Felipe was abiding and there would be no rest for any of them until she had ruined him.

A month later, the settlement was ready for habitation.

Carlotta and Juanita delved into sea chests brought from the galleon and began hanging tapestries on the wooden walls of the house which Carlotta was going to share with Manitas.

Much of the furniture already in the room, including a large tester bed, had also come from the Spanish ship. The fine silk brocades and highly-polished, ornately-carved chairs and tables looked at odds against the simple log cabin style of the house, but Carlotta loved the contrast.

There was a sense of the possessions she had lost to Don Felipe in the reddish tones of the dark wood furniture, the vibrant colours of silk thread, and the heavy almost oppressive style of the carvings. But the new house was unique, a total departure from her old

167

life, and that, more than anything else, made her aware of how far she had come from Spain – and not only physically.

These days she wore men's garments most of the time and her hair was caught at her nape in a leather thong. Sometimes Castile, the lost Mendoza estate, even Felipe himself, seemed like a dream.

'That fat banker must have been carrying these goods back to a mistress,' Juantia said, cutting into Carlotta's thoughts. 'He would not have been taking such riches back to a wife.'

Carlotta nodded agreement as she finished pinning up the wall hanging. Most men and women married for family connections or to elevate their status. Love and pleasure was sought outside marriage.

'Let's hope that Antonio's paramour is so displeased by his lack of gifts that she throws him into the street and empties the privy-pot onto his head from an upstairs window!'

Their voices joined in laughter. Juanita pinned up her full skirts as she began making up the bed. Unlike Carlotta, she chose to wear a pair of leather stays over a blouse and a number of skirts. Her hair was covered by a square of clean linen. She looked fresh and pretty.

Carlotta marvelled at how unspoilt Juanita appeared. Some of the women, brought by the men from Hispaniola, affected bright silk dresses, low over the shoulders and bosom and sewn with flashy jewels. Juanita, as neat as a new pin, might have been a maid in a great house in Spain, instead of a pirate's doxy living in a roughly-built stockade.

Juanita smoothed down the linen sheet and tucked it into place, then began slipping an embroidered and silken case onto a pillow. Her face was turned away from Carlotta, but Carlotta sensed that there was something on her friend's mind. She decided not to prompt her. Juanita would often take a while to speak out, being more thoughtful and deliberate in her words and actions than she was herself.

Carlotta did not have to wait for long.

'There is some talk amongst the men,' Juanita said in a tone of somewhat forced lightness.

'And what is it they say?'

'Just that you and Manitas intend to raid another Spanish ship,' Juanita said. 'I told Stow that it was idle talk. What need have we of more goods? The settlement is groaning under the weight of crates and trunks of jewels.'

Carlotta paused in sorting through a huge trunk of gowns, but did not glance up.

'The men speak the truth,' she said calmly. 'In a sennight another galleon will pass close by. We are to take her. She's loaded with wool, spices, and dyes.'

'But why risk your life a second time? Surely we have riches enough on this island?'

'You know why I must do these things,' Carlotta said slowly as if speaking to a child. 'One blow to my enemy's purse is not enough. This next loss will wound him sorely.'

Juanita gave a snort of disgust. 'Don Felipe Escada. Always him. God rot the man. Even here his presence casts a dark shadow over our happiness.'

'That is why I want this finished. After this merchant ship, there will be another. We'll take that too. I do not think that Felipe's finances can recover from three losses so close together.'

'And what then? Another ship and another? You are obsessed by the man. Can you not see that he holds power over you if you let this go on? Why not forget him now and be happy with Manitas?'

It was the longest speech Juanita had ever made. Carlotta was hurt by her friend's disapproval. She had assumed that she had Juanita's full support. Throughout all their years together as maid and mistress Juanita

169

had been loyal, never once questioning Carlotta's words or actions.

During the past weeks the relationship between them had undergone a subtle change. As Juanita spent more time in Stow's company, Carlotta's protective role over her friend weakened. She sensed that, for the first time, Juanita was beginning to think about what she wanted for her own future, without seeing her choices reflected solely through her mistress's wants and needs.

Disappointment and an unexpected flare of jealousy made Carlotta strike out.

'Stay here and be happy with Manitas, eh? As you are with Stow?' she said sharply, dumping the gowns back into the trunk and sitting back on her heels. 'What a perfect meeting of minds and bodies is *that* match! Or do all new lovers wear such a sour expression as I've seen on your face these past weeks?'

Juanita coloured and her lips thinned.

'Stow's my business and none of yours. I'll thank you not to speak of things you know nothing of!'

Carlotta looked taken aback. Juanita had never raised her voice to her before. Her fingers itched to slap the other woman's face. That would teach her her place. She smiled, her dark eyes glinting with suppressed anger.

'It's always amusing to see a kitten scratch, but take care to keep your place.'

'And where is that?' Juanita said. 'Tell me pray, how I am to know what "my place" is? In Castile you were my mistress and I was always at your side. All my life I have taken care of your needs. When I agreed to go with you I did not think that we would throw in our lot with pirates.'

There was a streak of colour across each cheek, but the rest of Juanita's face was pale. Her breasts rose and fell with agitation and she clenched one hand to her heart as if she could still the rapid beating of it. Her voice rose as she went on.

'You leave me to fret and worry while you go off raiding ships with Manitas! And what shall I do on this island while I wait to see if they bring you back alive or dead? Why I should continue to wash your linen, starch your ruffs, and mend the sword cuts in your hose!'

'You're good for little else!' Carlotta snapped back. 'Unless it is complaining. Where would you be now, if I had not taken care of you? Probably married to some foul lout who would eat your share of the food, beat you on weekdays, then cover you with his malodorous body and swive you on the Lord's day. Would you rather be back in Castile, with a snot-nosed brat clinging to your threadbare skirts? Go then if you've a mind to!'

Juanita's face crumpled. 'You wish me to leave you?' she said, her voice a horrified whisper.

At the evidence of her friend's distress Carlotta softened. She was shocked by the argument. It was unbearable to even think of being without Juanita.

'Oh, Juanita. Forgive me. I did not intend to speak so sharply. Dearest friend. I have been selfish. I did not realise that you were unhappy. I thought that you had begun to settle here. I struck out in anger. I'm happy that you are content with Stow – '

She broke off as Juanita gave a strangled groan and pushed her knuckles against her mouth. Her eyelids fluttered as she strove to contain her tears. In an instant Carlotta was on her feet. She slipped her arm around Juanita's shoulders.

'What is it? Has he hurt you? If he has I'll – '

'No!' Juanita burst out, her face a mask of misery. 'He hasn't done anything to me . . . yet. That is . . . That is the problem . . .'

Carlotta looked at Juanita's crimson face and the tears rolling down her cheeks and she thought she understood. In fact she was relieved in some measure to find that there was another reason, beside her own selfishness, for Juanita's unhappiness. Drawing Juanita to one of the high-backed chairs of mahogany she bade her sit.

Juanita pulled the kerchief from her head and her soft hair tumbled around her shoulders. She sat with her hands clasped tightly together in her lap. It hurt Carlotta to see the shut-in expression on her friend's face.

'Come now, love. Tell me all about it,' she said, stroking the soft light-brown hair.

In between gulps and sobs, Juanita told her. It seemed that Stow had confessed his love for her, but was reluctant to bed her. Juanita burned with unsatisfied longings.

With her chin tucked into her chest, so that she need not meet Carlotta's eyes, she told Carlotta how she longed for Stow to caress her and take away the burden of her virginity.

'On . . . on that deserted island, where we went to hunt while you took the treasure ship, he kissed me and stroked my breasts. He pulled the blouse down over my shoulders and I was proud to stand there before him, all unclothed and with my nipples hard with longing. I could see by his eyes that he . . . he liked my breasts and I was glad of it. When he suckled me, I went weak. The pleasure of his warm mouth was so . . . intense.'

She stopped and began chewing at her bottom lip. Carlotta stroked her hair gently, a mixture of emotions moving in her chest. There was sadness and guilt that little Juanita had become a woman without her noticing. I have been remiss, she thought. She felt tender and protective towards her friend. The unformed longings, the half-innocent experience, and the ache of desire unfulfilled were in sharp contrast to her own earthy couplings with Manitas and the many lovers before him.

She wanted to help, so that Juanita too could learn the joys of lying with a man. And she wanted her first experience to be full of joy and guilt-free. So many women never found pleasure in the act of love.

'Go on,' she said softly. 'Tell me all that happened. Hold nothing back.'

Juanita nodded and looked up. She managed a watery smile.

'No man ever made me feel so excited. There was a sort of warmth in my belly and a sweet ache between my thighs. I was ready for him to enter me, right away. My . . . woman's place . . . my coynte was all swollen and aching – it had never been like that before. I wanted Stow badly. He was so beautiful, so strong with his skin all golden from the sun. If the others had not come back we might have . . .' She paused and sighed. 'He asked me to be his woman and I agreed. I could hardly wait to be alone with him again. I thought that, the next time he would . . . you know . . . But nothing has happened and I dare not ask for what I want.'

Carlotta was astounded. 'He has never touched you since then? But I thought . . . Everyone thinks . . .'

'I know,' Juanita said miserably. 'That's what makes it worse. Everyone thinks we are lovers. But Stow has some strange notion of honour. The woman he marries shall be a virgin still, he says. I love him for that, but oh, Carlotta I burn so that I cannot sleep. All I can think about is him, the way he smells, the look of his body. I can't forget what his mouth tastes like when it's pressed to mine.'

'He does kiss you than? I'm relieved to here it. I begin to think the man's a monk! You have pressed your hand to his breeches and felt a sturdy pizzle therein? I have heard of men whose male organ does not harden, though I confess I never met one. The problem with most of my lovers is that their staff of Adam will not lie down!'

Juanita threw her a reproachful glance.

'It's no jesting matter. And Stow's man enough for any woman. I've felt him hard against me.'

'Of course. Forgive me.' Carlotta took Juanita's hands between her own and pressed them sympathetically.

'I wish I could think of a way to help. In Castile we could have sought the village wise woman and had her make a love philtre. The foolishness of some men is unbounded. What *is* Stow waiting for?'

Juanita sniffed loudly and waggled her head from side to side.

'The Lord alone knows. I confess I'm at my wits' end.'

'God save me from honourable men,' Carlotta said with feeling.

They fell into silence. Juanita dabbed at her eyes with the hem of her under skirt. On her left hand she wore a large gold ring set with rubies and pearls; it had been part of Stow's share of the treasure. The jewels winked in the sunlight which streamed into the house through the open window.

Seeing the ring gave Carlotta an idea.

'He wants to marry a virgin, you say? Then I have it. We'll have a wedding. A pirate wedding. I've heard that there's a lapsed churchman amongst Manitas's buccaneers, though he's a Huguenot. Mayhap he can be persuaded to say the words over you both. It'll mean that a heretic will perform the ceremony. Does that matter to you?'

Juanita brightened a fraction.

'When have I paid heed to priests? I have you as my teacher. I care not whether a gimcrack pie-man says the words over us, as long as Stow believes that we are made man and wife. My immortal soul, like yours, has been more endangered these past months than ever in our lives, and yet we are hale and hearty. Let our church be the trees overhead and wine will serve for the holy water.'

Carlotta gave a peel of throaty laughter and threw her arms around her friend.

'Oh, Juanita. What a pretty pair of papists are we! I do declare that you and I are the happiest heretics in

174

the whole of Christendom! A pirate wedding it shall be then!'

When Carlotta told Manitas the news, he was delighted and set about making preparations at once.

'It is a good omen. A wedding is just the thing we need to set the seal on the new settlement. Think you that we should stand beside Juanita and Stow and make our vows also?'

Carlotta smiled up at him in astonishment.

'Stow seems to need the trappings of respectability before he will bed Juanita, but I've not found you slow in that quarter!'

He grinned. 'There are other reasons for getting wed.'

'None that are good, as I see them,' Carlotta said with spirit. 'Men treat their wives as dried-up chattels and their mistresses as cherished lovers. I've been both in my time and I know which I'd rather be!'

Manitas picked her up bodily and gave her a resounding kiss on the cheek. One of his hands cradled the back of her head, his strong fingers penetrating her hair to stroke her scalp.

'Aye, and I've no complaints, lovedy. You're the lustiest bed-mate a man ever had. Maybe you'd best give little Juanita a few lessons, lest Stow be disappointed in his bride. A man likes his woman to bite and scratch a little. Juanita's a mousey little thing. Think you that her blood is as cool as her colouring?'

Carlotta punched him playfully on the chest, squirming as he nuzzled her neck and tightened his arms around her.

'Stow will have no complaints,' she said, her breath quickening as Manitas's caresses became bolder. 'Juanita is a ripe peach ready for the plucking. And she's sick with love for him. We'll give them a wedding to remember and let nature take care of what happens between the bedsheets.'

Chapter Twelve

*I*nside the stockade all was activity. The idea of celeb-trating Stow's marriage to Juanita had caught the buccaneers' imagination and everyone made their contribution.

Three huge piles of wood stood ready, so that bon-fires would burn long into the night. Smells of baking perfumed the air as the ship's cook outdid himself, making a variety of spiced cakes, savoury tarts and custards. The women hung garlands of flowers on house doors and tied bright ribbons on the trees, which had been enclosed within the sturdy fence.

By late afternoon, a number of long trestle tables were set out with the cook's delicacies. Along with bread, roast meats and fish, and baskets of fruit, there were jugs of ale and rum. One table held an enormous bowl filled with a special punch made of mango juice, limes, and a liquor of fermented coco sap.

With the preparations complete, the women went to put on their best finery. For the first time that day the settlement was quiet and Juanita, free from any task save making herself beautiful, had time to think.

The single room of Carlotta's house was strewn with female garments. A froth of silk, velvet, and lace covered every surface. Boxes of jewels stood open on a coffer. A pirate's bride she might be, but Juanita was to be attired like a queen.

She was nervous now that the moment was almost upon her. Would Stow change his mind? Perhaps he did not wish to wed her at all. His reticence to make love to her might be more than shyness. Oh God, what if he was a lover of men? It was something known to be rife amongst sailors. She had heard the crude jokes about laying the youngest and prettiest boys across a barrel.

Agitated, she crossed the room and peered out of the window. This was just foolishness. Stow was as eager to wed as she. He had taken his leave of her the previous night, murmuring close to her lips, 'See you on the morrow, wife-to-be.' Just a few hours more and she would lie beside him in their new bed.

A number of men sauntered into view. Juanita recognised Julio amongst them; his mean little eyes glittered and his weasely face was flushed with drink. Many of the pirates had been drinking since morning and all of them were merry. They wore doublets of slashed silk or padded velvet, some of them sporting short full cloaks in the Spanish style. Wine stains spotted many a fine cambric shirt and more than one lace ruff was untied and drooping.

Juanita smiled at their tawdry elegance. She was touched that they had decked themselves out for the celebration. Their voices were raised in song now and some of them were capering around in a dance, arms linked, while two of them played a reed whistle and a drum.

As she smoothed her hands down the rigid front of her stays, Juanita realised that she was trembling. She looked over her shoulder at Carlotta and said ruefully;

'This is not how I imagined my wedding would be. I wish my family were here. This island is wild and full of dangers and the men are so . . . so . . . barbaric.

I know they cannot help the way they are . . .' She stopped, feeling ashamed at having criticised the buccaneers.

Carlotta came to stand beside her. She smiled.

'The men may be rough, but they wish you well. They are celebrating in their own fashion. A wedding is a blessing on us all. And, do not forget, that you are to be wed to one of them. You are sure you wish this? It is not too late to change your mind.'

Juanita shook her head and smiled.

'I've never wanted anyone like I want Stow. I know what my life will be like here and it's a better living than many could hope for. If our church is to be a canopy of trees and those gathered to bear witness are pirates and whores, then so be it. At least they are honest thieves and have done me no harm.'

'That, they have not,' Carlotta said, musingly.

By the look in Carlotta's eyes, Juanita knew that she was thinking of Don Felipe. That man was the other kind of thief, the kind who hid behind a cloak of respectability whilst he stabbed you in the back. To Juanita's mind, he was worse by far than the buccaneers, who had taken to piracy only because they had been persecuted by the Spanish and had their lands torn from them.

She sought for something to say, to distract Carlotta. Whenever her friend thought about Don Felipe, Carlotta's dark eyes hardened and her mouth became cruel. Juanita did not want any dark thoughts marring the day.

'I ought to finish dressing now,' she said. 'Make me look beautiful? I want to dazzle Stow, to show him what a fine lady I become with the right garments.'

Carlotta's lips curved in an affectionate smile as she secured the cumbersome farthingale around Juanita's waist. The heavy, figured-velvet outer skirts would be smoothed over the frame to form the fashionable bell-shape. It took a while to fit the bodice and sleeves, each secured by tying tapes together, and then arranging decorative, padded rolls to cover the joins.

A few final touches of jewellery at throat and wrist and Juanita was ready.

'There. You look splendid. Stow will find you hard to resist.' Carlotta kissed her cheek. 'But look. See for yourself. That deep-blue is wonderful on you.'

Juanita glanced towards the beautifully wrought looking-glass, which Carlotta had taken from Antonio Alva's cabin aboard the galleon. In the uneven, misty-green depths of the Venetian glass she could see herself reflected.

Carlotta had brushed out the front of her hair into a smooth, rounded shape and covered it with a network caul, sewn all over with pearls. The remainder of her hair streamed down her back. The gauzy white ruff at her neck framed the pale oval of her face and reflected light up to her small features. The gown of slashed and embroidered velvet was low across the bosom and the globes of her breasts were pushed up high by her stays.

She held a small puff-shaped fan of dyed feathers, Carlotta's wedding gift to her. Turning back to Carlotta she smiled tremulously.

'My wedding will change things between us. Do you mind?'

Carlotta gave one of her infectious husky laughs.

'Things were changed between us, long since. I doubt whether I'll suffer for the time you must spend on a husband and house!'

Although neither of them voiced it, it was understood between them that Carlotta would often be away from the island. Nothing would deter her from going along with Manitas whenever there was a ship to raid.

Outside the window the settlement was once again full of activity. People had gathered around the archway, which had been constructed of wood and draped with flowers and ribbons. A cheer went up as Manitas and Stow made their way towards the arch.

'I think they are ready for us,' Carlotta said. 'Come, love. Your husband awaits.'

Juanita's knees trembled as she walked towards Stow. She hardly heard the cheers and shouts of approval, having eyes only for him. He wore a doublet and breeches of soft, rust-coloured leather, the sleeves of his under-shirt visible through slashes in the doublet. How handsome he looked, with his sun-bleached hair freshly washed and brushed back behind his ears.

As she reached him, he took her hand, pressing her fingers gently as if he knew that she was fearful. She looked into his calm blue eyes and felt such a rush of emotion that her throat dried and she could hardly swallow.

The ceremony was short; the religious phrases less rich and musical than those she had listened to all her life. Instead of the scent of incense there was the peppery smell of exotic flowers. The sun glimmered on the green foliage and sparkled off the distant sea, the colours as pure as any in a stained glass window. To Juanita, it was a perfect service.

She raised her chin for Stow's kiss, blushing prettily when the pirates cheered. The afternoon passed in a welter of feasting, drinking, and good wishes. A viol and lute had been procured from somewhere and, as the light faded to a dusty-violet and the orange flames of the bonfires climbed into the sky, the dancing began.

Juanita had eaten little, being too nervous to do justice to the spread of food. Nibbling at the corner of a savoury tart, she laid it aside to sip at a third goblet of punch. There was a warm tingling in her belly and a swimming feeling in her head. She liked the sensation, but decided that this had better be her last goblet of punch if she wanted to keep her wits about her for the bedding.

Carlotta waved as she swept by in a swirl of crimson velvet, held close in Manitas's arms. For such a big man Manitas was light on his feet. Carlotta looked beautiful with her dark hair up-swept and covered by a net sewn with rubies. A split-ruff of white lace framed her face, emphasising the clean lines of her jaw and her flawless olive skin. The glimmer of New World gold was at her ears and throat, the design of it heavy and barbaric, suiting Carlotta's exuberant personality.

Juanita felt no envy, rather she was proud of Carlotta's striking good-looks. It was the first time in many weeks that her friend had worn a dress and she attracted many admiring glances. One of the men who watched her was Julio. Juanita saw the look on his face and shivered. Something about that man made her skin crawl. She was sure that he bore Carlotta no good will. A man like him would never forget a slight.

She must remember to warn Carlotta to be on her guard against him.

'What is it, love?' Stow asked. 'Are you cold? Here let me put my cloak around your shoulders.'

Juanita forgot about Julio instantly. Stow's touch sent a frisson of pleasure down her back. The punch warming her veins made her bold.

'Can you think of no other way to warm me, husband?' she whispered, delighted when his eyes darkened with desire.

'I'll think of many ways, to be sure. Just wait until the bed curtains are closed around us this night, and the revellers are gone away to their homes.'

Bending his head he placed a kiss on the swelling curve of her bosom. His hair tickled her skin and she breathed in his scent. He was newly bathed and anointed with some woody-scented perfume; underneath that, was the aroma of his unique maleness.

'I can hardly wait,' Juanita said, her voice trembling with passion. 'Can we not go to our house now? I'm fairly dying with need for you.'

Stow grinned, showing his even, white teeth. He shook his head, then picked up her hand and turned it over, pressing his lips to her palm and then folding her fingers over the kiss.

'We cannot deprive the guests of the ceremony of bedding. It is tradition and they expect it. But keep this kiss until later. I'll claim it back and demand of you many more.'

Charmed by the gesture and speechless with love for him, she leaned into his embrace. How was it possible that she had found such a perfect and sensitive lover inside the rough and manly form of a buccaneer? Let the night end soon, she thought. She felt desperate to lay with him.

Virgin or no, there would be no need for a smear of pork fat to ease the way for Stow's entry into her body.

The tips of her breasts were as hard as berries, pressing almost painfully into the flat, boned front of her stays, and there was an aching heaviness between her thighs. Every time she moved on the wooden bench, she could feel the puffiness of her coynte and the slippery moisture which seeped from between the thickened flesh-lips.

The drunken singing and dancing reached new heights as the moon rose in the sky. Faster and faster whirled the dancers, their shapes outlined against the red flames of the bonfires. Showers of bright yellow sparks pricked the ebony darkness, dancing like fireflies as they were swept away on the breeze which blew in from the sea.

In a while Manitas stood up. Swaying slightly, he banged on a table for silence.

'Time to put the lovers to bed. What say you?'

Before Juanita had time to react, there was a great surge of people towards her. She and Stow were lifted bodily and borne away towards their house. The door stood open and the guests swarmed inside the single living room and deposited the bride and groom next to the tester bed.

Candles flickered in the gloom, spreading yellow light

182

on the revellers and sending shadows to climb the walls. The room smelt of wax polish, new linen, and the heavier, brown scent of wooden furntiture.

The women gathered around Juanita, their hands plucking at laces, fastenings, and pins. Her headdress was removed and someone set to combing out her tresses, while others drew off her sleeves, bodice, and skirts. The men performed a similar service for Stow. Amid much ribald joking and comments on his prowess as a lover, he was divested of all his garments and bundled into a nightshirt.

Juanita crossed her hands over her breasts and blushed furiously as she was stripped down to her stockings. The women giggled and whispered encouragement, slapping her heartily on the buttocks. Now and then a man penetrated the huddle of women, his fingers pinching and squeezing. Wine-scented breath fanned her face as kisses were pressed to her mouth.

'Good luck to kiss the bride!' they shouted.

Juanita bore it all with good grace. She had been present at many similar beddings. They were bawdy occasions and it was expected that the bride and groom allow certain liberties. But when she felt a rough male hand slip between her legs, she kicked out.

'Unhand me, knave!' she cried, feeling her toe connect with a soft paunch.

Someone groaned and drew back.

'Lively little piece, ain't she!' another man sniggered, his voice thin and reedy.

She was sure it was Julio. At the thought of his hands on her or his mean little mouth on hers, her gorge rose. She searched for his face, but could not see him in the gloom. She shrank down, trying to shield herself behind the reassuring figure of the nearest woman.

Someone embraced her and she knew a moment's panic before she realised it was Carlotta.

'Oh, thank the Lord,' she groaned, relaxing against her. 'I lost you in the crush of people.'

'Won't be long now, Mistress Stow,' Carlotta grinned. 'Bear it just a while longer. Think of the long night ahead.'

Juanita gritted her teeth and tried to smile as someone pulled her stockings off and threw them into the air. A man caught them and waved his trophy high. Juanita shrank into herself, longing to cover her nakedness. She was sure that her blush extended over her whole body.

'Enough now!' Stow called out equably. 'I have need of my bride. Get you gone, all of you, so that a man can get to his work!'

The laughter and quipping re-doubled in volume. Juanita felt Carlotta slip the nightgown over her head. It was twisted and lodged around her shoulders, leaving her lower body exposed. She was beginning to feel panicky with all the noise and the smells of hot bodies, sour ale, and perfume. The hands that touched her were becoming more venturesome. Someone grabbed for her breast and a male voice was loud in her ear.

She squirmed as hard fingers closed over her flesh, pinching at her nipple. The pain of it made her cry out.

'Aw, don't take on so. Give us a feel!'

'Here now, get off! You muckle lout!' Carlotta said, slapping away the offending hand.

'What's to do? It's only a bit of a jest.'

'I'll jest you! Move off now, lest you favour a throttling or your ears slitting!' Carlotta glowered at the man and he slunk away, muttering under his breath.

Juanita thanked God for Carlotta and took advantage of the brief interchange to thrust her arms into the nightgown and pull away from the well-wishers. In a trice she was in bed and under the lemon-scented sheets. She slid down into the cool safety of the linen and pulled the covers up to her chin. Stow slipped in beside her and she gave a strangled sob of relief and sought the safety of his arms.

The wedding guests capered around the bed for a

while longer, but Juanita did not mind them now. With Stow's strong arm around her and her cheek pressed to his broad chest, nothing else mattered. Under the hardness of his muscles she could feel the steady, reassuring beat of his heart.

'Kiss your bride, Stow!' someone called.

There were groans of disappointment when he pressed a chaste kiss to Juanita's forehead. Juanita closed her eyes and willed them all to go away. It seemed that her prayers were answered. When there was no more response to their ribaldry, the guests became bored. With Carlotta's encouragement, they began leaving the house.

Throwing flowers from shredded garlands and good luck charms onto the bed, the revellers poured out into the night to continue drinking and dancing until dawn. Carlotta saw the last person out, blew Juanita a kiss and then, finally, closed the door behind her.

Stow leapt from the bed. In a single bound he was across the room and shooting the bolt across.

'Thank the good Christ. I thought they'd never leave,' he said with feeling.

Juanita sat up and pushed down the sheets to lie in a tangle around her waist. She was filled with excitement, hardly able to believe that the moment was here at last. They were alone, with the whole night for loving. She gazed at her husband, her heart in her eyes. Stow looked at her, his back pressed to the door. His blue eyes were dark and intense in the candle light.

Had she really doubted his potency? The desire on his face was so focused on her person that it made her a little afraid.

'So, Mistress Stow, 'tis time to obey your husband,' he said thickly. 'For you are to be an obedient wife, are you not?'

She nodded. 'What . . . what will you have me do?'

'Take off your nightgown, so that I may look upon you fully.'

185

Her fingers shook so badly that she fumbled with the lacing at her neckline, but she managed it finally. Holding eye contact with Stow, she lifted the hem of her nightgown and pulled it up over her body. Her loose hair fanned out over her bare shoulders, masking her breasts from his view. Straightening her back, she thrust her breasts out proudly, the erect, pinkish-brown nipples peeping through the tangle of her hair.

Stow swore softly and moved towards her. 'God, but you're beautiful,' he said hoarsely.

Taking her in his arms he kissed her shoulder, her neck, the slope of her breast. His fingers were strong and warm, leaving a trail of sensation wherever they touched. She arched towards him, scrabbling at his nightshirt and dragging the fabric up over his head.

'I want to see you too,' she murmured.

Stow shrugged off the garment and threw it onto the coverlet. Then he grasped the bedcovers and jerked them loose, uncovering her from the waist down.

'Come here,' he whispered against her mouth, pulling her onto the crumpled nightshirt to lie beside him.

With a little gasp of surprise, Juanita lay on top of the bed, pressed full-length against his strong naked body. The firm bar of his cock pressed into her thighs. She had not thought it would be like this. Surely Stow's reticence, up to now, had been because she was a virgin? His caresses had always been tender and restrained. In her imagination they would lie together under the sheets, caressing gently, almost shyly, then Stow would kiss her tenderly, ease her legs apart, and enter her.

But marriage seemed to have changed him. He was bolder, more demanding than she expected. And, if she was honest, it was altogether more thrilling to lie next to him, unclothed, and to have him look down at her, his eyes following the path made by his hands. She made a sound deep in her throat, when he encircled one breast and squeezed it upwards, making an offering

186

of it. His mouth closed over her nipple hungrily and her hips began to work as the sweetly pulling sensations spread down to her belly.

Stow's other arm was around her waist, pressing her against the firmness of his flat belly. She felt his cock jerk against her closed thighs. It was hard and burning hot. Surging against him, she rubbed herself against his member and then reached down and curled her fingers around his shaft.

Stow moaned softly and the sound of his pleasure inflamed her. She squeezed and stroked him, wanting to give him pleasure, but afraid that she was too inexperienced. Would he like it if she did thus and thus? Stow's reactions gave her encouragement and she smoothed back the tight cock-skin and rubbed her thumb in a small circle over the revealed glans.

His cock was thick and sturdy; the tip big and with a flaring ridge. She examined him with awe, absorbing the details of his member through her fingertips. What a wonder was this thing of pleasure, with its hard centre and silky covering. There was moisture on her hand now as Stow's cock wept at the pleasure of her touch.

His mouth covered hers and she writhed under the joint pleasures of so many sensations. He tasted of rum and tobacco and of his own clean self. It was hard to think with his fingers on her breasts, his tongue in her mouth, and his cock leaping within her hand. Then she felt his hand cover hers as he released himself.

'Nay, love. Best stop now or I'll be no use to you.'

He sat up and bade her lie back on the bed. Sweeping her body with eyes that were dark with love and lust, he reached out and stroked one hand over the slight rise of her belly. She quivered under him as he meshed his fingers in the soft curls on her Venus mound.

His fingers moved between her thighs and she adjusted position to admit him entry. Ah, he was smoothing the way for his cock. She was eager for him

187

to take her virginity. It would be soon now. But Stow seemed to be in no hurry.

A hot flush stained her cheeks as he parted the lips of her sex, caressing and investigating the moist folds, all the time watching her expression. She had not expected this either. Why did he not prenetrate her and have done? It was almost – unseemly, the way he was lingering over stroking her coynte. He seemed fascinated by the way she was made. Such curiosity.

Then she realised that the stroking, the gentle but firm manipulation, was for *her* benefit, not his. He wanted her to like it too. In fact Stow was demanding evidence of his new wife's pleasure. But surely all men took pleasure freely and the obedient wife received *her* pleasure in knowing that she had given her man satisfaction?

She was confused, and unsure how to react. His searching fingers grew ever bolder. She longed to hide her face against his shoulder, to veil the nakedness of her unseemly lust from him, but Stow insisted that she act like a wanton.

'Do you like this, love?' he asked. 'And this? Tell me what to do to please you.'

She made an inarticulate sound in her throat, half of pleasure, half of protest. Surely he did not imagine that she could bring herself to give him instruction? But the evidence of her enjoyment seemed enough for Stow. He smiled with satisfaction, obviously pleased by his power over her.

So be it then, if he wished to play her like a harpsichord. As an obedient wife, she must not fight against her husband's will. But, what was he doing? It felt wonderful.

As he stroked her, smoothing the slippery flesh of her coynte in a subtle, dragging sort of movement she felt her climax approaching. Oh no, she could not give way now, not with him watching her face. Would he know that she had felt this pleasure before – at her own hands?

But it was impossible to hold back. Tendrils of spiked heat spread outwards from his knowing fingers, the hard little bud of concentrated sensation quivered and pulsed in its purse of captive flesh. Stow pressed firmly on that bud and rubbed gently with a sort of tapping motion.

'Please . . . I can't stand any more . . .' she whimpered, but her body belied her words.

She sank down onto his hand, her legs lolling apart, quite beyond caring that she was panting and her eyes were squeezed tight shut. Her hips worked lewdly as she lost control.

Then she came. She threw back her head, so that the cords in her neck stood out. She moaned without restraint as wave after wave of pleasure spread over her and tears of shame pricked her eyelids. How awful it was to writhe so against his fingers. He would think her no better than a whore. She turned away from him and covered her face with her hands.

A sob lodged in her throat. She hated what he had made her do. Oh it was spoilt, all spoilt.

'Nay, love. Never hide yourself from me,' Stow said gently. 'It makes me proud to see you melt in my arms.'

She peeped out through meshed fingers, turning back towards him.

'Truly? You are not angry with me? You do not think me wanton and sinful?'

He chuckled. 'The only sin would be to leave me wanting. Look at the state I am in!'

He pointed to his cock which was flushed dark-red and throbbing fit to burst. Juanita laughed with relief and held out her arms to him. What had she done to deserve such a beautiful and caring man? She parted her thighs and tipped her hips up to meet him.

Stow pressed his cock to her entrance. Waiting for a moment to let her get used to the feeling of his flesh pressing into her, he kissed her deeply. In the midst of the kiss, he slid into her in a single smooth motion. There was hardly any pain and Juanita's eyes opened wide in surprise.

She placed her palms on Stow's lean hips and began to move, matching him stroke for stroke. The feeling of being filled by him was wonderful. He was at once strong and gentle. Oh, Lord. How to explain the exquisite sensation of his hot, hard flesh pounding into her?

Then she ceased to think as Stow's cock reached into some deep dark recess inside her. She became a mindless creature of singing nerves as he drew her towards another plane of pleasure.

Chapter Thirteen

*I*t was just past dawn when Carlotta, Manitas, and a group of other men left the compound.

The sky was streaked with a wash of peach and there was a silver line at the horizon where the sea met the heavens. The houses of the settlement were deep in shadow, their shutters presenting a blind face to the morning.

Carlotta passed Juanita's house and smiled. No doubt she slept in Stow's arms, worn out by a long night of love. It was just as well. Juanita had, no doubt, forgotten that this was the day when the pirates must leave to intercept another Spanish ship.

There was no argument amongst the men now about Carlotta going with them. They all accepted that she could hold her own in a fight. Their descent from the hills was swift and soon they reached the sheltered bay where the *Esmeralda* and the Spanish galleon, the *Bird of Prey*, lay at anchor.

Manitas greeted the men at watch.

'Is all ready? We sail with the tide.'

'Aye. All's ready. Just one last order to carry out.'

The man gave a piercing whistle and, when a figure

appeared on board the deck of the *Bird of Prey*, waved his arm in a pre-arranged signal.

As Carlotta watched, the ship ran up a flag. There was a great cheer as the flag unfurled and streamed out in the breeze. The pirates threw their caps in the air and called out with one voice.

'Hail. The *Crimson Buccaneer*. Hail Carlotta!'

Carlotta turned towards Manitas, her black brows dipping in a puzzled frown.

'What does this mean?' she said.

He gave a shout of laughter and clapped her on the back. It was all she could do not to stagger under the vehemence of the blow.

'Do you not recognize the flag?' he said, his voice booming out in the stillness of the morning. 'It's your red petticoat! We have re-named the galleon in your honour. From this moment forth she's to be the *Crimson Buccaneer* – your namesake. The men have taken you to their hearts, love. This is their way of showing you that.'

Carlotta was speechless and horrified to find that she was perilously close to tears. She finally managed to get a few words out.

'So, I'm the crimson buccaneer, am I? I've been called a lot worse. Oh, Manitas. I'm deeply honoured. What can I say?'

He chuckled. 'Say nothing. Just give those aboard a wave and a smile. Then let's get aboard. Your crew await your command and we have a rendezvous to keep.'

The captain of the Spanish merchant ship did not know what was happening until the pirates were upon him. Duped by the innocent sight of the Spanish galleon coming alongside, he only became alarmed when he saw the flag she was flying. There was hardly time to let fly with a single broadside, before grappling irons were thrown over the ships's rail and the pirates swarmed aboard.

Carlotta was amongst the first to board the merchant ship. Immediately she set about cutting a path across the crowded deck. The sailors gave way before her, many of them horrified by the sight of a woman with a sword in her hand. Spotting the ship's captain, Carlotta left the huddle of fighting men on the lower deck and sprang up to the poop deck.

Manitas followed her, laying about him left and right. Disabling the first officer who challenged her, Carlotta pushed forward until she stood beside the captain. Manitas took care of the other officers.

'What in God's name? Who let a woman on board my ship?' the captain grated.

Before the man could gather his shattered wits, Carlotta had taken him prisoner.

'Give the order to surrender and I'll let you live,' she said, pressing the point of her rapier to the big artery in his neck.

His eyes flicked over her contemptuously. But when he saw her expression he handed over his weapons and did as she asked. After the sailors were secured safely, Manitas and Carlotta examined the cargo hold. It was packed with wool, dyes, rare spices and a goodly amount of luxuries.

Carlotta opened chest after chest and dug out handfuls of emeralds, pearls, topazes. There were vases and mirrors of polished obsidian and a great many pieces of silver. The hoard was not as rich as that from the galleon, but it would still make a dent in Don Felipe's pocket.

'Where is your ship's master?' she asked the captain.

He was eager to save his own skin and led her to a cabin, where a middle-aged man sat at a desk. He was writing in a ledger as calmly as if the ship lay at anchor.

Carlotta admired the man's composure. He was slender and dressed in dark garments of a rich but restrained design. His close-cropped hair and beard were iron-grey, a great beak of a nose dominated his

193

narrow face, which gave him an expression of natural arrogance.

He stood up as they entered the cabin, his pale-grey eyes narrowing as he bowed mockingly.

'Ah, the black-haired, sea-witch and the giant pirate. Your fame has spread. I am honoured to meet you, though you have me at a disadvantage. May I introduce myself. I am Pedro Las Casas. I trust that you will not harm me. My patron Don Felipe Escada will – '

'Pay handsomely for your safe passage back to Spain,' Carlotta interrupted. 'Yes, I know. You can relax. Your life is not in danger.' She smiled, rather liking this man with his dry self-effacing humour.

Pedro's eyes narrowed as he looked from one to the other. 'I assume you speak for both of you. Then what do you want with me? I suspect that I am not to be bundled into the lifeboats with the rest of the crew, otherwise, why seek me out personally?'

Carlotta smiled thinly. 'You are astute, señor. I have a task for you. I wish you to carry a message back to Spain for me.'

'May I ask, for whom?'

'For Don Felipe. He and I are . . . well known to each other. He owes me a debt. And I shall see that he honours it fully.'

Pedro's eyes sparkled with interest. He stroked his chin and she saw that his hands were long and slender.

'Is this . . . message to be specific?'

She nodded, annoyed to see that he was looking her over with coolly appraising eyes. Suddenly she wanted to shatter his composure. He was a little too self-contained and rather too arrogant for a man whose ship was about to be stripped of all its goods.

'Come here,' she said.

Ah, that surprised him. A shadow of unease passed over his ascetic face. Pedro stood up slowly. He was very tall and as thin as a priest who has taken a vow of abstinence.

'Kneel before me,' Carlotta said.

Pedro glanced uneasily at Manitas. Manitas grinned.

'Best do as she says, señor. She has a fearful temper.'

Pedro sank down slowly. There was a spot of colour high up on each cheek, otherwise he was grey to the lips.

'What . . . what would you have me do?' he said.

'I wish you to write the letter to Felipe yourself. Tell him that we met and the full circumstances of our meeting. Leave out no detail. I wish to make certain that he knows there has been no mistake. Felipe has seen me . . . intimately and will ask you specific questions. Now, you will disrobe me, stroke my skin, taste me if you will, and commit your impressions to parchment.'

Pedro's eyes opened wide with shock. He looked again at Manitas.

'But . . . this man, your lover? will kill me, if I lay a hand on you. Is this some trick to humiliate me?'

'No trick, señor. Manitas will do nothing, I assure you. He will enjoy watching another man make obeisance to me. Is that not so, my love?'

Manitas chuckled. 'Whatever makes you happy. But this spindle-shanks is slow. Is he not aware of the honour you do him? Mayhap he favours being hauled around the keel? Let's see what damage the barnacles do to his fine doublet. Or I could cast him overboard.'

'No!' Pedro burst out. 'I cannot stand pain and I cannot swim. Please. I . . . I'll do it.'

Carlotta stood with her feet apart and her hands on her hips as Pedro edged forward on his knees. Reaching up he began unlacing her doublet. His hands shook badly as he fumbled with the fastening but, at last, the garment dropped to the cabin floor. It was followed by her loose cambric shirt. Underneath she wore straight-fronted stays, shaped like a sleeveless bodice with a low pointed waist.

Pedro crawled around to the back of her and

unthreaded the lace which drew the stays in to her waist. The back of the garment parted and Carlotta held her arms crossed over her breasts, holding the loosened stays close to her skin.

Pedro looked disappointed that she kept hold of the stays. His eyes seemed fastened to the rounded tops of her breasts and the deep, shadowed cleavage between them.

'My boots and breeches now,' Carlotta said.

Pedro was breathing hard, his earlier composure having deserted him completely. As Carlotta leaned back against the desk, he reached for her boot. One hand was at her ankle, while with the other, he cradled her foot. His fingers stroked the leather and swept over her high instep. It was taking some time and Carlotta gave a sigh of impatience.

Suddenly, in a swift movement, Pedro swooped and pressed his lips to the leather. She was so surprised that she just gaped at him. It seemed that he was getting some kind of sexual thrill out of touching and kissing her boot. She watched in fascination as he began mouthing and licking the toe. After a moment he pressed his nose to the leather and inhaled deeply.

Glancing up at Manitas, Carlotta threw him a questioning glance. He shrugged and grinned. Pulling her foot out of Pedro's grasp, she said: 'Stop that now. You're enjoying yourself too much. Pull off my boots. You'd best stand to do that.'

Pedro made a sound of disappointment, then stood up and turned his back to her. He took hold of one boot and Carlotta pressed the other foot against his skinny rump and pushed. Both boots slid free in turn and Pedro placed them neatly side by side. He glanced at them longingly, gave a sigh of regret, and turned his attention to Carlotta's leather breeches.

She lifted her bottom up off the desk so that he could pull the breeches free. Pedro's eyes almost popped out of his head when he saw that she wore nothing under them. He could not look away from her rounded thighs and the triangular patch of curls at her groin. Apart from her stays, Carlotta was naked.

With a triumphant grin, she lifted the final garment away from her body and threw her stays in Pedro's face. He caught them and pressed them to his face, inhaling her perfume, then he gave a low moan and fell to his knees. Clutching the boned fabric to his chest, he rubbed his cheeks against the curved top where it was still warm from her body.

Carlotta sensed what Pedro wanted. It amused her to grant him his wish. Oh, how she wished she could be present when Pedro related the details of this day's events to Don Felipe!

'Lick me,' she said, imperiously. 'Every part of me from my neck to my toes. Pay special attention to my breasts and coynte, but leave my feet until last.'

Pedro's mouth worked, but he seemed incapable of speech. There were beads of sweat on his forehead and top lip. From the doorway, Manitas gave a low chuckle.

'You're a sea-witch indeed. Have you heard the tales of the sirens who drive sailors mad? You could probably teach them a thing or two!'

Carlotta laughed, threw back her head and stretched luxuriously. The rich tones of her laughter rang around the cabin. Pedro seemed spell-bound. He seemed to have forgotten that Manitas existed. It was as if he was locked in a private world of his own. Carlotta closed her eyes as he drew near and stretched over her, his body curving into a bow-shape.

His hair had a dry, dusty smell spiced with spikenard. It was not unpleasant. Trembling he reached for her, but she brought him up short.

'No hands!'

He mumbled an apology and stretched out his neck. The first touch of his tongue on her flesh sent a jolt of heat to her groin. It was far more pleasing than she had expected it to be. Pedro bent to his task with a will,

197

pushing out his tongue and trailing it lusciously over her chest and breasts.

He licked the under-swell of each breast, mouthing the generous globes of flesh so that they trembled slightly. Carlotta looked down at the movement of his grey head as he concentrated on her nipples, polishing them with his saliva and pressing the extended flat of his tongue against their cherry-red tips. When he moved between her breasts, pushing his nose into the vale of her cleavage, the air played quite maddeningly across the taut wet morsels he had now abandoned.

It was all she could do to stop herself laying hands on her breasts and pinching her sensitised nipples. But, by the look on Manitas's face, there would be no lack of pleasuring after Pedro had completed his task.

With a soft moan, Pedro bent to lick her belly. Starting at her ribs, he licked downwards until he came to rest at her navel. He spent some time mouthing the depression and darting the point of his tongue into the tiny, fleshy well. Carlotta dug her fingers into the wooden desk and arched her back, anticipating the hot spiked pleasure of the moment when he would push his head between her thighs.

Pedro seemed in no hurry and she smiled dryly. Damn the man. He knew that she was enjoying this as much as him. Manitas too had not spoken since Pedro began his ministrations. He leaned against the doorway, one hand at his waist. The fingers of his hand pointed towards the pronounced bulge in his breeches. Carlotta's pulse quickened as she pictured the half-slumbering cock which was awakening more with every moment.

She held the image of it in mind as Pedro's tongue trailed over her flesh. Manitas's big fleshy cock, lengthening, stiffening into its impressive blood-flushed glory. Delicious. As if he sensed that her concentration had slipped from him, Pedro nipped her navel playfully.

She fetched him a slap across the head. The blow was none too gentle.

'Your tongue and lips only,' she said, containing her smile with difficulty.

In any other circumstances, she would have found Pedro likeable, but as a friend of Felipe's he was beyond the reach of friendship.

Pedro's hot tongue moved down to the rounded bowl of her belly. The ticklish wetness spread out over her skin as he mouthed her flesh, his lips loose and relaxed. He was crouching down now and moving forward to quest between her legs. Carlotta held her breath as his smooth-shaven cheeks brushed the insides of her thighs. The contrast between hot mouth and cool cheeks, with just the slightest rasp of new beard growth, was intoxicating.

She opened her thighs and heard the inrush of his breath as he took a deep draught of her musky female scent. Then he began licking and sucking in earnest. His tongue lolled against the moist folds, searching out her intimate creases and the delicate frilled edges of her inner lips. She sighed as he found the throbbing bead that was the source of concentrated sensation and began to lip it gently.

Gradually her hips began to work and she ground herself against his mouth as he used the tip of his tongue to press the tiny hood of flesh up towards her belly, freeing the exquisitely sensitive morsel of flesh. It was a pleasure that bordered on discomfort and she pulled back from him. He drew back a little and she felt his breath fanning over her exposed pleasure-bud. That was enough to tip her over and her climax swept through her.

Bracing her legs, she closed her eyes, centering on the sensations, and enjoyed the pulsing fade gradually. Pedro looked up at her and grinned, his face alight with pride. He seemed genuinely glad to have given her such pleasure and she could not force herself to be short with him.

'Complete your task,' she said, her voice soft and almost caressing.

He bent to it with a will, licking down the inside of each creamy thigh and kissing her knees. Even though the pleasure of her climax had faded, her skin remained sensitive and the touch of his tongue was more than pleasant. Now he worked down each calf in turn, adjusting his position until he lay prone on the cabin floor.

She sensed his gathering excitement as his mouth moved down to her feet. Even whilst mouthing her coynte he had been contained, slightly aloof, but his presence deserted him utterly when he brushed his lips against each foot in turn. Gently he encircled each ankle bone, licking and sucking with a curious reverence.

His tongue tip moved over each foot, tasting and exploring each slight ridge, each prominent vein. When he took the first toe into his mouth and began to suck, he made an odd little sound in the back of his throat – a similar noise to that made by babes when suckling at their mother's breast. Carlotta was fascinated by Pedro's sudden intensity.

As he sucked each of her toes in turn, licking between them and nuzzling them with relaxed lips, he began to buck and writhe. God's bones, he's going to spend any second, she thought. What a thing – to be so aroused by her feet that he reached a climax!

Pedro let out a strangled groan and went rigid, his mouth clamped around two of her toes. His lips worked feverishly as he absorbed the taste of her, then he rolled onto his side and curled into a ball. His face was bound by an expression of pained-pleasure. After a moment or two he recovered and pushed himself to his knees, fumbling in the pocket of his jerkin for a kerchief. Mopping his forehead and wiping his mouth, he rose to his feet. He seemed composed now and used one hand to smooth back his rumpled grey hair.

Carlotta made no move to cover her nakedness. She regarded him coolly from her seated position.

'So, señor Las Casas, are you clear about the message you will carry to Felipe?'

He nodded. 'You wish me to relay everything that has happened here?'

'Everything. In the greatest detail.'

Pedro's expression was one of mixed respect and awe. 'Mother of God. This is not the first such message, is it? You must hate Felipe very much. Do you wish to drive the poor man mad?'

Carlotta's lips compressed into a smile.

'I wish to ruin him completely. But madness would be a good enough beginning, señor.'

Pedro drew in his breath. His pale-grey eyes were suddenly icy.

'I do not know what to think of you, señora. You are like no one I have ever known. Either you are an angel of retribution or the Devil's temptress.'

Carlotta laughed in his face.

'I am neither of those things. I am simply a woman as God made me! But I am my own woman and I bow to no man's will. Perchance that is what you find so strange? Felipe tried to bend me to his will and could not. Tell him that I have not changed? And I have not finished with him yet.'

Pedro bowed his head, his hand pressed to his heart in a gesture of submission.

'I will carry your message, señora. And I thank the martyred Christ that you are not my enemy.'

Felipe stood in front of the entrance to the cathedral at Santiago de Compostela.

The journey, made on foot, had been long and arduous; yet he had made it gladly. He was tired and in need of food and a bath, but he would not rest or eat until he had completed his pilgrimage. His rough woollen robe brushed against his bare legs and the dust from the road felt gritty between his toes. He had wound rags around his feet where they were blistered and he limped slightly as he started forward.

All around him other travellers, many of them ragged, their clothes powdery with dust, pressed towards the door. Each of them looked pale and drawn, their eyes hollowed and bright with religious fervour. Did he look like that too? Many of the pilgrims fell to the ground and kissed the stone floor, crying out with gladness at having reached their goal, the tears pouring down their thin cheeks.

Felipe felt somehow removed from the other pilgrims, as if he was watching himself from some distance away. Their voices were raised now in prayer and it seemed to him that the air thickened as the backwash of their devotion brushed past him. He prayed that he too might find release from his inner torment.

As he stepped into the cool stone interior, he felt peace of a sort descend on him. The cathedral was vast, a work of man's love and fear. His heart must surely be uplifted by the beauty all around him. Here he would purge himself of Carlotta, consign her image to some cold and dark place; out of reach of his senses.

He passed through the Portico de la Gloria and bent his head before the triple arches of the twelfth-century sculpture by Mateo. Like thousands of others before him, he stretched out his hand towards the smiling, animated stone figures, which encrusted the sculpture. There were smooth places on some of the figures, where the worshipful hands of the faithful had worn the stone away.

A shiver snaked down his sprine. Surely he had glimpsed Carlotta's face on a figure. Impossible. He shook his head to clear it. Now he saw that he had been mistaken. He must be so weak and hungry that he was having delusions.

He moved on and walked through the nave and transept. The presence of God seemed to permeate every stone, every fold of rich drapery, and every jewel-bright sliver of stained glass. The murmur of prayers filled the air. He raised his eyes to the chapterhouse and upper galleries, hung with sumptuous tapestries embroidered with silk and gold threads.

Gold and silver work decorated almost every surface around the high altar. And there was the great silver shrine with the richly attired statue of the saints.

Felipe waited in turn to make his offering to St James, St Theodore, and St Athanasius. The pilgrims filed past the altar, running the beads of their rosaries through their fingers and accepting the blessing of the priests. With his head bowed Philipe murmured his prayers, accepted a sip of wine and held the wafer of the host on his tongue until it dissolved. Then he moved away, lit a taper, and touched it to the wick of a costly beeswax candle.

He closed his eyes, still able to see the flickering yellow light of the many candles through his eyelids. The cold of the stone floor penetrated his robe and seeped into his knees. He squeezed his eyes shut, trying to centre his thoughts.

But, try as he might, he could not completely lose himself in the ritual around him. A small voice within him kept reminding him of the reason why he had made the pilgrimage.

Carlotta – her beauty of the Devil; her tainted woman-flesh which held him in thrall. Could it be possible that her witchcraft was so great that it defied even the church? He groaned aloud.

Would her face never fade from his mind?

Even here, she tormented him. He was filled with desperation. Was there any place he might find salvation?

He backed away from the shrine, his devotions completed, and began walking back through the cathedral.

The glory of the altar and shrine was behind him. The body of the cathedral was filled with a mass of common people intent on their daily business. Now, instead of the majesty of his surroundings, the aura of holiness around the shrines, he was aware only of the mundane nature of human endeavour.

Work was in progress on a new side chapel and the sound of hammers on stone split the air. The workmen sweated as they toiled, their faces bronze in the candle-light. Two of them shared a joke and their rough laughter rose above the murmur of prayer and the reedy notes of a choir boy's voice.

Felipe walked on, his perceptions coloured by his troubled thoughts. Many dark shapes, wrapped in tattered cloaks were curled against the walls, their packs and staves beside them. He realised that they were pilgrims who could not afford lodgings. The stench of them was only partly masked by the scent of incense, which wreathed out from a number of censers suspended over the transept.

Felipe's mouth thinned disapprovingly. He had come to the shrine of the saints to try to rise above his own human frailty, but the reminders of his state were all around him. All men and women were sinners and he was weaker than any of them, beyond being saved. When he left this place he would be alone with himself – unchanged. What had he really expected? To be cauterised by the fire of God?

He sighed. Perhaps it was not possible for him to resolve the dichotomy between flesh and spirit. The cathedral had offered solace of a sort. The priest, whom he had paid to say prayers for him and to light a candle on all the Saints' days, had also given him a measure of comfort.

But his pilgrimage had been in vain, for he knew now with a dreadful certainty, that the failing was within himself. He was unable to reach out and take God's comfort. There was a dark flaw on his soul. And that was the place Carlotta reached.

It was a revelation of sorts. There was freedom in accepting that he must continue to look within himself, not without, for the answer. He was clear now about what he must do. The mortification of the flesh was the only true way to banish sinful lusts. But he needed help. His own methods were not stringent enough. He needed the ministrations of experts.

Luckily such help was at hand.

It was known that, at the convent where he was to spend the night, the nuns were well versed in the practice of chastisement. For a generous donation to the poor fund, he could avail himself of their services. He had discovered that the Abbess had a reputation for being more than willing to attend to sinners such as he. She was a strong-minded woman who would ignore any pleas for mercy.

As he left the cathedral, a cloud passed over the sun and he began to shiver – whether with cold or anticipation, he could not say.

Chapter Fourteen

The cell Felipe was allotted for the night was small and cheerless. A wooden bench covered with a straw mattress was the only furniture. A thin, woollen blanket was folded on top of the mattress and there was a wooden hook on the wall where he might hang up his pack.

Apart from his plain robe and heavy cape, he wore only sandals and a wide-brimmed hat. It was the rule in the convent that everyone go bare-foot. Felipe hung up his sandals and hat, along with his pack. His feet were still rubbed raw by his long journey, so he left on the rags which bound them.

In the refectory he took the evening meal with the other pilgrims who were lodging overnight. The nuns who served them were all young and fresh-faced, their hair covered by snowy wimples. They moved around the room in silence, their black habits making soft whispering sounds as they brushed against the stone floor. Felipe was fascinated by their grace. They seemed to glide rather than walk.

The meal was plain; a wooden bowl of soup and a hunk of black bread. There was watered wine to wash down the meal. Felipe was still hungry when he went back to his cell, but his stomach burned with excitement and it was probably best that he did not eat too much.

Bunching up the woollen blanket to form a pillow, he lay on the straw mattress and linked his hands across his chest. There was an hour and more before compline, after which he would be sent for. He closed his eyes and tried to rest. Behind his eyelids it felt scratchy, as if the dust of the road had penetrated even there. The straw from the mattress pricked his skin and he welcomed the small discomfort as an echo of what was to come.

His self-inflicted punishments would be nothing to what the Abbess would order inflicted on him. His flesh quivered in an agony of helpless anticipation. It was no use. He would never be able to sleep.

He woke to find someone shaking him. It seemed impossible, but he had slept for two hurs. Rubbing his eyes, he sat up.

'Come with me,' the nun said, shortly.

Felipe rose at once and followed her. He wanted to ask the woman her name, but he knew that she would not reply. She kept her head bent and he could not tell her age. She moved smoothly down the dark stone corridors, a figure in trailing black robes and spotless white veil.

After a while she stopped by a low stone archway and indicated that he should enter a room. Flares in iron sconces were positioned on either side of the doorway, but all was dark and silent within. Felipe felt a prickle of apprehension. Was this place to be his prison? Perhaps the Abbess would demand that he be chained and left alone.

Then, in the purple-black of the room's interior, he saw a candle flicker into life, then another. He moved forward and had to bend his neck to get under the archway. Once inside the doorway the room opened out, the walls were slightly curved and uneven and the ceiling swept upwards into shadow. It was a cellar of some kind, he thought. There was a feeling of age about the place.

The room was occupied. Two female faces were illuminated by two small pools of candle-light. One of the women wore the white wimple and dark robes worn by all the nuns. She had a smooth, plain face. Her jaw was square and her lips firm and ruddy.

The other woman wore a dark wimple, surmounted by a stiff band of white linen. Her face was a perfect oval, her features sharp, but well-formed. A chased gold crucifix gleamed against her black robes. Felipe would have known that this was the Abbess by her bearing alone. Her severe handsome face caused mixed reactions inside him.

The Abbess lifted one slender white hand and beckoned to him.

'Don Felipe, enter. You are welcome. We are most grateful for the donation you have given to our order. It is generous indeed and will be put to good use.'

Felipe crossed the room and knelt before her. He took the hand she held out to him and pressed his lips to the silver ring she wore on the third finger.

'Reverend Mother,' he whispered.

Her mouth curved in a smile. Her face was enlivened by her expression and he saw that she was almost beautiful. So much the better. It would be easier to give himself over to her.

The nun who had been sent to collect him came into the room and stood by his side. She glanced at his feet, which were still bound by dusty rags, and threw a questioning look at the Abbess. The Abbess lifted her eyebrows and nodded.

'If you will sit, Don Felipe, sister Maria-Theresa will tend your wounds before we begin. Sister Concepta will get all else ready.'

Felipe sank onto the wooden bench, which apart from a few dark shapes in the shadowed corners of the room, seemed to be the only furniture. Sister Maria-Theresa's hands were cool on his skin as she bathed his feet and smeared some herb-smelling unguent on them.

While she did this, sister Concepta lit more candles and placed them around the room. The dark shapes of furniture resolved themselves into a table and chairs. One chair held his attention. It was built all of heavy, carved wood and had arms and a high back. He had seen a similar object in the cathedral earlier, a bishop's chair. But this chair had one curious feature. In the centre of the wooden seat was a large circular hole. For some unknown reason his pulses quickened when he looked at that chair.

'Is all ready?' the Abbess asked. 'Then you may disrobe, Don Felipe.'

Felipe rose from the bench. It seemed that he was to strip in front of the three nuns, there being no screen or clothes press. Sister Maria-Theresa held out her arms for his robe. He smiled shakily as he gave it to her and saw her face for the first time. She was the youngest of the three and had the face of an angel.

Her features were almost child-like in their purity, her expression blank and innocent. She did not return his smile and her eyes were pale and cold, her lips compressed into a single line. Felipe felt that the young nun despised him and his suspicion was confirmed when sister Maria-Theresa swept his nakedness with a measuring glance, her lip curling with distaste as his cock twitched into life. Oh, God how awful it was to be naked before the three of them and how humiliating that he could not control his body's responses.

'You are sore in need of our help,' the Abbess said coolly, tapping his hardening shaft with the tip of one slim white finger.

Felipe managed to nod, trembling with fear and anticipation. Did the Abbess realise that a dart of concentrated lust had centred in his belly at that slight touch?

'The flesh is weak. It was ever so,' the Abbess said,

209

her voice detached and toneless. 'Many things are sent to test our faith. Have no fear, Don Felipe. We shall drive all lustful thoughts from your mind and the foul, devilish humours from your body. You will empty yourself completely, I promise you. I am well schooled in these matters and will not fail you.'

'Thank you. God bless you, Reverend Mother,' he murmured, knowing, with absolute certainty in that second, that he could expect no mercy at the hands of the three women.

How many sinners had they punished? He imagined all the men and women who had stood naked and shivering in the dank cellar. Perversely he found the idea stimulating and felt his erection burgeoning, the blood pounding at his groin. He hunched over and brought his hands down to cover himself. But he could not hide the evidence of his arousal. They must think him a monster of depravity. The shame of it made his cheeks burn.

If the Abbess had noticed his state, she gave no sign of the fact. She ordered him to move towards the chair of carved wood. And he did so, noticing what he had missed at first. On the table there was a sort of wooden tray with separate compartments. In each of them there was an instrument of punishment. The array of beautifully made flails, whips, and paddles took his breath away.

In one compartment were a number of small objects which he did not recognise. They were made of carved wood and there was the glint of metal in the compartment also. What could be the purpose of these strange things?

'Tether him,' the Abbess ordered. 'First position, to begin with.'

Felipe shivered slightly when the two nuns laid hands on him. He allowed them to push him down onto the seat of the carved chair and to secure his wrists to the arm-rests. His legs were pulled apart and his ankles secured to iron rings, set into the front legs of the chair.

Now he was entirely at their mercy. Being bound made him afraid, but far worse, was the way his bottom and ballocks hung through the cut-out of the seat. His thighs were spread widely and that was all that prevented his lower body from slipping through the hole. What could be the purpose of such a seat? He must tense his leg muscles if he wished to remain in an upright position. Wedging himself against the back of the chair helped him keep his balance, but then sister Concepta lowered the chair back – which must have been hinged – and he gave a grunt of dismay.

Now he must lean forward at the waist and keep the whole of his upper body rigid. Already his muscles were beginning to burn with the strain. Yet, despite his discomfort, his erect cock pressed upwards against his taut stomach. He was concentrating so hard on just sitting upright that he was unprepared for the first blow.

His breath left his lips in a hiss as he felt the lash curl around his shoulders. Sister Maria-Theresa, her lovely face cold and expressionless, drew back her arm for another blow. She had folded back the sleeve of her dark robes and her slim white wrists and small hands looked shockingly exposed in the candle-light.

Felipe could not take his eyes from her hands. They were as small as a child's and were curled almost tenderly around the handle of the leather whip. A thin line of fire spread its heat across his skin every time the lash connected. But he was used to such punishment. He did not cry out, although the sweat started from his pores.

Sister Maria-Theresa concentrated on his back and shoulders. The old scars and thickened skin there, offered him some protection and he was barely breathing hard when she stopped. He let out a great sigh of relief, thinking that sister Maria-Theresa had finished, but she had only paused long enough to take something from the box on the table.

Her cool hands moved across his chest and he almost cried out at the smooth silky feel of her skin. Tenderness was not something he had expected from her and he was momentarily lulled into a false sense of security. Then twin starbursts of pain bloomed within him as she attached two wooden pegs to his nipples. For a moment he could not catch his breath and closed his eyes to gather his wits.

The sharp, pinching sensation receded to be replaced by a hot throbbing pain. He hardly had time to absorb the new sensation of discomfort, before she attached two more pegs to his throbbing paps. Then two more. Shaking his head from side to side he gnawed at his bottom lip.

'Have you no words for sister Maria-Theresa?' the Abbess asked.

'Thank you, sister,' Felipe said, amazed to hear that his voice was level.

Sister Maria-Theresa gave him a cold smile. Her lips were as pale as a shell and her skin gleamed like a pearl in the candle-light.

'I am pleased to do God's work,' he said piously, stepping back to allow sister Concepta to take over.

Sister Concepta took up a flail and walked over to stand beside Felipe. Her strong, square face was flushed and her mouth was curved into a smile. Unlike sister Maria-Theresa, the older nun seemed to relish her work and she spent a few moments trailing the loose leather strands over his back and chest, stroking his skin gently.

The oiled leather brushing against his pinched nipples was delicious and his cock twitched and jumped, the glans swelling until it pushed half-free from the tight cock-skin. Sister Concepta glanced down at his straining organ and trailed the flail over it. The tip of her tongue protruded through her parted lips.

212

Felipe closed his eyes, enjoying the soft, almost silky caress on his shaft. The tension built inside him and he knew that his cock-mouth was weeping a salty fluid. The leather strands stroked across his glans, capturing the clear seepage and carrying it away.

The first blow, when it came, was all the more shocking after the nun's gentleness. One sharp blow to his cock had him wincing and bending almost double. Needles of pain seemed to penetrate down to his cods and up into his belly. Sister Concepta beat him up and down his shaft, using the flail in a back and forth motion.

When his cock was a burning pillar of tormented flesh, she stopped for a moment and encircled him with her cool fingers. Felipe gasped and surged into her hand. Oh, God let her keep up the stroking. He felt the seed gathering in his cods as they tightened. He was ready to erupt. Soon, oh, soon. But she loosed him and began to lay about him with the flail.

She placed each blow a little above the previous one and began working up and down his sides. Then she concentrated on the tender skin under each arm. Felipe writhed and groaned softly, but could not escape the many stinging strands. She was thorough and pitiless and he found himself murmuring his thanks as she administered her blessing of pain.

The Abbess watched, nodding her approval as sister Concepta used the flail on his belly. Felipe pulled against his bonds and caught his lower lip in his teeth. His entire back, chest, and belly were sore and burning. Each new stroke of the flail was an agony. Surely she would stop soon; all his senses had become condensed into one sizzling throbbing ache.

When he knew that he must either start to beg, or scream, the beating stopped. The Abbess had given some signal he had missed.

'The salve now, if you please, sister Maria,' the

Abbess said, 'A moment's respite, I think, before we begin again. Don Felipe?'

'Thank you, Reverend Mother,' he whispered, flopping forward and taking deep steadying breaths.

He did not know how much more he could stand. What would have happened if he had begged for mercy? The beating had stopped because the Abbess ordered it. With a thrill of horror he knew that his wishes were immaterial to the ritual. If he pleaded for mercy they would pay him no heed. At that thought, he felt a pulse within him – deep and red and abiding.

Was it possible that he would always be content to be a sinner and to be punished? Surely not. The thought was too awful to contemplate.

Sister Maria-Theresa's cool white hands moved over him, smoothing the herb-scented salve over his sore flesh. The stinging pain lessened almost at once, to be replaced by a sensitised warmth. Having finished anointing him sister Maria-Theresa stood clear, her head bowed with respect as the Abbess approached.

Felipe avoided the Abbess's piercing eyes. Those eyes seemed to be able to strip away flesh and bone and see into his very soul. Of the three women, it was the Abbess who he feared the most, her punishing touch he desired most of all. Somehow he knew that, whatever she planned to do to him, it would be no ordinary beating.

Even knowing that, his eyes widened in puzzlement as she secured a wide leather belt around his waist. She reached down to his groin and took a firm hold of his cock and balls, her touch efficient and dispassionate. Ignoring his indrawn breath, she wrapped a leather thong tightly around the loose skin above his sac and then bound up his member. Having finished wrapping him, she drew the whole package up toward his belly and fastened his cock and balls to a metal ring set in the front of the belt.

Too shocked to do anything but observe the Abbess's

actions, Felipe bowed his head. His tightly wrapped member pulsed and throbbed unbearably and there was an ache in his trapped ballocks. What could be the purpose of such a punishment? Was this a way to seal-in his lust?

Then he realised that the Abbess was protecting the most sensitive part of his body from what was to come. A thrill of horror made his cods prickle and swell.

Picking up a flat, leather paddle, the Abbess took up position to one side of the chair. Sister Maria-Theresa and sister Concepta, each took hold of a lever, pre-viously unnoticed by Felipe, and began to wind up a mechanism. The chair was cranked up until the seat was raised to above waist height. Now the Abbess could reach Felipe's exposed buttocks without having to bend.

'That will do,' she said. 'Now, Don Felipe, to the final part of your discipline. The evil humours will be driven from your body and the demon lust will no longer have a hold on you. I wish you to give yourself over com-pletely into my hands. I demand instant obedience and expect nothing less. That is the only way you will benefit fully. Do you understand?'

Felipe nodded, beyond words, Sweet Christ, what else could she be planning?

The crack of the paddle against his buttocks was loud in the cellar. Felipe let out a yell. He couldn't help it. The skin of his bottom was tender, virgin territory to the lash. And, stretched and forced to gape through the seat-hole as he was, he was spared nothing. The Abbess had chosen her target well.

As she laid to with the paddle, Felipe's eyes watered and the tears ran freely down his cheeks. He jerked against his bonds, trying to wrench himself free, but the leather binding held. Crack, went the paddle. And again. It was a most satisfying sound, more terrifying than the whistle of the lash or flail.

Nothing existed outside the pain. Felipe could only

look inwards. He whimpered as the redness within himself bloomed and opened. In the very centre of the pain, Felipe saw Carlotta's face, her white body, her red mouth. No. It could not all have been for nothing. She should be gone. He lost control. Sobbing and shaking, he began to plead for the Abbess to stop.

'She is there, mocking me! Please . . . no more . . .' Spittle flecked his lips and his eyes rolled back in his head.

Oh, merciful God, the witch-woman was part of him. How could she be torn from his soul when he wanted to keep her? Impossible. He was surely damned.

'Ah, now I hear the voice of your demon,' the Abbess said, her voice ringing out with zeal. 'We make excellent progress. Let the voice of your unclean lust ring out. I shall master it and drive it forth into the void!'

'Stop! I beg you. Stop!' Felipe panted, his buttocks simmering and throbbing. 'I don't want to lose her.'

But she ignored his pleas. The paddle slapped against his flesh again and again. He twisted and lurched upwards, succeeding only in exposing the top of his thighs to her merciless hands. Sinking down hard, he tried to escape that way, but his buttocks gaped at the movement and her next blow caught him squarely between them.

'Be merciful,' he moaned, wedged tight now by the wood surrounding him as she spanked him expertly, flicking against his anus until it too was a hot well of suffering.

The air rang with Felipe's entreaties. He begged, cursed, offered bribes, but the punishment went on. The Abbess was indeed practised and ruthless in her treatment of sinners. In the midst of it all, when his whole world seemed to have narrowed to a black maw of suffering, he thought only of Carlotta.

If only it was she who punished him, she who drove the demons from him, she who taught him the majesty of pain.

He hardly realised that the Abbess had stopped beating him. Gentle hands smoothed salve on his buttocks and he had not the strength even to wince at the touch on his abused flesh.

He closed his eyes. That must be all. There could be nothing left to suffer. But the Abbess bent close and said coolly, 'I require now that you cleanse your demons from your lustful flesh. Soon you will void them and your travail will be over.'

He did not understand and turned to look at her, his brows dipping in question. Then he gasped as sister Maria-Theresa's slim, cold fingers penetrated his anus, smoothing the salve deep inside him. He winced at the soreness as her fingers probed and stroked, opening and softening the tight ring of muscle.

Sister Concepta was at his side also and now she pressed a cold object to his loosened orifice. She began pushing and he felt his flesh give as it accepted the intrusion. The awful sensation of being penetrated went on and on. Whatever it was it was made of metal and was shaped to fit inside him.

'No . . . Oh, no . . .' he ground out, twisting to escape as the cold object slid more deeply into him. 'Stop that. Oh . . . don't . . .'

A moment passed and he tried to adjust to the feeling of being violated. Was this how a woman felt when a man forced her? He had no time to develop his train of thought. There came the sensation of liquid flowing into him. It was icy cold and he clenched his teeth against the indignity of it.

'Try not to resist,' the Abbess said, her voice almost kind now. 'Your demons will resist strongly and give voice to their anger through your words. But this is a most efficacious treatment and has great benefits. Just a little longer now.'

Felipe's bowels churned as the liquid was pumped inside him. He clenched his buttocks and tried not to fight the urge to bear down, but it was impossible. The

217

sensation was so strange, so horribly arousing. Incredibly his leather-wrapped cock stirred against his belly and slivers of pleasure spread up his shaft and centred in the enclosed glans.

As the nozzle was removed slowly his anus convulsed, and he bucked and fought the lust which raged through him. Oh God of mercy. Nothing he had asked the whore to do to him in his private chapel compared with this. This was sublime. This was the ultimate in pleasure-pain. He knew now that he had been born to suffer.

He threw back his head as his orgasm approached and rose up against his bonds. His body was stretched into a bow and every nerve end trembled and suffered. He was hardly aware of the Abbess's voice, of the other nuns' cries of satisfaction as the semen burst from his imprisoned cock in hot stinging jets.

And, following on so swiftly from that first eruption that it seemed part of it, his body gave in to the impetus to empty itself. Shaking with the shameful pleasure of it, Felipe bore down and voided his body's wastes onto the stone floor of the cellar.

The journey back to Castile was undertaken in sombre mood. Felipe rode on horseback. His whole body bore the marks of his punishment, but it was his feet which pained him the most. They were still swollen and blistered and he smeared on herb salve whenever he stopped to rest.

Mentally he felt calm, clear-headed for the first time in many months. The nuns' treatment had purged him as completely as the cathedral had left him unmoved. He knew that he could fight Carlotta no longer. He was wholly hers and he had no choice now but to take responsibility for that fact.

He did not care what she was – the instrument of Satan, Lilith, a succubus sent to drive him wild with lust. She was as much a part of him as his breath and blood.

On arriving back at his house, he found the letter from Pedro La Casas. Breaking open the seal, he scanned the parchment. As he read, he smiled. Pedro could hardly contain himself, his writing was loose and sprawling; and the terms he used to describe Carlotta's charms, comparing her to a siren and calling her 'dangerously fascinating', made Felipe smile knowingly.

Carlotta had actually made the poor wretch *lick* her from head to foot and then promise to recount every detail of the exchange. Once he would have been enraged beyond reason by the account of Carlotta's wantonness. But now he was only glad that she had seen fit to send him this message – for it proved that she too felt the bond between them.

Had she not made it obvious that she could not forget him? Her attacks on his ships, the blows to his finances, the way she taunted his associates, and the letters – all these were her ways of assuring that he remember her. She had told Pedro that she would not stop until she had ruined Felipe and taken her full revenge.

And why? because she was as besotted with him as he was with her. They were united in hate and lust.

It seemed an eternity since that day in her bedchamber when she had taunted him with her nakedness. The painting by El Greco still hung in his private chapel, a constant reminder of her beauty, the vibrant colours and the shocking pose a testament to her wayward character. Carlotta was stronger than any warrior, her weapons of the flesh more potent, more dangerous than a whole magazine full of arms.

By the ever-living God, *she* was his salvation. Why had he not seen that before? He had been wriggling on the end of a line, trying to avoid his destiny. Well, no longer.

No one but Carlotta herself could grant him absolution.

In his imagination he saw himself facing her, then falling to his knees and reaching out for the hem of her gown. If he begged her to forgive him, would she? or would she devise some humiliating punishment, something which would shame and degrade him?

Pedro had been made to lick her, Antonio Alva had pleasured her with his mouth and then been forced to commit the sin of Onan, while she watched and beat his buttocks with the flat of her sword. And Felipe wanted to do those things, and more.

Oh, yes. Sweet Jesus, yes. He would do anything she asked. He wanted to suffer at her hands, to show her that he was sorry for what he had done. And it was not a mere indulgence on his part; he *needed* to worship at the fount of her womanhood. Otherwise he would go completely mad.

But what of the giant pirate she had taken up with? By all accounts the man was fearsome. Might he not wish to please Carlotta by removing the object of her rage from the face of the earth? He trembled at the thought of it, but Manitas was not really a consideration.

This was something between himself and Carlotta which must be laid to rest. Neither of them would know a moment's peace until that was done. And, knowing her as he did, he knew that she would let no man fight her battles for her. It was clear then what he must do.

Felipe stood still for a moment, stroking his long jaw, then he crossed the room and opened a chest which stood on a table beneath the mullioned window. Taking out the bundle of lists and charts, he slid his finger down a page until he found what he wanted. Ah, that was the one. On a date three months hence, one of his galleons was to return from Puerto Caballos, loaded with silver, silks and linens.

Carlotta and her pirate friends would not be able to

resist taking the ship. And this time, she would get the shock of her life.

His heart was light as he replaced the chart in the chest. He had little time to make preparations before he left. Best get to it.

Chapter Fifteen

Carlotta stood up in the prow of the pinnace and waved at Juanita and Stow who stood on the shore. The other women from the settlement were also gathered on the beach, waiting to welcome their men home.

As the longboat breasted the breakers, Carlotta jumped into the shallows and helped pull the boat above the high tide line. The green forested slopes, further inland, were still wreathed in a thick mist. Sunlight streamed through the sea-grape trees nearest the shore and gilded the gentle rolling waves.

Carlotta's spirits lifted as she looked at the natural beauty all around. This was their own island, a sanctuary from all that the world had taken from them. Each of the buccaneers and most of the women had been victims of some injustice. It seemed only right that they should have fashioned their own haven.

Stow stepped forward to greet his friends.

'Give us a hand then, man! If you have strength left after your nightly endeavours,' Manitas called out.

The others cheered and clapped Stow on the back. He began to unload the boat, laughing good-naturedly at the bawdy comments.

Juanita threw her arms around Carlotta. Carlotta

returned the embrace, touched by such an open display of affection. It was not like Juanita to show her emotions in public.

'You are a happy wife, I see,' she said.

Juanita nodded, her cheeks turning pink. 'Perhaps you should try it,' she said.

Carlotta grimaced. 'I have, remember?'

Juanita smiled knowingly. 'But you did not marry the right man. Perhaps Manitas – ' she broke off, seeing the warning light in Carlotta's eyes. She changed the subject hurriedly. 'Was it a good haul? Though I hardly need ask, judging by your expression.'

Carlotta gave a husky laugh. 'Oh, it was good enough. We have silver and jewels aplenty. Mirrors too. Not a house in the settlement need go without a looking-glass. We've enough to buy food and supplies for many a year. But my greatest satisfaction was in sending a message back to Don Felipe. His man, Pedro La Casas, was on board the galleon and I gave him a lesson he won't forget in a hurry.'

'How so?'

'Let's walk back along the hill track and I'll tell you all about it.'

Arm in arm Juanita and Carlotta walked up the beach. As Carlotta told her the details, Juanita brought her hand up to her mouth to hide her scandalised expression. Then she started to laugh.

'Oh, Carlotta. You're truly dreadful! That poor man. Did you really make him lick you . . . there? And he reached his peak of pleasure by sucking your . . . toes?'

'You don't sound nearly so shocked as you usually do,' Carlotta joked. 'But, of course, you're an experienced woman now, Mistress Stow!'

Julio paused in loading the booty into a cart and straightened up to watch Carlotta walking away.

'Putana,' he spat under his breath.

Carlotta was just a pirate's whore and yet she gave

herself such airs. Whoever this Don Felipe – the man she was obsessed by – was, Julio admired the man. He must have great strength of character if she hated him so much.

In Julio's opinion, Carlotta needed subduing. The other men looked on her as some kind of a Madonna of the sea. They blessed her for making them all rich. Could they not see that she was just using them all to her own ends? Now they had named the captured Spanish galleon after her.

The *Crimson Buccaneer* – for the love of Heaven! Whoever heard of a pirate ship flying a red petticoat? He had been the only man to speak out against it, but no one had heeded him.

His breast burned with hatred. It was time he did something about Carlotta. No one else had the guts to do it. They were either afraid of Manitas or half in love with the black-haired witch themselves. It was as if she had woven a silken web around them all. Even the poor sots she tormented on board the captured ships adored her.

Well he, Julio, had not fallen under her spell. He spat into the sand. It was enough to give anyone the belly-grubs.

As he turned back to the long-boat and took hold of a sack of silver, he began plotting. There would be a celebration that night. Wine and rum would flow freely. There would doubtless be a chance for him to be revenged upon her; then, in the confusion after the act he would slip away.

He'd had a bellyful of Manitas and the others. With his share of the booty he would travel to one of the larger islands, buy himself a few native wives and settle down to farm the land whilst the women waited on him.

But first he would have Carlotta. He wanted to know why she had such a hold over Manitas; the poor fool had never been so besotted over a woman. Perhaps she was not made like other women. Witches were reckoned to have extra paps – teats by which they suckled their familiars. These were often hidden inside a witch's coynte.

His breath quickened as he imagined sticking his fingers into her, searching her hot female orifice for unnatural protuberances. He grew even more excited at the thought of fondling her breasts, searching every intimate fold for other tell-tale signs of Devilry. Witches had areas on their body which were immune to pain. He would press the point of his knife to her flesh, just hard enough to prick the skin and watch her eyes as they widened in fear and panic. She would not bleed nor feel any discomfort.

Then she would know that he had discovered her secret. How she would plead with him not to reveal what she was. She would offer to pleasure him in diverse ways and he would let her think that he would spare her. Then, when he had slaked his lust, he would kill her.

'Here, Julio,' one of the men called out, 'What's the hurry? Slow down. You're working like all the hounds of Hell are pursuing you!'

Julio glanced over his shoulder and grinned narrowly. If only he knew.

Carlotta clapped her hands in time to the drum beat. The stockade blazed with the light from many flares, and the dancing and singing had been going on for some hours.

To celebrate their safe homecoming and rich haul she had dressed in a gown of emerald murry-cloth, overlaid with silver lace. The gown was beautiful and suited her dark colouring, but it had been some time since she wore stays and the constriction around her waist made her feel breathless.

When there was a lull in the dancing she would go

back to her house and change into a simple kirtle and blouse.

Manitas scooped her up and bore her into the midst of a dance. They whirled together in a quadrille, Carlotta finding that she fell into step with ease. Touching toe and heel to the ground, she passed around the square, linking arms with the other dancers and exchanging partners.

When it was her turn to dance in the centre of the formation, she lifted up her heavy skirts to show neat ankles clad in embroidered stockings. Her shoes were of brocade with heels of red wood. As she clicked her heel and straightened her back in the posture of the Spanish dancers from her home region of Castile, the other dancers took up the rhythm, clapping and shouting encouragement.

Each man placed a kiss on her cheek as she wove her way back to Manitas, freeing the next woman to take her turn in the centre. Catching her eye, Juanita smiled with pure happiness. Carlotta returned the smile, feeling light-headed with wine and contentment.

Manitas caught her arm and whispered in her ear, 'You look beautiful tonight, love. Dance all you wish, and kiss whomever you like, for you're my partner between the bed-sheets.'

She sparkled at him. 'I never forget it,' she said, kissing him passionately. 'It's where I want to be.'

Mantias's arm encircled her waist and she lay back against his broad chest. The delicious smell of roasting pig filled the air and her mouth watered. She went across to the roasting pit and carved a large juicy slice of meat. Back at the table she cut it into slivers. She and Manitas took turns feeding each other from the point of his knife.

Trickles of sweat ran down inside her chemise and she could feel the heat blooming in her cheeks. If she was to do any more dancing she really must take off some of the suffocating layers of petticoats. She moved away from Manitas, who seemed content to slump on the bench, drink wine, and make conversation with the man sitting next to him.

'I must go and change,' she said. 'I'll be back in just a moment. The night is too warm for such a heavy gown.'

He lifted his wine goblet and grinned at her over the rim.

'Need any help with your laces?'

'No. I'll manage. Besides, the help you offer would likely hold me back for some time!'

His laughter followed her until she reached the edge of the light. Away from the flares and the cooking fires it was as black as pitch. She stood still for a moment, letting her eyes become accustomed to the darkness. Feeling her way around familiar objects and buildings, she found her way to her house.

How stupid not to have brought a flare. She would bring one to light her way back. The house door was unlocked. No one amongst the pirates stole from their own kind. There was no need, they all had so much now.

Leaving the front door ajar, she searched for a tinder box and touched a taper to an oil lamp. A soft-yellow light filled the room as she placed the lamp on a table. Turning back to close the door, she felt a hand close over her wrist. She cried out as someone pushed her hard and she went sprawling across the bed.

There was the click of the door closing and the sound of the bolt sliding into place. Carlotta whipped around and brushed the tousled curls out of her eyes. Before she could sit up, Julio had crossed the room and was standing over her. His thin mouth was stretched in a smile and the light glinted off the skinning knife he held pointing towards her.

'How now, bitch-woman,' he hissed. 'Here's your destiny come calling, devil-woman.'

Carlotta felt an icy hand grip her heart. She knew with dreadful certainty that he meant to kill her. Her throat dried. Even if she was able to call for help, no one would hear her above the sound of revelling. She was alone with a madman.

Julio smiled, showing his blackened teeth, secure in his power over her.

'Well, is this not cosy? You and I all alone. And you not armed with that pig-sticker of a sword. What shall we do?'

She fought against the blinding panic. The wine fumes clouding her brain evaporated. She was cold sober. Think, think. She must do something, anything. If only she had been wearing breeches and shirt, she would have stood a chance against him. But the heavy folds of the gown, the ornate padded sleeves, served to hamper her movements. The only thing she could hope for was that the thick fabric would deflect the blade.

Then she saw Julio's mean little eyes stray to the low, square neck of her gown. His expression was unmistakable. Pure, distilled lust. So, he did not intend to kill her right away. She lowered her eyes so that he would not see the spark of triumph.

She did not move as Julio bent over her, although the stench of his breath made her gorge rise.

'Turn over,' he ordered. 'I don't want your witch's eyes looking at me. You'll not cast one of your cursed spells.'

Slowly she did as he asked. It took a great deal of self control not to flinch away when he moved her hair aside and trailed his fingers across the back of her neck. She held herself rigid as he reached around and thrust one hand inside her bodice.

His fingers clawed at her flesh and she shrank inside herself, putting distance between her mind and body. Whatever he did she was determined not to be affected by it. Julio seemed intent on forcing a response from her. He dragged her breasts free of her gown and squeezed at them roughly, bruising the tender skin.

'Too well-bred to cry out with pleasure, are you? I'll

wager that you're not so cold when lying beneath Manitas! Well let's see what it is that holds him so in thrall.'

As he moved away, his weight was removed from her back. She tried to ignore the pain in her breasts and took a deep shuddering breath, holding herself tensed ready for the moment when he would lower his guard. Then she felt the back of her bodice loosen and heard the sound of laces being cut.

Julio intended to cut the clothes from her back.

The thought of being naked and defenceless was so awful that she began fighting her way up the bed in a mindless attempt at escape. She clutched at the bed covers, trying to gain purchase, and saw with some part of her conscious self – the hook on the wall where her men's clothes hung.

Her sword belt was under her doublet. If only she could distract Juilo long enough to reach for it.

'No you don't! Come here,' Julio groaned, springing onto the bed and straddling her.

He meshed one hand in her loose hair and pressed her face down into the cover. She thrashed and fought for breath, while he held her down, using his free hand to slit the laces up her bodice and to slash at the fastening of her sleeves and stays. Although he was smaller than her, he seemed to possess an unnatural strength.

She felt the warm air on her skin as the slashed fabric gaped. Breathing hard, Julio paused.

'I'm going to let you up now. Don't try any tricks, hear me?'

She nodded, gasping for breath, her lips bruised by being ground against the embroidered velvet.

'If you try to escape, I'll cut you, understand? You won't be so pretty then. Now, take off your garments and lay on your back.'

Slowly she drew her legs under herself and kneeled on the bed. Her mind was clearing and she had the beginnings of an idea. Turning to Julio she smiled shakily and drew one ruined sleeve down her arm. Julio watched her, his thin lips working.

'I know what you want,' she said, her voice gaining in volume after the first few words. 'You want me to use my whore's tricks on you, just like I use them on Manitas. Isn't that right?'

He looked at her with suspicion. 'You admit that you're a witch?'

She forced herself to laugh. 'Oh, yes. How else do you think I bind him to me? The devil has given me special powers. I can give men pleasure beyond their wildest dreams. I have a salt teat which my lovers get to suck. I'll show you, if you'll let me live.'

Julio's eyes almost popped out of their sockets. He stammered as he promised to spare her, his mouth slack with lust. So, I told you what you were prepared to believe, she thought. She hid the contempt she felt for him and continued to disrobe, pulling each garment off slowly. Julio sank back on the bed, resting against one of the carved pillars.

After a moment he laid the knife down and began to unbuckle his belt. Naked now, Carlotta faced him. She pulled her stomach in and thrust out her breasts. Julio swallowed, his eyes roaming over her smooth limbs and coming to rest at her groin.

Slowly she changed position, sitting down with her knees bent and her feet flat on the bed. Julio pushed down his breeches and rose up, beginning to move towards her. Carlotta made herself smile with welcome and opened her knees, just long enough to give him a glimpse of what was between her legs.

'Is this what you want? Come, look upon the wound of womanhood. This is the altar at which all men worship.'

Julio gave a tortured moan.

'Christ save me. I am bewitched. Show me then. Do those Godless things to me.'

'Oh, I will. Come closer,' she said, her voice like honey. 'Let me see your male staff.'

Inside she was quivering with fear and tension. A moment more. Just let him come nearer. Julio loomed over her, his cock standing out in front of him, his back arched as he prepared to mount her. This was it. There would not be another chance.

Carlotta brought her knees in toward her chest and in one swift motion kicked out hard. Her feet caught Julio square in the chest and, such was the force of the blow, he was thrown off the bed and across the room. He fell heavily and stayed down. It seemed that he was stunned. She had only seconds before he recovered.

In a trice, Carlotta was off the bed and reaching out for the clothes' hook. She shoved the doublet aside, fumbling for the sword belt.

Sobbing with relief she felt her hand close around the handle of her rapier. The sound of metal sliding free of leather was loud in the room. She straightened and faced Julio, taking up the fighting stance which was second nature to her.

'Give me one good reason why I should not send you straight to Hell,' she said, in a voice that dripped ice.

Julio rose slowly to his feet. His face was grey.

'I did not mean . . . It were only a bit of fun . . .' he stammered, backing against the door.

'Don't move,' she rapped. 'You're not getting away this time. I should have finished you that time on board the *Esmeralda*. You're a poisonous little bastard, Julio. We don't need your sort.'

'What . . . what are you going to do?' he said.

'I'm taking you outside, so that your buccaneer friends can judge you. I've heard that they have a rough code of justice. Manitas can pass sentence on you.'

Julio's eyes sparked with malice.

'Then it'll be your word against mine. We'll see who comes off best.'

'That we will,' she said, and to his complete shock ordered him to open the door and step outside.

Julio was too dumbfounded to utter a word of protest as she marched stark naked through the stockade, holding him at sword point.

Manitas stroked Carlotta's hair, his huge hands gentle as he held her to him.

They lay in bed, curled together in the peaceful aftermath of their loving. He had so nearly lost her, the thought terrified him. From this moment on, Manitas would never again take their happiness for granted.

'I must have been blind not to notice what was happening,' he said. 'Julio was maddened by envy and hate. Yet he had everything he wanted. What makes a man act like that?'

Carlotta shrugged sleepily and he smiled. She was too sated with pleasure to answer. Remembering how beautiful she had looked as he thrust into her, her eyes wild with passion and her fingers trailing bonelessly over his hips, he smiled.

They had come together fiercely as man and woman, no games, no refinements – Carlotta as eager as he for the shattering consummation of their pleasure. The room smelt of sex, a mixture of perfume, sweat, and the subtle musk which was hers alone.

God, how he loved this woman: this spirited, brave, infuriating woman.

He kissed her cheek, whispering, 'Sleep then, lovely. Rest easy knowing that Julio will never harm anyone here again.'

They had set him adrift in a longboat, after taking him far out to sea. He had water for a few days, but nought else. It was possible, but not likely, that he would be washed up on one of the small habitable rocks that peppered the area. He felt no regrets. The man had made his choice. Now he must take his chances.

Manitas pulled the covers over his broad shoulders.

Carlotta was sleeping, her face as peaceful as a child's. He chuckled, recalling the moment when she strode into the midst of the celebrations. What a glorious sight she had been, naked as the day she was born, and as proud and unashamed as a Greek warrior of old.

There was not a man amongst the buccaneers who did not envy him.

Manitas was content. There was only one thing needed for his complete happiness and that was for Carlotta to give up her quest for revenge against Don Felipe Escada. But that, he knew, was a vain hope.

Chapter Sixteen

Carlotta stood in the doorway and watched Manitas chopping wood.

He wore only leather breeches and knee-high boots. His muscles rippled and the skin was pulled taut across his massive shoulders as he brought the axe down onto a log. The wood split open with a dull thud and the two halves rolled apart.

Manitas looked up and smiled, wiping his forehead with the back of his hand. She returned his smile, thinking that he looked magnificent with the tight leather hugging his slim hips and delineating his long legs. His face and body were bronzed and healthy and his dark hair was glossy and freshly-washed.

For the past few months they had lived together in simple contentment. Rich they might be, but there was the daily round of tasks to perform, animals to care for, food to be prepared, and, as now, wood to be chopped. Manitas preferred to do a task himself, rather than ask someone to do it – a legacy of his solitary life as a buccanner on Hispaniola.

Carlotta had discovered that she enjoyed certain domestic tasks, a revelation, since she had been attended by an army of servants since birth and had never even lifted a finger to dress herself before leaving Castile. Now that Juanita had a husband to care for, she came less often to wait on Carlotta.

It seemed natural that this should be the case as Juanita was more friend than servant.

Carlotta was honest enough to admit that, although it was a novelty to cook and keep their one-room dwelling clean, she would be glad when work started on the larger house.

Manitas had shown her the plans he was drawing up. The house would be built of stone, have two stories and a gracious sweeping staircase leading up to the second floor. The rooms would be grand in scale. There would be white pillars flanking the front door and balconies with wrought iron railings at every window.

She smiled inwardly as she dusted flour from her hands and shook out her calico apron and cotton skirts, knowing how readily she would fall back into the role of being mistress over the house and the servants who would be needed to run it.

Manitas carried a pile of logs around the side of the house and stacked them with the others in the wood pile. Carlotta dipped a ladle into a covered pail of spring water and took him a drink.

He drank deeply, then reached up to brush away a smudge of flour from her cheek.

'Happy, love?' he said, kissing her on the mouth.

She returned his kiss, feeling the desire for him, which was always just below the surface, rise up within her.

'That I am,' she murmured against his mouth. 'Have I not everything I wish for?'

He seemed pleased by her answer and pulled her into his embrace, kissing the tip of her nose, the point of her chin, and then trailing kisses down her neck. His hands slid down to cup her buttocks and she leaned into him, feeling his cock hardening against her thigh.

'Perhaps I can think of something else I want,' she

said. 'Why don't you leave chopping that wood until later and come into the house?'

Manitas affected shock. 'Can it be that you've designs on my body? You're a bold wench.'

She laughed huskily. There was that certain look in his eye, which heated her blood. She knew what he intended. How she relished it when Manitas took her without preamble, bending her over the table and flinging her skirts above her waist. The feeling of his great strength, contained and distilled into passion, was part of his attractiveness for her.

Sometimes all she wanted was a lusty swiving, no soft words or lingering kisses, just the knocking of his hard flat belly against her buttocks and his cock thrusting deeply inside her. Her coynte was already softening and swelling and her pleasure bud throbbed as if anticipating the touch of knowing fingers.

Then, over Manitas's shoulder, she saw Bartholomew Stow approaching. She made a sound of disappointment. Their loving would have to wait.

'I think you are needed,' she said, indicating Stow.

Manitas cursed under his breath and moved away reluctantly, but not before slapping her on the rump.

'I'll see what's amiss. Why don't you go into the house and wait for me? I'll not be long.'

'I'd best get back to my baking then,' she said, giving him a wry grimace, her eyes sparkling with mischief. 'There'll be a hot apple pastry ready for you when you get back.'

He burst out laughing. 'That's the first time I've heard it called that!'

She laughed too. His ready wit was another of the things she liked about him.

'You're a wonder to me, love,' Manitas called over his shoulder, blowing her a kiss. 'Of a certainty, you are the only woman I've ever met who's as handy with a cook-pan as she is with a sword!'

He walked up to Stow, exchanged a few words, and

they moved off together. Carlotta watched the two men thoughtfully until they were out of sight and then went into the house. Behind Manitas's smiles and easy manner she detected a trace of tension. Something was bothering him.

She knew that he had been watching her lately when he thought she was not looking, his eyebrows drawn in with concentration. And she thought she had the answer. He was still worried that she would return to Spain and challenge Felipe's claim on her house and lands and, once in Castile, she might decide to stay there.

In fact she had been feeling for some time that it was fruitless to keep her hate for Felipe alive. Better to let it go, before it tainted her soul. In a few days time, they were to set out to intercept another Spanish ship; this time it was leaving Puerto Caballos on the coast of Nicaragua, its cargo one of silver, silks, and linens.

This would be the last time she need set out to wreak revenge on Felipe. She did not think that he could sustain three heavy blows to his finances. He would be ruined and her task would be over.

The desire to go to Castile was less strong than it once had been. The house and lands she had owned were tainted now, imbued by Felipe's presence. She did not know if she wanted her properties back, even if it was possible to regain them.

And what of Manitas? She owed him so much. He accepted her just as she was. All of her previous lovers had disapproved of her outspokenness, her independent manner, her irreverence and personal code of morality. Only Manitas did not demand that she change to suit his perception of perfect womanhood. She knew that he would remain loyal to her, whatever she did.

In Manitas she had found the perfect mate. On their island she was content. It was a most unexpected thing. Perhaps this had wrought the change in her; for contentment and a quest for revenge made for disagreeable bedfellows.

She smiled wryly, 'Carlotta Mendoza,' she said aloud. 'Can it be that you are growing soft?'

The red petticoat, atop the main mast of the *Crimson Buccaneer*, fluttered in the sharp sea breeze as the ship bore down on the Spanish galleon.

Carlotta leaned over the ship's rail, the salt spray stinging her face and settling in a fine silver mist on her braided hair. The sea was a heaving mass of grey slopes, flecked with white spume. Intoxicating. She was always moved by the fierce beauty of the wind and waves.

How she loved the chase and the few moments before they boarded the other ship. It was as if the fear, excitement, and blood lust was an elixir which ran through her veins.

Her fingers strayed to her belt and she rested her hand on the pommel of her sword as the *Crimson Buccaneer* drew broadside-on to the Spanish ship. As before, the galleon had no time to fire her cannons. Only now did the sailors realise that they were in danger.

Carlotta could see the startled faces of the Spanish sailors. Many of them were crossing themselves, others shouted curses and waved cutlasses. The grappling lines were thrown out and the ships drew together, their timbers creaking and grinding. Already sailors were swarming up the rigging, engaging in hand to hand combat. The first of the buccaneers leapt aboard the galleon and the deck became a seething mass of men fighting for their lives.

'Time to go,' Manitas said at her side.

His craggy face was alight with the joy of fighting. She flashed him a smile, knowing that she wore a similar expression. They leapt onto the galleon's deck together. Carlotta let out a cry of triumph as she closed with one of the Spanish sailors. She and Manitas fought their way to the poop deck where the ship's officers were gathered.

It was a matter of moments to disarm them and corner the captain. As before, the element of surprise had assured them victory.

'This is almost too easy!' she said to Manitas.

The captain crossed himself hurriedly, his face grey and his lips moving in a prayer as if he expected to be killed at any moment. Sinking to his knees he began begging to be spared.

'Get up man and stop your babbling. Take us to the orlop deck,' Carlotta ordered. 'You'll not be harmed if you do as we say. Come now. We wish to inspect your cargo.'

The captain's eyes bulged. He seemed dumbfounded, both by the fact that his captor was a woman and that she knew her way around a ship. He was a well-built handsome man, in his middle years. After a pause, when his colour came back and his eyes swept appreciatively over her person, he managed a shaky grin.

'You'll not need to hold me at swordpoint, señora. I'll give you no cause to kill me. Where's the sense in bailing out a sinking ship, eh? I know when the fight is lost. So, why not put up your sword before you cut your pretty finger?'

'Very wise of you to give way,' Carlotta said dryly. 'Nevertheless, I'll keep my sword ready and trust in my instincts.'

The captain glanced over his shoulder as he descended the ladder leading below deck.

'Instincts? Is it not better for a wench to put her trust in God?'

'God is not here, he is inside the minds of men. But I am here,' Carlotta said, enjoying the look of shock on his face. 'I suggest that you put your trust in *my* word and keep your piety for your confessor.'

'Mary mother of Jesus save me. I have been captured

by heretics!' the captain moaned. 'You must be the sea-witch men speak of.'

Behind her, she heard Manitas's deep rumble of laughter. He enjoyed these exchanges. It gave him pleasure to see the outrage on men's faces when they saw her male garments and heard her scandalous words. How it galled these proud and God-fearing coves to take orders from a woman.

'Have you passengers aboard?' Carlotta asked the captain. 'And do not trouble to lie, I will find out soon enough and then it will be the worst for you.'

The captain nodded, having recovered himself somewhat. 'There is one. The ship's owner. He is using my cabin for the voyage. You'll not harm him?'

Carlotta froze. Surely she had not heard right. Her heart began to beat fast. She ignored the captain's question.

'Take me to your cabin, at once,' she said.

'But . . . Do you not wish to inspect the cargo?'

'Yes, yes. Later. First I wish to speak with this passenger.'

'Carlotta?' Manitas said. 'Is something amiss?'

She smiled reassuringly. The situation needed careful handling if Manitas was not to rush into the captain's cabin and kill the man he found there.

'Don Felipe Escada is on board. I cannot imagine why, but I intend to find out. I have been waiting for this, for so long.'

Manitas nodded. 'I know it. Do what you must,' he said, evenly. 'I'll not interfere, lest you ask for my help.'

'Thank you,' she said softly. 'I know how to deal with him.'

The captain looked from one to the other, his eyebrows raised. 'You know the man in my cabin?' he said and gave a mocking laugh. 'I wish you well of him!'

'What mean you? Tell me at once,' she said, her voice cold. 'The man *is* Don Felipe Escada, is he not?'

The captain shrugged. 'Aye. It's him right enough.

240

But I fear that his wits are addled. You'll not get much sense out of him. Ever since he boarded ship in Nicaragua, just after the mule train arrived from the silver mines, he's been muttering about – destiny and fate. Something about a Spanish woman who bewitched him. He says that she condemned him to a life of self abuse and unholy lusts. The crew laugh at him and call him a madman.

Carlotta felt the blood drain from her face. It really was Felipe. Had he arranged to be on this voyage in the hope of meeting up with her? It seemed impossible. To take such a step he must be mad indeed. She could hardly believe that they were to speak at last, face to face. It was almost a year since she left Castile. A year since her life had been torn into shreds.

She found that she could not remember Felipe's face clearly. He had loomed so large in her life, that he had taken on the image of a monster. He had haunted her dreams and waking hours for so long. Never a day had passed when she did not think of him.

There was a bitter taste in her mouth. She could feel the anger and the hate gathering pace inside her as she remembered Felipe's insufferable arrogance, his absolute belief that she could be tamed and bent to his will. Had she really thought that she no longer thirsted for revenge?

'Carlotta? Do you wish to speak with Don Felipe alone?' Manitas asked. His voice was cool and calm and it exerted a steadying influence over her.

She knew that Manitas wished Don Felipe a speedy passage to Hell. His self-control was admirable. In his dark eyes she saw the longing to kill Felipe. It was only his regard for her which made him willing to allow her to settle matters in her own way.

'I wish to have no secrets from you,' she said. 'Secure the good captain here and let us go in to the cabin together.'

* * *

Felipe clasped his hands together and prayed for all he was worth. Above him he could hear the clash of metal and the screams of the wounded. Soon the pirates would swarm below deck and examine every space for treasure.

Let her be amongst them. Dear God let her find him and do her worst.

And if she was not amongst the pirates, then let him perish at the hands of her cut-throat friends. He could not stand any more of this miserable existence. His eyes were gritty from lack of sleep and the fresh marks of the scourge across his chest burnt like fire. It was two days now since food had passed his lips and his knees hurt from so much kneeling.

He felt like a hollow shell, as if all of his vitality had been sucked out of him slowly over the past year. Carlotta had done this to him. She had set her mark on him. Ensuring that his body burned with lust for her, day and night. No matter what privations he forced himself to endure, his staff of Adam stood rigid – a turgid, fleshy testament to the power of her spell over him.

Nothing had been the same since first he glimpsed her in her father's house, a dainty, thirteen year old maiden with large dark eyes and olive skin. She had seemed innocent then, but he had glimpsed the touch of wilfulness in the set of her crushed-flower mouth, the imprint of a sharp intelligence – so displeasing in a woman – on her smooth brow.

Years later when he went to the Mendoza estate and found her at sword practice in the barn, he saw that the early promise of beauty had been realised. But he had been unprepared for her strength of character, her amused contempt for the morals and beliefs which he valued and enforced in his own life.

Such women were born to torment and enslave men. They were willing vessels for the Devil's designs; how pleased the horned deceiver must be with Carlotta.

242

Felipe sighed. He no longer fought against destiny. He accepted the fact that he was a weak sinner, the willing victim of a creature from the pit. Since the Abbess and the holy sisters had not been able to cast out his personal demon, despite all the painful refinements they wrought on his flesh, he had known that he was lost indeed. The Devil's bride, his tormentor, was the only person who could grant him salvation.

Ah, there were footsteps outside. Two people approached. Felipe remained on his knees, facing the door. Was she really here? Were all his long months of suffering about to be rewarded?

The longing within him rose up until it lodged in his chest. There it burned, like a hot coal.

'Carlotta, free me. Give me succour, release me,' he whispered, and then louder 'Oh, sweet martyred Christ – Carlotta.'

The first thing Carlotta heard when she pushed open the door was Felipe calling her name.

For some reason that made her angry. He had no right to colour her name with such an agony of longing, to make the single word sound like a prayer. It was as if he felt that he owned something of her, when the very opposite was the case.

Her anger seemed like a live thing in her belly. There was a red haze over her vision. She blinked hard and the kneeling figure came gradually into focus. It was him. She had known it would be, but it was still a shock to see him.

This was the man who changed her life. She had the strangest feeling that the room drew in around the two of them, enclosing them in shadow.

'Carlotta. Thank God. Oh, thank God,' Felipe whispered hoarsely. 'My prayers have been answered.'

'Be silent!' she ordered and was surprised when he obeyed instantly. Had he become so meek?

She studied him intently. Was this the creature she

had hated for so long? He did not look so terrifying. On his face was a beatific expression, the sort of look she had seen only on priests of an overly zealous nature and on those who had been granted a vision. He wore a doublet and breeches of black velvet, a simple white ruff at his throat.

The changes in his appearance startled her. He had always been slim, but he had lost so much weight that he looked gaunt. There were hollows at his cheekbones, a pinched look to his nostrils, and his eyes – heavily lidded as they were – burned with an unnatural fervour. The only thing which had remained the same was his mouth. She remembered now that it had always been surprisingly firm and sensual.

Surely his dark hair had been only lightly streaked with grey? Now great wings of white were smoothed back behind his ears, the effect rather striking against the black hair which was brushed straight back from his brow.

'How now, Don Felipe. I did not expect to see you again in this world,' she said coldly. 'Well? It seems that you have crossed the world to find me. What have you to say?'

Felipe's mouth opened and closed. She knew that she looked startling in her doublet of padded red leather and black trunk-hose. Her sword belt was worn low on her hip. Shiny black boots reached to her thighs and her hair was plaited and pinned tightly to her skull.

She recalled that Felipe had always been shocked by her immodest dress. That day in the barn, when she was taking lessons in sword fighting . . . How she had teased him. Her lips curved as she remembered Felipe's expression. He wore a similar look now.

'Donna Carlotta,' Felipe stammered. 'I . . . hardly know how to begin. I have done you a great wrong in taking your lands and properties for my own. I have thought long and hard about this and now . . . I wish to make amends . . .' he tailed off and glanced at Manitas who stood at her side, towering over them both.

Carlotta saw Felipe's eyes spark with dislike and something else – envy? So, he is not entirely the humbled creature he appears to be, she thought. In a strange way she was glad. It was easier to hate him when he showed traces of his old arrogance.

'Must we speak in the presence of your over-sized pirate lover?' Felipe said, his lip curling. 'Dismiss the man if you please. With all that is between us, you surely wish to settle matters in privacy.'

Carlotta laughed shortly at this haughty speech. Did Felipe presume to give her orders?

'Manitas is much more than my equal partner in crime,' she said. 'He is privy to my innermost thoughts and emotions. He stays in the room. And you delude yourself. There is nothing between us, Felipe, nothing, besides the fact that you cheated me out of everything I owned. Damn you for a thieving rogue. I've hated you for so long. Mayhap I should cut you up and feed you to the sharks.'

Felipe blanched. 'Very well. If you insist that your trained giant stays, then let him witness this.'

Manitas gave a grunt of rage and made a move towards Felipe, but Carlotta held him back.

'Nay, love. Let him not provoke you. He's not worth killing. Let's see what he has to say.'

Felipe gave Manitas a look of withering contempt, rose from his knees and crossed the room. Extracting a roll of parchment from a small coffer, he turned and held it out towards Carlotta. She took the documents and studied them closely. After a few moments she threw them contemptuously onto a table.

For a moment Felipe seemed stunned.

'Have you nothing to say?' he said. 'I have made over all your lands and properties. The documents have been duly witnessed and signed. They are legal. You can return home now. There is no need to stay amongst these barbarians. Come home, Carlotta. I promise that you will not regret it.'

Carlotta saw the look on Manitas's face and spoke quickly.

'It is too late, Felipe. I want nothing from you. Everything I need, I have. My life in Castile seems like a dream. I have a new home and family – Juanita too.' She laughed. 'Your ships have made me rich. Is that not a fine irony? Once I hated you and wished you dead. I would have given anything to be revenged upon you. But now, seeing you before me, I realise that I am free of you.'

'But . . . but this is impossible,' Felipe stammered. 'You cannot refuse my offer. You must take everything back.'

His voice was tinged with desperation. She thought of the captain's words earlier. Felipe did indeed have a brittle quality about him, as if he teetered on the brink of madness.

'You *must* forgive me and take back what is yours,' Felipe repeated, his long pale face filled with confusion. 'Don't you understand? I cannot find peace unless *you* grant it me. How else can I forget everything that is between us?'

'But there never was anything,' she said slowly and clearly. 'It was all in your mind, a creation of your distorted perceptions. You could not accept the fact that you desired me, wanted me so badly that you were prepared to marry me – flawed and in need of correction as I was. No. That would have been too easy. So you blamed me for your lust. It was ever the way with weak men.'

Felipe seemed to come to life. His head reared back, his eyes narrowed with malice.

'You lie! Do you deny that you bewitched me, taunted me with your Devilish beauty until I was near consumed by unholy lusts? I have not known a moment's peace since you left the house in Castile. My flesh burns for you day and night and my staff of Adam is stiff with shame. You *must* admit to having cast a shadow over my soul! God alone knows how I have been in torment.'

'I cast no shadow over you,' Carlotta said evenly. 'Your demons are your own and the hell-wain you ride is of your own making. Do you think me a priest that I can grant you absolution? Your arrogance still sickens me. If this is all you wish to say to me, then you have had a wasted journey. Better for you to have stayed in Spain and battled with your guilt there. I want nothing more of you, Don Felipe. Not your twisted ravings, nor your false sorrow, nor your pride which is steeped in self-pity. You are nothing to me. Less than nothing. Keep my lands and properties, or give them to the poor. I care not.'

She turned away and Felipe moaned and fell to his knees. He held out his hands, plucking at the hem of her doublet.

'You cannot mean to walk away and leave me in torment. Do not spurn me. Punish me for my sins, I beg you. Do to me what you did to Pedro and Antonio. They wrote and told me how you served them. I desire only to be your slave, to worship you and to do your bidding.'

Carlotta eyed him with distaste. She saw through his mask of humility. He did not desire her forgiveness, he still wanted her as badly as ever, but his lust had turned inwards. Over the past year he had driven himself to the brink of insanity with his repressed and fanatical desires. And now he wished to be her slave and to season his unclean passions with the heady spice of servitude.

Would Felipe never understand that he was the instigator *and* the master of his own lusts?

She felt drained suddenly. Perhaps Felipe did deserve her pity, since her anger against him seemed to have faded. But it was impossible to feel charitable towards him. She felt only a withering contempt. He really expected her to absolve him of his sins and to lift the spell she was supposed to have cast over him.

It would be easy to indulge him and to free herself of him by lying. But she decided that he needed a lesson he would not forget. A different sort of lesson to that which he had in mind.

'I have nothing left – pride, honour, any sense of worth – all gone,' Felipe said, rushing on before Carlotta could speak. 'Everything has become channelled into the obsession you placed within me. I am ruined. Beyond redemption. Will you not take pity on me? Do whatever you wish with me. Berate me, humiliate me. Spit on me. Press your foot onto my neck and grind my face in your body's wastes. I deserve your wrath.' His voice was hoarse and quivering with restrained excitement.

Carlotta glanced at Manitas who was staring at Felipe with amused disbelief.

'What say you?' she said. 'Shall I give this wretched sinner a lesson?'

Manitas grinned and nodded. He understood what she was about to do. Felipe saw the look which passed between them and she knew that it hurt him. She was glad.

'Take off your garments,' she said to Felipe.

Felipe closed his eyes and gave a shudder of ecstasy.

'Oh God be thanked,' he murmured, his fingers trembling as he fumbled with the hooks and laces on his doublet and breeches.

Carlotta suppressed a gasp as he took off his cambric shirt and his torso came into view. His skin was marked by stripes and scratches; some of them old and faded to silver lines, others new and barely scabbed over. When he was naked she saw that his whole body was marked in the same way. His buttocks bore the stigmata of his most recent beating.

Against the thinness of his limbs and the spareness of his form, Felipe's erection looked huge and dark purple-red in colour. It loomed up from his loins, lying almost flat against his hollow belly. His cods were gathered into a tight purse at the base of his cock. By the look of him, he was ready to burst.

She had been right about him. Felipe thrived on abuse. If she was to take him at his word and treat him as she had Pedro and Antonio, then she would only be fanning the fire of his most base passions. He would continue to demand more and more suffering and she was not prepared to grant him that.

'You have fed your passions with suffering and gloried in your unclean lusts whilst blaming me for your travail,' she said. 'And now you wish me to punish you still more. I intend to deny you that. I want you to realise that I will *never* lay a hand on you, neither will I heap abuse on your head. There is to be no more excuse for this behaviour. *You* must face your demons and accept or defeat them in your own way. I am not responsible for the state you are in.'

Felipe's shoulders sagged and tears squeezed from the corners of his eyes. He encircled his cock-shaft with both hands.

'How cruel you are,' he said brokenly. 'How deliciously heartless. Touch me. Beat me. Take pity on me. Do whatever you wish to me. Only touch me. I need to abase myself before you. I need to.'

'I have told you. I will not be part of this,' she said. 'I never was. It was all *you*, Felipe.'

While Felipe watched her hungrily, she walked across the room and into Manitas's arms. Glancing over her shoulder at Felipe, she said, 'Now, you shall watch and see what it is for a man to love a woman. This is what your stiff pride will not allow you to do. Believe me at last, Felipe. You are not bewitched. You are simply misguided. Face your obsessions and learn from this.'

Felipe let loose a cry of utter despair. 'No. Don't give

249

yourself to him! I cannot stand this. Why do you deny me the comfort I beg for?'

Carlotta did not answer him. She had nothing more to say. Felipe must find his own salvation. She gave herself up to Manitas's caresses. At the touch of his skin, the familiar scent of him, her passions stirred.

'I did not know that you were so wise,' Manitas whispered against her mouth.

'I have some secrets from you still,' she said huskily, as she allowed him to unfasten her doublet and slide it from her shoulders.

When he cupped her breasts in his huge hands she moaned softly, the desire blooming liquidly within her. Naked to the waist, she took Manitas's hand and led him across the cabin past the still-kneeling figure of Felipe. Felipe seemed to be praying, while his hands were at work on his cock.

Carlotta laid herself belly-down on a table, her breasts hanging down over the far side. As Manitas took off her belt and dragged down her breeches, she held eye contact with Felipe. His face was white and drawn and his deep-set eyes were pools of exquisite suffering.

He had begged for cruelty, well now he had it. The ultimate cruelty was to be ignored, rejected totally, while still able to view the object of his obsession taking her pleasure with the man she loved.

Felipe's hands stroked and kneaded his rigid flesh. He grunted and sweated, his buttocks and thighs tensed so that the muscles stood out like cords. Beads of sweat appeared on his forehead and top lip. His eyes never left her face.

'So beautiful,' he murmured. 'So cruel.'

Carlotta sighed as Manitas covered her with his remarkable body. His cock was hot and hard against her skin. She pressed back against him eagerly, but he did not enter her at once. Reaching over, he took hold of her breasts, his fingers massaging the nipples into hard peaks. Carlotta arched her back and parted her thighs, longing for the feel of his flesh sliding into her.

Manitas eased her buttocks apart with his hands and stood back before he nudged at her intimate folds with his big glans. She knew that he was watching her coynte enfold his cock and imagined what he could see – the red-brown lips of her sex stretched around the shiny purple plum. How she loved the sensation of being opened by him, the way he pushed past the closure of her flesh into the slippery warmth within.

As he began thrusting into her, she groaned with pleasure, feeling her body move back and forth in a rhythm as old as time. Her breasts swung free, the pulling of his fingers against her sensitised nipples adding to her enjoyment.

She was conscious of Felipe watching her changes of expression. He seemed to be absorbing her every sigh and moan. His bottom lip was caught up in his teeth. As he pulled at his cock he sobbed, the tears making silver tracks down his thin cheeks.

'Carlotta,' he whimpered, in a voice that held grief and, she hoped, understanding. 'Oh, Carlotta.'

Felipe cannot help but know that he is an observer only, she thought. He meant nothing to either of the two people who were totally absorbed in giving pleasure to each other.

As Felipe's climax approached, he threw his head back and screwed his eyes shut. His hand pumped energetically at his cock. His uncovered glans looked engorged, the skin stretched and shiny. A drop of clear fluid trembled at the tip.

Carlotta let out a breathy moan as Manitas drew partway out of her body and began to thrust quickly in and out of her entrance. The pulling against her sex-lips exerted a gentle tugging on her pleasure bud and she threw back her head in total abandonment.

That was enough to tip Felipe over.

'Dear God,' he cried, his whole body jerking as his

251

semen spurted from him to lie in creamy droplets on the cabin floor.

A few seconds later, with a great cry, Manitas came. Carlotta felt him surge into her and his cock lodge against her womb, pulsing as he emptied himself. Her inner flesh convulsed around him and the orgasmic pleasure spread through all her nerve ends.

It was silent in the cabin, but for the sound of breathing. Carlotta and Manitas remained joined, Felipe forgotten, as they kissed and exchanged endearments.

How she loved this giant of a man. He had no need to prove himself, no need to punish his flesh or to blame others because he could not face the dark side of his nature. In a while Manitas separated from her and began to dress himself.

'We'd best get back to the others, before Stow sends out a search party,' Manitas said.

Carlotta nodded and crossed the cabin. She bent down to pick up her doublet. Juanita too would be waiting for her, worried as usual until they all returned safely. At the thought of the settlement, she felt a surge of happiness. She was truly content now. The spectre of Felipe would no longer cast a shadow over her life. She was finally free of her hatred. Now, at last, she allowed herself to feel a little pity.

Felipe was still kneeling, hunched over and with his head bowed. Shudders wracked his body. He looked sad as if he had woken from a dream and found that he had lost something precious. He looked up slowly and his eyes met hers. She saw they were bright with tears, but he looked sane for the first time since she set foot inside the cabin.

'What of me? What am I to do?' he asked in a small voice.

'I suggest that you return to Spain and begin living,' she said. 'There is nothing for you here, Felipe. There never was.'

Perhaps, this time, he would believe her. She hoped so, but it was no longer her concern. He must find his own way. She turned away and Manitas slipped his arm around her waist.

'Come love, we have the ship's hold to inspect,' he said, grinning. 'Shall we see what treasure the Don here has brought the Crimson Buccaneer?'

Carlotta smiled up at him. At the door she glanced over her shoulder.

'God go with you, Don Felipe,' she said, surprised to find that she meant it.

Felipe watched Carlotta and Manitas walk away. It seemed that he was free to go. Free indeed.

He dressed slowly, his mind full of all he had seen and heard.

Oh, Carlotta was clever, a most practised sorceress. Her wiles were subtle and refined. It was obvious that she had bewitched her pirate lover. That was why she had finally released Felipe from her spell.

For her hold over him had gone. No longer was he aware of her presence within him. He felt strangely empty and at peace. The sorrow, left behind by the void, was still fresh enough to sting like a raw wound, but that would lessen as the days passed. Crossing the cabin, he uncovered the large square object which leaned against the wall.

The painting, his constant companion for so many months, did not seem so luminous somehow. In fact it wasn't all that good. The artist had made Carlotta's features a little too soft, her lips too thin. El Greco did not execute many portraits and he did not excel at them. He was more famous for his religious paintings.

Felipe began packing a trunk. He would leave the painting in the cabin when he reached Spain. He had no need to keep Carlotta's image alive.

It would be the start of Spring by the time he reached Castile. On the Mendoza estate there was much work to be done. His finances had taken a severe blow. It would be a while before they recovered and there would be much time for contemplation.

Fleetingly he thought of Carlotta locked in a passionate embrace with her pirate lover. His cock stirred against his leg as if seeking the warmth and comfort of a female orifice.

In his mind he saw an image of soft white arms reaching for him, a deep breast which held the promise of comfort. For the first time in many months he wondered how it would feel to hold and pleasure a woman, to stroke her silky hair and smell her skin.

Perhaps it was time he looked for a wife.

NO LADY
Saskia Hope
30-year-old Kate dumps her boyfriend, walks out of her job and sets off in search of sexual adventure. Set against the rugged terrain of the Pyrenees, the love-making is as rough as the landscape.

ISBN 0 352 32857 6

WEB OF DESIRE
Sophie Danson
High-flying executive Marcie is gradually drawn away from the normality of her married life. Strange messages begin to appear on her computer, summoning her to sinister and fetishistic sexual liaisons.

ISBN 0 352 32856 8

BLUE HOTEL
Cherri Pickford
Hotelier Ramon can't understand why best-selling author Floy Pennington has come to stay at his quiet hotel. Her exhibitionist tendencies are driving him crazy, as are her increasingly wanton encounters with the hotel's other guests.

ISBN 0 352 32858 4

CASSANDRA'S CONFLICT
Fredrica Alleyn
Behind the respectable facade of a house in present-day Hampstead lies a world of decadent indulgence and darkly bizarre eroticism. A sternly attractive Baron and his beautiful but cruel wife are playing games with the young Cassandra.

ISBN 0 352 32859 2

THE CAPTIVE FLESH
Cleo Cordell
Marietta and Claudine, French aristocrats saved from pirates, learn that their invitation to stay at the opulent Algerian mansion of their rescuer, Kasim, requires something in return; their complete surrender to the ecstasy of pleasure in pain.

ISBN 0 352 32872 X

PLEASURE HUNT
Sophie Danson

Sexual adventurer Olympia Deschamps is determined to become a member of the Légion D'Amour – the most exclusive society of French libertines.

ISBN 0 352 32880 0

BLACK ORCHID
Roxanne Carr

The Black Orchid is a women's health club which provides a specialised service for its high-powered clients; women who don't have the time to spend building complex relationships, but who enjoy the pleasures of the flesh.

ISBN 0 352 32888 6

ODALISQUE
Fleur Reynolds

A tale of family intrigue and depravity set against the glittering backdrop of the designer set. This facade of respectability conceals a reality of bitter rivalry and unnatural love.

ISBN 0 352 32887 8

OUTLAW LOVER
Saskia Hope

Fee Cambridge lives in an upper level deluxe pleasuredome of technologically advanced comfort. Bored with her predictable husband and pampered lifestyle, Fee ventures into the wild side of town, finding an outlaw who becomes her lover.

ISBN 0 352 32909 2

THE SENSES BEJEWELLED
Cleo Cordell

Willing captives Marietta and Claudine are settling into life at Kasim's harem. But 18th century Algeria can be a hostile place. When the women are kidnapped by Kasim's sworn enemy, they face indignities that will test the boundaries of erotic experience. This is the sequel to *The Captive Flesh*.

ISBN 0 352 32904 1

GEMINI HEAT
Portia Da Costa

As the metropolis sizzles in freak early summer temperatures, twin sisters Deana and Delia find themselves cooking up a heatwave of their own. Jackson de Guile, master of power dynamics and wealthy connoisseur of fine things, draws them both into a web of luxuriously decadent debauchery.

ISBN 0 352 32912 2

VIRTUOSO
Katrina Vincenzi

Mika and Serena, darlings of classical music's jet-set, inhabit a world of secluded passion. The reason? Since Mika's tragic accident which put a stop to his meteoric rise to fame as a solo violinist, he cannot face the world, and together they lead a decadent, reclusive existence.

ISBN 0 352 32907 6

MOON OF DESIRE
Sophie Danson

When Soraya Chilton is posted to the ancient and mysterious city of Ragzburg on a mission for the Foreign Office, strange things begin to happen to her. Wild, sexual urges overwhelm her at the coming of each full moon.

ISBN 0 352 32911 4

FIONA'S FATE
Fredrica Alleyn

When Fiona Sheldon is kidnapped by the infamous Trimarchi brothers, along with her friend Bethany, she finds herself acting in ways her husband Duncan would be shocked by. Alessandro Trimarchi makes full use of this opportunity to discover the true extent of Fiona's suppressed, but powerful, sexuality.

ISBN 0 352 32913 0

HANDMAIDEN OF PALMYRA
Fleur Reynolds

3rd century Palmyra: a lush oasis in the Syrian desert. The beautiful and fiercely independent Samoya takes her place in the temple of Antioch as an apprentice priestess. Decadent bachelor Prince Alif has other plans for her and sends his scheming sister to bring her to his Bacchanalian wedding feast.

ISBN 0 352 32919 X

OUTLAW FANTASY
Saskia Hope

On the outer reaches of the 21st century metropolis the Amazenes are on the prowl; fierce warrior women who have some unfinished business with Fee Cambridge's pirate lover. This is the sequel to *Outlaw Lover*.

ISBN 0 352 32920 3

THE SILKEN CAGE
Sophie Danson

When university lecturer Maria Treharne inherits her aunt's mansion in Cornwall, she finds herself the subject of strange and unexpected attention. Using the craft of goddess worship and sexual magnetism, Maria finds allies and foes in this savage and beautiful landscape.

ISBN 0 352 32928 9

RIVER OF SECRETS
Saskia Hope & Georgia Angelis

Intrepid female reporter Sydney Johnson takes over someone else's assignment up the Amazon river. Sydney soon realises this mission to find a lost Inca city has a hidden agenda. Everyone is behaving so strangely, so sexually, and the tropical humidity is reaching fever pitch.

ISBN 0 352 32925 4

VELVET CLAWS
Cleo Cordell

It's the 19th century; a time of exploration and discovery and young, spirited Gwendoline Farnshawe is determined not to be left behind in the parlour when the handsome and celebrated anthropologist, Jonathan Kimberton, is planning his latest expedition to Africa.

ISBN 0 352 32926 2

THE GIFT OF SHAME
Sarah Hope-Walker

Helen is a woman with extreme fantasies. When she meets Jeffrey – a cultured wealthy stranger – at a party, they soon become partners in obsession. Now nothing is impossible for her, no fantasy beyond his imagination or their mutual exploration.

ISBN 0 352 32935 1

SUMMER OF ENLIGHTENMENT
Cheryl Mildenhall

Karin's new-found freedom is getting her into all sorts of trouble. The enigmatic Nicolai has been showing interest in her since their chance meeting in a cafe. But he's the husband of a valued friend and is trying to embroil her in the sexual tension he thrives on.

ISBN 0 352 32937 8

A BOUQUET OF BLACK ORCHIDS
Roxanne Carr

The exclusive Black Orchid health spa has provided Maggie with a new social life and a new career, where giving and receiving pleasure of the most sophisticated nature takes top priority. But her loyalty to the club is being tested by the presence of Tourell; a powerful man who makes her an offer she finds difficult to refuse.

ISBN 0 352 32939 4

JULIET RISING
Cleo Cordell

At Madame Nicol's exclusive but strict 18th-century academy for young ladies, the bright and wilful Juliet is learning the art of courting the affections of young noblemen.

ISBN 0 352 32938 6

DEBORAH'S DISCOVERY
Fredrica Alleyn

Deborah Woods is trying to change her life. Having just ended her long-term relationship and handed in her notice at work, she is ready for a little adventure. Meeting American oil magnate John Pavin III throws her world into even more confusion as he invites her to stay at his luxurious renovated castle in Scotland. But what looked like being a romantic holiday soon turns into a test of sexual bravery.

ISBN 0 352 32945 9

THE TUTOR
Portia Da Costa

Like minded libertines reap the rewards of their desire in this story of the sexual initiation of a beautiful young man. Rosalind Howard takes a post as personal librarian to a husband and wife, both unashamed sensualists keen to engage her into their decadent scenarios.

ISBN 0 352 32946 7

THE HOUSE IN NEW ORLEANS
Fleur Reynolds

When she inherits her family home in the fashionable Garden district of New Orleans, Ottilie Duvier discovers it has been leased to the notorious Helmut von Straffen; a debauched German count famous for his decadent Mardi Gras parties. Determined to oust him from the property, she soon realises that not all dangerous animals live in the swamp!

ISBN 0 352 32951 3

ELENA'S CONQUEST
Lisette Allen

It's summer – 1070AD – and the gentle Elena is gathering herbs in the garden of the convent where she leads a peaceful, but uneventful, life. When Norman soldiers besiege the convent, they take Elena captive and present her to the dark and masterful Lord Aimery to satisfy his savage desire for Saxon women.

ISBN 0 352 32950 5

CASSANDRA'S CHATEAU
Fredrica Alleyn

Cassandra has been living with the dominant and perverse Baron von Ritter for eighteen months when their already bizarre relationship takes an unexpected turn. The arrival of a naive female visitor at the chateau provides the Baron with a new opportunity to indulge his fancy for playing darkly erotic games with strangers.

ISBN 0 352 32955 6

WICKED WORK
Pamela Kyle

At twenty-eight, Suzie Carlton is at the height of her journalistic career. She has status, money and power. What she doesn't have is a masterful partner who will allow her to realise the true extent of her fantasies. How will she reconcile the demands of her job with her sexual needs?

ISBN 0 352 32958 0

DREAM LOVER
Katrina Vincenzi

Icily controlled Gemma is a dedicated film producer, immersed in her latest production – a darkly Gothic vampire movie. But after a visit to Brittany, where she encounters a mystery lover, a disquieting feeling continues to haunt her. Compelled to discover the identity of the man who ravished her, she becomes entangled in a mystifying erotic odyssey.

ISBN 0 352 32956 4

PATH OF THE TIGER
Cleo Cordell

India, in the early days of the Raj. Amy Spencer is looking for an excuse to rebel against the stuffy morals of the British army wives. Luckily, a new friend introduces her to places where other women dare not venture – where Tantric mysteries and the Kama Sutra come alive. Soon she becomes besotted by Ravinder, the exquisitely handsome son of the Maharaja, and finds the pathway to absolute pleasure.

ISBN 0 352 32959 9

BELLA'S BLADE
Georgia Angelis

Bella is a fearless, good-looking young woman with an eye for handsome highwaymen and a taste for finery. It's the seventeenth century and Charles II's Merrie England is in full swing. Finding herself to be the object of royal affections, Bella has to choose between living a life of predictable luxury at court or following her desire to sail the high seas – where a certain dashing young captain is waiting for her.

ISBN 0 352 32965 3

THE DEVIL AND THE DEEP BLUE SEA
Cheryl Mildenhall

A secluded country house in Norfolk is the setting for this contemporary story of one woman's summer of sexual exploration. Renting a holiday home with her girlfriends, the recently graduated Hillary is pleased to discover that the owner of the country estate is the most fanciable man in the locale. But soon she meets Haldane, the beautifully proportioned Norwegian sailor. Attracted by the allure of two very different men, Hillary is faced with a difficult decision.

ISBN 0 352 32966 1

WESTERN STAR
Roxanne Carr

Maribel Harker is heading west, and she's sure grown up since the last wagon train moved out to California. Dan Cutter is the frontiersman that Maribel's father has appointed to take care of his wilful daughter. She is determined to seduce him – he is determined not to give into temptation. Thrown together in a wild and unpredictable landscape, passions are destined to run high!

ISBN 0 352 32969 6

A PRIVATE COLLECTION
Sarah Fisher

Behind an overgrown garden by the sea, a crumbling mansion harbours a tantalising secret: a remarkable collection of priceless erotica belonging to a fading society beauty and her inscrutable chauffeur. When writer Francesca Leeman is commissioned to catalogue the collection, she finds herself becoming embroiled in a three-way game of voyeurism and mystery.

ISBN 0 352 32970 X

NICOLE'S REVENGE
Lisette Allen

Set against the turmoil of the French Revolution, opera star Nicole Chabrier faces a life of uncertainty now that angry hordes are venting their wrath on the aristocracy. Rescued by a handsome stranger and taken to a deserted palace, Nicole and her insatiable lover, Jacques, seek a reversal of their fortune using charm, sexual magnetism and revenge!

ISBN 0 352 32984 X

UNFINISHED BUSINESS
Sarah Hope-Walker

As a financial analyst for a top London bank, Joanne's life is about being in control. But privately, her submissive self cries out to be explored. She has tried to quell her strange desires, but they insist on haunting her. There is only one place where she can realise her desire to be dominated: the *Salon de Fantasie*, run by her enigmatic Parisian friend, Chantal. Soon, the complexities of Joanne's sexuality begin to take over the rest of her life.

ISBN 0 352 32983 1

Forthcoming titles

WE NEED YOUR HELP . . .
to plan the future of women's erotic fiction –

– and no stamp required!

Yours are the only opinions that matter.

Black Lace is the first series of books devoted to erotic fiction by women for women.

We intend to keep providing the best-written, sexiest books you can buy. And we'd appreciate your help and valued opinion of the books so far. Tell us what you want to read.

THE BLACK LACE QUESTIONNAIRE

SECTION ONE: ABOUT YOU

1.1 Sex (*we presume you are female, but so as not to discriminate*)
Are you?
Male ☐
Female ☐

1.2 Age
under 21 ☐ 21–30 ☐
31–40 ☐ 41–50 ☐
51–60 ☐ over 60 ☐

1.3 At what age did you leave full-time education?
still in education ☐ 16 or younger ☐
17–19 ☐ 20 or older ☐

1.4 Occupation _____

1.5 Annual household income
      under £10,000 ☐   £10–£20,000 ☐
      £20–£30,000 ☐   £30–£40,000 ☐
      over £40,000 ☐

1.6 We are perfectly happy for you to remain anonymous;
but if you would like to receive information on other
publications available, please insert your name and
address

_____

_____

_____

_____

SECTION TWO: ABOUT BUYING BLACK LACE BOOKS

2.1 How did you acquire this copy of *Crimson Buccaneer*?
      I bought it myself ☐   My partner bought it ☐
      I borrowed/found it ☐

2.2 How did you find out about Black Lace books?
      I saw them in a shop ☐
      I saw them advertised in a magazine ☐
      I saw the London Underground posters ☐
      I read about them in _____
      Other _____

2.3 Please tick the following statements you agree with:
      I would be less embarrassed about buying Black
      Lace books if the cover pictures were less explicit ☐
      I think that in general the pictures on Black
      Lace books are about right ☐
      I think Black Lace cover pictures should be as
      explicit as possible ☐

2.4 Would you read a Black Lace book in a public place – on
a train for instance?
      Yes ☐   No ☐

SECTION THREE: ABOUT THIS BLACK LACE BOOK

3.1 Do you think the sex content in this book is:
Too much ☐ About right ☐
Not enough ☐

3.2 Do you think the writing style in this book is:
Too unreal/escapist ☐ About right ☐
Too down to earth ☐

3.3 Do you think the story in this book is:
Too complicated ☐ About right ☐
Too boring/simple ☐

3.4 Do you think the cover of this book is:
Too explicit ☐ About right ☐
Not explicit enough ☐

Here's a space for any other comments:

SECTION FOUR: ABOUT OTHER BLACK LACE BOOKS

4.1 How many Black Lace books have you read? ☐

4.2 If more than one, which one did you prefer?

4.3 Why?

SECTION FIVE: ABOUT YOUR IDEAL EROTIC NOVEL

We want to publish the books you want to read – so this is your chance to tell us exactly what your ideal erotic novel would be like.

5.1   Using a scale of 1 to 5 (1 = no interest at all, 5 = your ideal), please rate the following possible settings for an erotic novel:

Medieval/barbarian/sword 'n' sorcery ☐
Renaissance/Elizabethan/Restoration ☐
Victorian/Edwardian ☐
1920s & 1930s – the Jazz Age ☐
Present day ☐
Future/Science Fiction ☐

5.2   Using the same scale of 1 to 5, please rate the following themes you may find in an erotic novel:

Submissive male/dominant female ☐
Submissive female/dominant male ☐
Lesbianism ☐
Bondage/fetishism ☐
Romantic love ☐
Experimental sex e.g. anal/watersports/sex toys ☐
Gay male sex ☐
Group sex ☐

Using the same scale of 1 to 5, please rate the following styles in which an erotic novel could be written:

Realistic, down to earth, set in real life ☐
Escapist fantasy, but just about believable ☐
Completely unreal, impressionistic, dreamlike ☐

5.3   Would you prefer your ideal erotic novel to be written from the viewpoint of the main male characters or the main female characters?

Male ☐   Female ☐
Both ☐

5.4 What would your ideal Black Lace heroine be like? Tick as many as you like:

Dominant ☐   Glamorous ☐
Extroverted ☐   Contemporary ☐
Independent ☐   Bisexual ☐
Adventurous ☐   Naive ☐
Intellectual ☐   Introverted ☐
Professional ☐   Kinky ☐
Submissive ☐   Anything else? ☐
Ordinary ☐   _____

5.5 What would your ideal male lead character be like? Again, tick as many as you like:

Rugged ☐
Athletic ☐   Caring ☐
Sophisticated ☐   Cruel ☐
Retiring ☐   Debonair ☐
Outdoor-type ☐   Naive ☐
Executive-type ☐   Intellectual ☐
Ordinary ☐   Professional ☐
Kinky ☐   Romantic ☐
Hunky ☐
Sexually dominant ☐   Anything else? ☐
Sexually submissive ☐   _____

5.6 Is there one particular setting or subject matter that your ideal erotic novel would contain?

_____

SECTION SIX: LAST WORDS

6.1 What do you like best about Black Lace books?

_____

6.2 What do you most dislike about Black Lace books?

_____

6.3 In what way, if any, would you like to change Black Lace covers?

_____

6.4 Here's a space for any other comments:

_____

_____

_____

_____

Thank you for completing this questionnaire. Now tear it out of the book – carefully! – put it in an envelope and send it to:

Black Lace
FREEPOST
London
W10 5BR

No stamp is required if you are resident in the U.K.